Daredevils

'Relentlessly enjoyable, surprising, inventive, and just plain heartwarming... a bona fide marvel... I couldn't put it down as I cheered on Loretta until the very last page. A real wonder'

Scott Cheshire, author of *High as the Horses' Bridles*

'A speeding stunt bike of a novel, propulsive and daring. Vestal's prose feels born of the southern Idaho landscape, as fleet and muscular as the jackrabbits swarming the desert floor... The characters' desires and aches – for love, for glory, for freedom – strain within their confines and burst off of the page. A lucid, bright gem'

Sharma Shields, author of *The Sasquatch Hunter's Almanac*

'Daring, moving, and tender... Beautiful and at times heartbreaking, this book will knock you out'

Nina McConigley, author of *Cowboys and East Indians*

SHAWN VESTAL was born in 1966 in Gooding, Idaho. His story collection *Godforsaken Idaho* won the 2014 PEN/Robert W. Bingham Prize and was shortlisted for the Saroyan Prize. His stories have appeared in *Tin House*, *Ecotone*, *McSweeney's*, *Southern Review* and other journals. *Daredevils* is his first novel.

Daredevils

SHAWN VESTAL

★

ONE

AN IMPRINT OF PUSHKIN PRESS

ONE
an imprint of Pushkin Press
71–75 Shelton Street,
London WC2H 9JQ

First published by ONE in 2016

1 3 5 7 9 8 6 4 2

ISBN 978 0993506 20 8

www.pushkinpress.com/one

Printed and bound by CPI Group (UK) Ltd, Croydon, CR0 4YY

For my brothers and sisters

TWO DESERTS

EVEL KNIEVEL ADDRESSES
AN ADORING NATION

When did we first think of jumping a canyon? It seems now that we always thought it. That it was always there for us to think. What do you call that, when the world guides you toward its purpose? We believed, America. We believed we could do anything we tried to do. We believed we could do anything we said we would do. We believed in ourself and the things we were saying. We believed that in saying these things, we were already making them true.

July 6, 1974

SHORT CREEK, ARIZONA

Loretta slides open her bedroom window and waits, listening to the house. She pops out the screen and slowly pulls it inside. The summer night is blue and black, filled with plump, spiny stars and the floral waft of alfalfa and irrigated fields. She swings one leg out, then the other, and sits on the sill. A tiny, muffled creak sounds, and she can't tell if it comes from the house or the night or inside her jangled mind. She spends every day now thinking about the night, and this moment is always the same—the exhilarating passage from here to there. To the brief, momentary future. To Bradshaw.

She drops to the ground and sets off across the lawn, hunched as if trying to stay below the searching beam of a powerful light. She is wearing her jeans, the one pair her father lets her keep for chores, and her clogs. Her Gentile clothes. The mountains, red by day, stand black and craggy against the rich ink of night. Their home is on the edge out here, on the edge of the Short Creek community just as she and her family are on the edge of it—half outsiders, not yet inside the prophet's full embrace—but that makes it easier to sneak away without being spotted by the prophet's men. The God Squad, Bradshaw calls them. If she sees car lights, she crouches in the ditch grass until they pass, but tonight she sees no car. She walks the barrow pit for a quarter mile, grass cool on her bare ankles, to where the dirt lane runs into county road and she sees Bradshaw's Nova on the wide roadside, pale luster along the fender, signal lights glowing like the hot eyes of a new beast coiled against the earth.

As she comes to the car, the passenger door opens, as if on its own, and the interior light blares, and there he is, Bradshaw, smile cocked on his hard, happy face. She feels it again, the sense that she doesn't know if she loves him, or even if she likes him, because sometimes she yearns for a glimpse of him and sometimes she feels desperate to get away from him—Bradshaw, sitting there with his wrist draped on the steering wheel like a king—but what is certain is that she cannot resist his gravity. She falls toward him at a speed beyond her control.

"*There* she is," he says as she slides in. "Holy hell, Lori, you are a vision."

He leans over and presses his chapped lips against her mouth. He tastes of beer, yeasty and sour. He pulls away and looks at her searchingly, ghostly eyes somehow alight, head tilted, one curly sideburn grazed by the green dashboard glow.

"Did you miss me, sweet Lori?"

"I missed you."

"Did you think about me a whole bunch?"

"I thought about you all the time."

6

She loves how much he seems to love her. He kisses her again, cupping the back of her head with a hand. She puts her hands on his back, feels the knots of muscle there. Sometimes she thinks he is trying to press his face through hers. To consume her. She wants this, always—this sin—but when it arrives she does not enjoy it, because he loses himself. He spreads a palm on her rib cage, thumb an inch from her breast. Then closer.

They part. He breathes as if he's been sprinting.

"Did you think any more about it?" he says.

He wants her to leave with him. To take off for good and put The Crick in the rearview mirror. To be together, he says. *Together* together.

"I did," she says. "I want to. But I don't think yet. I don't think now."

"Aww, Lori," he says. "Don't say that. Don't you say that to me."

She wants to go. She wants to fly into her future, but she feels she must be very careful, must be precise and exact, or she will miss it. She is sure that her future is a specific place, a destination she will either reach or miss, and it awaits her out there somewhere away from all that is here. Away from the long cotton dresses. Away from the tedious days in church school, studying the same scriptures they study all day on Sundays. Away from her father's stern but halfhearted righteousness and her mother's constant acquiescence. And, mostly, away from the looming reality that no one ever says a word about: she is fifteen, she is eligible, she is a means now for her father to pursue his own righteousness. He cannot take another wife himself, but he can still serve the Principle— the principle of plural marriage. *Celestial marriage.* They have been welcoming certain brothers for dinners in their home. The men are always bright with questions for Loretta.

Bradshaw wrestles her to the seat for a while, and then they drive and talk. He loves to be listened to. He loves to tell her about the way he has handled something, the way he has put someone in their place. He is talking about his new boss, the turf farmer outside St. George.

"So he keeps handing me the eleven-sixteenths, and I keep asking for the thirteen-sixteenths, and then he does it again," he says, slapping a hand on the dash. "I say, bud, you got your glasses on?"

His laugh is like a chugging motor. Why does he think she wants to hear this? The strange thing is, she does. She loves listening to him talk, to his strange locutions, his crudeness. *So hungry I could eat the ass out of a cow,* he'll say. *Shit oh dear. That smarmy bastard.* He never utters a righteous word. It wasn't all that long ago that Loretta thought he was her savior, the one who'd rescue her. She has been heading out into the night since she was thirteen, she and her friend Tonaya, meeting up with the Hurricane boys, the St. George boys, the boys the prophet had exiled. They were the crowd Loretta and Tonaya chased around whenever they could, sneaking out at night, joyriding on dirt roads, drinking beer, building bonfires in the desert, shoplifting at the grocery store, riding in the backseat as the boys bashed mailboxes or keyed cars, coming home before dawn, climbing back in that bedroom window, back into the world where no one watched television, where they prayed constantly, or sat over scripture, or sang hymns, or walked to the neighbors to weed a garden. Out there, into the worldly world, and then back home, to reverence and boredom.

The night she met Bradshaw, she and Tonaya were wedged in

the backseat of an old Rambler station wagon owned by one of the boys, parked outside the 7-Eleven in Hurricane looking for someone to buy them something—a six-pack, a bottle of sweet wine. That night, it was Bradshaw. Almost immediately, when he came around the side of the store and handed the bag into the car, he looked into the back and found Loretta's eyes. He was older than the boys she was hanging around with, but younger than the men in Short Creek, the men whose eyes she felt on Sundays at church, the men who blushed if she returned their gaze. Bradshaw didn't blush, ever. Everything about him announced that he did not harbor a doubt—his quick, bowlegged walk, eyes of washed-out blue and angular face, and the way he was always doing something handsome and prominent with his jaw, cocking it this way or that. Soon she was meeting him alone, and every time she climbed into his car he looked thrilled and he said, "*There* she is," like he was announcing something the world had long awaited.

Now, tonight, Bradshaw turns onto a dirt road and guns it, fishtailing the Nova into the desert. They drive up into a bump of low hills where he will find a reason to stop again. It's past midnight, almost one, Loretta guesses, and she remembers that tomorrow is Fast Sunday, the first Sunday of the month, and she has forgotten to stash something to eat.

"There's probably nothing open now, is there?" she asks.

"Open for what?"

"Some food. Anything. Tomorrow's Fast Sunday."

"Tomorrow's *what* Sunday?"

Does Bradshaw not know what Fast Sunday is? The day of fasting? He's lived down here all his life.

"Fast Sunday. No eating. I get headaches if I don't sneak something."

9

Bradshaw brays laughter. "A day of no eating. You Mormons. I swear."

You Mormons. Loretta doesn't think of herself—of her family, of Short Creek—as Mormon, exactly, although everyone here thinks of themselves as the only true Mormons. In her mind, Mormons were what they were before they came here seven years ago. Mormons were what they were when they lived in Cedar City, went to the church on Main Street, the tan-brick wardhouse on a street with ordinary homes and a grocery store and a gas station. Mormons, she thinks, live in the real world, or at least closer to it. They had a television back then, and a radio in the kitchen. Her mother listened to country music. They dressed like real people, like worldly people—though, she knows, they were farmier and more country than Salt Lake City Mormons, the rich, blond Mormons, the ones you can barely tell are even Mormons at all. Mormons, she thinks, marry one person at a time.

They came here when she turned eight—the age for her baptism. Her father had grown up in Short Creek, on the desert border between Utah and Arizona, among the polygamists and fundamentalists, but he had left as a teenager, a rebellious boy encouraged by the prophet to leave. They had lived in Cedar and Loretta's parents raised eight children, and he worked fixing cars at the town's auto dealership. Loretta came late and unexpected, as her father had begun turning back toward the faith he had departed and hardening against the soft ways of the mainstream church. When it came time to baptize Loretta, he found he could not do so. They moved back to The Crick—where his brothers lived, where his parents had died. You cannot exactly join this church, Loretta knows; you cannot simply show up and convert to the Fundamentalist Church of Jesus Christ of Latter-day Saints, but because of his family and his history and his willingness to submit, her father was allowed to return, half-caste. Still, all these years later, they are not yet fully in the United Order—the inner circle of the most righteous, those living in the Principle of plural marriage—and yet are allowed to hope, to strive, probationary.

She remembers the spring night her father told them they were returning. They sat around the small kitchen table, the smell of cut grass pungent through the screen door. A Pyrex dish of hamburger casserole, a meaty stew run through with ribbons of noodle and brownish clumps of tomato, sat before them. Her mother wore an ankle-length dress, nothing like she would usually wear. An exhausted pall shadowed her face, and she did not say one word. Loretta's father, stout and slow, spoke in the deliberate voice that made him seem dumb; his hands were flat on the table beside his plate, grooved in engine black. He answered all of her questions in a tone that made it clear the decision had been made.

"It is for your eternal soul, Loretta, that we do this," he said. "Even if you can't see that."

Loretta's mother sat twisting her hands, galaxies of red dots spreading across her face and neck. They were both so old, Loretta knew even then—like grandparents. Her father was always wearily heaving himself up and around, always groaning toward the next task, and her mother moved with slow, weary resignation. And now there she was, dressed like a sister wife, dressed the way you would see the Short Creek women dressed when they came to town. Loretta wanted her mother to say something then, to say anything at all.

Loretta has never felt right here. She hates to braid her hair. She hates to sit quietly while the boys run and shout. She does not want to live in one of these strange, huge families, the men orbited by constellations of wives and children. She imagines her future as something like the ads in magazines she has glimpsed in stores, in the hair salon in St. George, those times her mother has let her go. Modern clothing and fast cars and makeup and shining tall buildings that glow at night and cigarettes and cocktails and every forbidden thing. She loved the lipstick ad with the beautiful girl in black jeans lying on the hood of a pink Mustang and smirking into the camera. The name of the lipstick like a password: Tussy.

Bradshaw's hand is inside her blouse, crawling over her back. Her mouth is sore, her neck is tired. He puts his hand on the inside of her thigh and squeezes. He takes the skin of her neck in his teeth and bites gently, but not gently enough. "Some night I won't be able to stop myself," he says, breath like a furnace. "I can't be responsible."

Sometimes he holds her wrists so hard he leaves small bruises. He says he can't help it, and she believes him because he acts like he can't help it. She wants to do it, too, although she's also scared it will create something unstoppable in Bradshaw, and she resents the way he pressures her. Still, she spends her days thinking about coming out into the night with Bradshaw and so she wonders if he is not a savior after all but a demon, since she will keep coming to him even as she wants it less and less.

Finally, they stop. He begins to ask her again about leaving.

"Not yet, baby," she says. "Not now." She calls him baby because she wants to calm him, like a baby, and because she knows that this is how people talk to each other out in the world where her future lies.

"Well, holy shit, Lori, what are we waiting for?"

"Money," she says. "A plan or something."

"I got your plan right here," he says, taking her hand and placing it on the stiffening in his jeans.

She yanks it back and says, "I'm serious."

If they leave now, all she'll have is him.

Pink light is etching the hilltops when she returns. It is the coolest time of the day, the very early morning, and she yearns for sleep, wondering how she will steal slumber today. She crosses the lumpy, wormholed backyard and comes to her window. The house, the small Boise Cascade rancher in light blue and navy blue, is silent. Stepping between her mother's paper flower bushes, she uses a finger to open the slider, hoists herself into the bedroom, and takes up the screen and replaces it. When she turns at last she leaps and gasps, startled by the sight of her father sitting on her bed.

"I had not guessed you to be such a rebellious harlot," he whispers.

Loretta is frozen, her mind a storm.

"Can you say nothing? Can you not invent some lie?"

She is somehow not terrified, though she can't think what to say or do. Her father stands. He comes toward her slowly, his sore-hipped walk, rage purpling his face. Her mother watches from the doorway. Loretta could outrun them, overpower them, probably, but she does not. He seizes her ponytail and slaps her on the side of the head. A slow-motion slap. It hurts less than she expects. He is large bellied and top-heavy, ready to tip, and it is this that she seizes on as he swings his arm slowly again and again, each strike hurting less than she expects, each blow breaking through whatever is happening now and making a path forward, she thinks, toward her future. He is speaking to her, growling, grunting, but she doesn't hear him, and soon she can't feel his blows. The flesh on the side of her face fills and puffs, rising like dough. He is old, he is old, and she is on her way to somewhere else.

The day follows, still and silent. It is unspoken that she will remain in her room. Awaiting what, she does not know. Her father does not go to his brother's ranch, to care for the livestock they raise for the United Order. They do not go to church. Her father comes to put a lock on her bedroom door, a toolbox in his left hand and the lock in the other. He doesn't look at her, canting his head away as if from light of punishing brightness. He mutters and fumbles. Her mother comes in with toast and eggs on a tray, red eyed and pale in her housecoat. Loretta wonders if they have forgotten it is Fast Sunday.

She should have gone with Bradshaw. Should she have gone with Bradshaw? Which unknown path should she choose, and how should she choose it? All she knows is that while she waited for an answer, the paths closed down. Bradshaw won't even know why she will stop showing up.

Her father finishes and leaves. Then she hears him outside her bedroom window, doing something to the slider. Hours pass. Loretta, still clothed in her jeans and work blouse, lies on the bed. Everything has a thickened feel, as if all of life will be reduced now to this: a room, some food, and time. She falls asleep hard, and when she awakens to the clicking of the lock on her door, she is groggy and disoriented. She sits up to see her mother entering.

As she sits on the bed, Loretta notes that she is still in her housecoat, the pilled flannel plaid. Loretta doesn't speak. She has not said one word to them since climbing back in that window. She wonders if she will ever say another word to them. Her mother's face looks older than Loretta has ever seen it, collapsing like fruit that's turned. She speaks tentatively, tearfully.

"Your father has made a decision," she says.

The words come at Loretta as if through water.

"What you've done—" Her mother stops. "He feels—"

She smooths her trembling hands outward along her legs, as though brushing crumbs to the floor.

"We feel that you are in peril. That your soul is in peril."

Neither she nor her mother has anything to do with this. Neither has any part in it but to obey. Her father has agreed to place her with Brother Harder, with Dean Harder, the man who runs Zion's Harvest, the food supply, a righteous man, a faithful member of the Order, who is ready to add to his heavenly family.

"Place me?" Loretta asks.

"You know," her mother says, so quietly that Loretta can barely hear her over the sound of a sprinkler fanning the lawn outside. "You've known."

September 8, 1974

TWIN FALLS, IDAHO

A little mischief is good for the soul," Grandpa tells Jason, leveling a thick, crooked finger toward the road ahead, as if that were mischief right there, fat and smiling on Highway 10.

He says, "There's nothing so wrong with this."

The highway plunges as straight as a pipe through the desert and into the horizon. Inside the old Ford pickup, warm air flaps loudly past the open windows, drowning Grandpa's low growl.

He says, "Your dad never was much of a listener." Chuckles. Bits of whirling hay prickle Jason's ears. It's Grandpa's work truck—floor mats worn through, seats split and stained. A mess of empty parts boxes, hand tools, and baling twine is pressed into the cove where the dashboard meets the windshield. He is telling stories, and in the blast of the truck cab, Jason can hear only scraps of them, disconnected pieces.

Grandpa says, "By the time we got there, that Packard was all but sunk in the canal."

He is telling stories about Jason's father. The time five-year-old Dad was caught shoplifting butterscotch candies. How wildly he fought with his older brother, Dean, when they were teenagers. How he took the family car without permission once and drove it into the canal.

Jason doesn't understand this unloading of family lore. It seems significant. Announced. He looks at his grandfather—face and neck scorched with crosshatched sunburn and drooping ears red and thick as ham. He's saying something but the wind blasts it away. The land skims by, a flat plain broken with lava rock and spotted with sage. Thin sky, rags of cloud. The early coat of autumn shows its bright tans and shorn fields, the first scent of bitter dying in the air.

He says, "I thought your dad was going to bite his ear off."

On the seat between them, balanced atop a pair of hardened leather work gloves and two V-belts, is Grandpa's set of scriptures, zipped into a leather case: the Bible, the Book of Mormon, the Doctrine and Covenants, the Pearl of Great Price.

They are wearing their Sunday suits, but they are not going to church.

They pass through Wendell and onto Interstate 84, bound for Twin Falls. Grandpa pushes the Ford to seventy, seventy-five, and stops trying to shout above the noise. He is handsome, better looking than the rest of the Harder men: tall, neat, sun chapped. Beside him, Jason feels thin and soft. He hates the way he looks, his dense scrub of auburn hair, his freckles, his gangling knobbiness. Grandpa's dark gray hair is oiled, rows of comb tines as neat as a barley field, and his suit smells of Old Spice and perspiration.

An adrenal flutter passes through Jason, then comes again.

They are not going to church, though they have told Jason's parents they are driving to Rupert so Grandpa can speak to the ward there. It is a plausible lie—Grandpa is a high councillor and he often goes to speak at the Mormon wards around southern Idaho—but Jason is astonished that Grandpa told it.

"This oughta be something," Grandpa shouts.

Jason nods. He wants to say *More than something,* but then he doesn't want to say it anymore. This day wears a skin around it, a membrane that might burst with the wrong word. They are going to watch Evel Knievel jump the Snake River Canyon in a steam-powered rocket.

Grandpa says, "What do you think? He gonna make it?"

"Not sure."

"Well, Judas Priest. Of course you're not sure. But what do you *think*?"

Who could say? Jason sees every jump he can, worshipping at the Panasonic each time Evel Knievel climbs onto a motorcycle and flies into the air. It began when Jason watched the Caesars Palace crash on *Wide World of Sports* when he was nine: Evel Knievel bouncing off the ramp, body rippling and bike roaring after him like an angry bull. Surely that was a vision of death. But Evel Knievel survived and went out and did it again and again.

This jump today, though—rocket ship, canyon—this is something else.

"What do *you* think?" Jason shouts.

Grandpa laughs.

"He might just do it. He might. I mean, all's he's got to do is sit there and get shot a long way."

"That's all an astronaut does, too, but that don't make it easy."

This is something Evel Knievel himself has said, in one of the articles Jason razored from the *Times-News* and taped into his scrapbook.

"Well," Grandpa says, like he's not going to fight about something so silly with such a junior opponent. "It's not exactly the moon launch."

Jason wants to ask Grandpa about their lie. To pin down why it might be acceptable, given what he and the other elders always say in church: Thou shalt not bear false witness. Jason's parents had cited another commandment when they initially told him he couldn't go to the canyon jump: Thou shalt keep the Sabbath holy. He was pissed off for days, until Grandpa approached—in his shoulder-to-shoulder, gazing-at-the-horizon way one morning while Jason was feeding calves—and asked if he'd heard of this fella Knievel.

He could understand Grandpa wanting to see the jump. He used to race motorbikes in the desert and drive to Boise for the stock cars. The lie, though. Why would he do it, and then just wink about it? Jason wonders, though he thinks he's starting to know: the rules are the rules are the rules, the eternal truths unchanging, but inside the brotherhood of men are passageways and tangents, compartments and exceptions.

They leave the freeway and cut south through the desert. Soon the canyon comes into view, a great gray crack in the land. Crowds swarm on the far rim, and behind them a dome of trees cloisters a ranch house.

The bulge of the launchpad stands at the far end of the crowd, a mound of earth with a metal, spirelike ramp, flanked by TV trucks and a white trailer. Below, the cut basalt walls of the canyon turn back afternoon light at strange angles, silvered here, ashen there. The walls crumble downward into piles of boulder, and then stone, and then earthen slopes of weed and duff at the canyon bottom, split by the heavy, swirling Snake River.

They turn east, away from town, and enter a line of cars inching forward. Soon they hear the sound of a marching band—the harsh tin of the horns, the thump of drums. Grandpa guns the sputtering engine. To the left, in the hundred yards or so between the road and the canyon rim, crowds mill and clump; motorcycle engines whine. Beyond them is the ramp. Already, there is the Skycycle, the steam-powered rocket ship, cocked toward heaven, in red, white, and blue and with EVEL KNIEVEL spelled in golden letters and the numeral 1 on the tail fin.

"Skycycle," Grandpa scoffs. "Nothing cycle about it."

They come to the gate, and the man standing there with a bulging belly and hands full of bills gives their suits a second look. Grandpa hands him a fifty, then drives in, bumping across the field.

"Isn't this ridiculous?" he asks happily as he parks.

Ahead Jason can see tent tops. People have been camping here all week, partying, drinking, fighting, skinny-dipping in the canyon pools, frightening the citizens, and upsetting the chamber of commerce.

Grandpa waves his hand at the scene. "A lot of this is exactly the sort of thing you've got to avoid, now that you're getting older. Drinking and whatnot. Rowdy nonsense. But you can't hide yourself away. You've got to live in this world, and keep it off you somehow. But"—and here he pats the leather block of scriptures absently, with the heel of his fist—"you ought to have a little fun when you get a chance. This ought to be fun, don't you think?"

"I guess."

"You guess."

Jason blushes. He feels bashful before this strange day.

They take off their coats and ties, leave them folded on the seat, and head into the crowd. Grandpa veers toward the ramp in a stiff trot, winding past guys in trucker hats and cowboy boots, long-haired kids throwing Frisbees. The crowd tightens as they draw closer, but Grandpa slips through, making a way, until they are about thirty yards from the ramp. The scene looks like something out of *Billy Jack*—shirtless men with long hair and beards, blurry tattoos on their forearms; women in cutoffs with wild hair; the smell of cigarettes and marijuana. It's like nothing Jason has ever seen around here, where men wear their hair short and women wear their skirts long and most people think Richard Nixon got a raw deal. A couple of guys wearing leather vests carry girls on their shoulders, girls in tank tops without bras, and Jason studies the shift and jiggle inside those shirts. Someone calls, "Fuckin'-A!" and Jason feels embarrassed for Grandpa, imagining that he has not experienced such worldliness or that he may feel Jason has not, and Jason worries that his grandfather might regret bringing him here, might change his mind, but then the noise of a helicopter rises, a growing *thwuk* and drone, and a great cheer bursts forth, and it's too late to change anything because it's happening.

The copter tilts and drops toward the open desert on the other side of the satellite truck. TV cameras scan the crowd with their gleaming eyes. The marching band, in two shades of blue, blasts away as the copter settles, a skirt of dust billowing. Then he emerges: Evel Knievel, flanked by two frowning men in mirrored sunglasses and cowboy hats. All attention and energy fly to him, like metal shavings to a magnet. He passes along the outer edge of the crowd, dressed like anyone at the co-op on a Saturday—jeans, snap-button shirt, cowboy boots—but for a cane with a silver knob. He grasps the shaft and holds it up and the silver ball burns in the sun, channeling a pillar of light. The crowd cheers, shouts his name, and Evel Knievel and his entourage enter the trailer. The cheers fade, the band lurches to a stop.

"Well," Grandpa says. "There he is."

Jason can't stand the waiting but he doesn't want it to end. He feels a ludicrous faith, a sense that his future will be more like this day than anything he has experienced—all the holy Sabbaths, the constant prayer, milking and feeding, thresher and combine. The smell of cow shit rising from everything, all the time, even him, announcing his association with the lowest things. He wants to screw down this moment, keep it in front of him. The clamor, the humid press of bodies, the vault of pale sky, and the humming behind it all, the idling motor, gentle but irrevocable, the thing behind the thing, the thing behind everything, the thing that brings us what we get.

The bikers holler and pump their fists to the Rolling Stones, "Under My Thumb" now leaking from the speakers on the TV truck. The crowd is vulgar and filthy and unspeakably beautiful. In front of them, a man in worn jeans sways to the music. His shoulder-length hair is the color of hay, the hair of Jesus Christ, and he wears a red, white, and blue headband. A cigarette dangles from his lips, goes tight as he drags, dangles again. A brown-haired girl beside him in cutoffs and a threadbare Boise State T-shirt cranes her head. She says, "Is he gonna come out or what?" and the entranced hippie says, "Are you gonna shut the fuck up or what?" and Grandpa shifts back and forth, one foot to the other, irritated.

All this waiting, all this pressure. The Sabbath feel of stalled time. And then the trailer door bangs open, and Evel Knievel hops down, glorious in the white jumpsuit with red and blue bands of stars crossing his chest like bandoliers. White boots. Tall Elvis collar open at the neck, and swooping golden-brown hair. He waves again with the cane, and plunges toward the crowd, which parts before him. The loudspeaker narrates, crackling. He seems to float, though his gait is hitched. He passes just yards from Jason and Grandpa, and they feel the backward swell of bodies. Evel Knievel comes so close Jason can see the lines on his face and his quartzite stare, and his scanning eyes stop on Jason's. He thrusts the cane skyward, mouths something Jason cannot make out, and the gesture seems meant for him.

Evel Knievel comes closer, and Jason reaches toward him, as those around him are reaching. He waits for him to reach back, to put his hand into the striving mass of worshipping hands and to grab Jason's one hand.

Which Evel Knievel does.

A quick grasp, one shake. The bones in Evel Knievel's hand feel like a bundle of green branches. His eyes find Jason's again—"Thanks for coming, buddy"—and glide away. A shout goes up: "Good luck, Evel," and he says without turning, "It's in God's hands now."

He strides into the cleared space by the ramp. The helicopter rises, dangling a basket to Evel, his hands out to the crowd as though he is blessing them. He sits in the basket and ascends, rising to the rocket ship on the ramp. Information flies, static, from the speakers. Grandpa squeezes Jason's shoulder and Jason sees his face is wild, reverent, as he nods toward the Skycycle. *Don't miss a bit of it.* The rocket reminds Jason of something from *The Jetsons* but cooler, finned in the rear and sleekly pointed, with the name huge on the sides and colorful ads painted around it: Mack Trucks, Chuckles candy. Evel flashes a thumbs-up from the cockpit. The crew retreats, and the Skycycle sits alone. A hushed pause, and then a revving, a sharp whine rising and rising, pressure building to a flash—the Skycycle bursts up the ramp and off, rotating gracefully, screwing itself into the atmosphere. Jason feels pinned to the earth, and his stomach fills with slither. It is like prayer, like hope, and he'll make it, of course he will. Jason can see that in the arc of the rocket. It reigns over the earth and all its servants, a brilliant bullet aimed for the heart of the desert sky.

Something pops from the back of the Skycycle. What is it? The chute? A change ripples through the air. A pinprick in the pressure. The rocket slows, slows, and a white parachute drags behind it.

"Oh, my word," Grandpa says. "For heaven's sake."

The rocket noses downward, drifting now toward the bottom of the canyon like a bit of burst cattail above a canal. Jason feels slapped, flattened. People race to the canyon rim, but Grandpa and Jason stay back. An eddy of body odor and cigarette smoke swirls around them. Jason fears he might cry.

Later, they drive in silence for a long time. No stories. The day has reoriented itself earthward, toward the dull and the disappointing. The truck smells like dirt. Gray dust films Jason's shoes and socks. He stares at the delicate hem of rust lining the heater vents.

As they approach Wendell, Grandpa chuckles.

"That'll be good for him," he says. "Starting to believe his own bullshit."

January 13, 1975

SHORT CREEK, ARIZONA

Ruth brushes Loretta's hair like she's haltering a horse, yank, yank, hold. Loretta stiffens against each pull. In the dim, round mirror above the dresser, Loretta watches Ruth's face, the same determined, resigned look as always. Her dough-kneading face. A weak scent of paint lingers, and from downstairs comes the smell of Ruth's carob-and-date sheet cakes. Loretta's eyes drift downward, and then her head drifts downward, and Ruth places one palm firmly over each ear and sets Loretta's head roughly back in position. She divides Loretta's hair neatly, an ivory line along the scalp, and begins braiding, her mouth tightened into an insistent little fist.

"I think it's prettier long," Loretta says, because she cannot help herself.

Ruth turns a braid tightly against Loretta's scalp.

"It is a joyous day, Aunt Loretta," she says, "but a sacred one as well. It is important to remain modest before the Lord."

Something tries to rise from Loretta's stomach. *Aunt Loretta.* This is what the children will call her.

"I believe you know this," Ruth says. She looks into the mirror, into Loretta's eyes, without changing her expression. Loretta returns the look, mimicking Ruth's flatness. At first, Loretta thought Ruth's expression revealed anger or frustration, but she has come to see that Ruth has merely emptied herself and adopted the aspect of duty in all things. Even with her children. Even the night she and Dean had come to the home of Loretta's parents, and they had all knelt in prayer on the porch. "The Lord has given me a testimony of the righteousness of our choice," Ruth had said, her face blank. "I know that we will be exalted in the celestial kingdom." As if she had willed herself out of herself. Dean had blushed, his enormous ears luminous with blood, and though Loretta hardly knew him, and though she was just fifteen, she could see in his rabbity eyes that it wasn't the celestial kingdom he had on his mind.

The room's walls are bare and clean, the late morning sun somewhere outside the window's brightening rectangle. Bed, dresser, carpet of bronze. Loretta has a hard time seeing this as her room, this empty corner of this barnlike house. She has all that is hers packed into a single shoebox in the back of the closet: two Christmas ornaments that were her grandmother's, a silver star with red piping and a snowflake twinkling with glitter; a diary she wrote in seventeen times when she was eleven, including a page listing the qualities of "The man I will mary"; three photographs with worn, curled edges and hazy yellow orbs shadowing the images—her parents holding her as an infant, Loretta standing in a dress at three or four and squinting somewhere out of frame, and a Border collie they'd had as a child, snout buried in the lawn, digging; a greeting card with a picture of a stork and a silver dollar taped inside; two pewter rings and a set of earrings with tiny emerald cut-glass gems, still in the paper backing; a small leather pouch with arrowheads and rock chips she collected in the desert; and an embroidered handkerchief her mother made that reads *Loretta Sara Buckton* above her date of birth, *May 21, 1959*.

Nothing else, anywhere, is hers.

Ruth finishes weaving a braided crown around Loretta's head, which gathers into a single braid down her back. Ruth runs her hands over Loretta's hair, over her dress, smelling of heat and borax. She looks Loretta over, everywhere but her eyes. Picks a thread from her shoulder. Ruth wears the same white dress as Loretta, the starched white cotton, boxy bosom, lacelike moth-holed embroidery at the collar, wrists, and ankle-length hem.

Ruth says, "I'll leave you to pray."

They stand. She takes Loretta by the shoulders and looks into her eyes like she's trying to ram something into her brain. How old is Ruth? Forty? Older? She has seven children, and often seems like their grandmother. She is thin, dry skinned, mouth sketched in faint wrinkles. The sisters whisper about her close-cropped hair, call it mannish, rebellious. In this, she is like Dean, who wears a beard though the brothers discourage it. *Sister wife*, Loretta thinks, and the phrase lands in her mind with a false weight, words she's heard all her life without recognizing their deep contradictions.

Loretta will never call Ruth "Sister," but she sees in her the way to do this: be stronger than the thing against you.

"We will raise up a glorious seed unto the Lord," Ruth says, and encircles Loretta in a fencelike hug, barely touching. Loretta insists to herself that it is not true. *I will not raise any seed.* She will hold herself inside herself, away from everyone.

"Welcome to our family," Ruth whispers over Loretta's shoulder, in a voice that could not possibly be less welcoming. "Our eternal family."

They await Uncle Elden, the prophet. The living room is insistently plain, with beige carpet and two long sofas, parallel and facing, and two love seats boxing them in, all upholstered in navy blue cloth patterned with small white flowers. The whole place seems uninhabited, Loretta thinks, though Dean and Ruth and the kids have lived there for going on three years. When the Harders first moved to this huge new house on the north edge of town, about a hundred yards from the Utah border, it had started talk even then that Dean would take a new wife.

Loretta's father and mother sit on a sofa, deferential to the day's events. She feels her mother's eyes seeking hers. Her father does not look at her, she knows. He made all the arrangements without her, including Dean's promise to wait until she turns sixteen before consummating their union. It sickens her, how far outside of it all she stood.

Loretta, Ruth, and Dean stand between the sofas, in front of the fireplace, and Ruth holds a small pillow at her waist, as if she were preserving a treasure. Loretta knows it is the three-strand ring of silver she will wear on the third finger of her left hand. The children line up tallest to shortest. Samuel, the oldest at thirteen, scowls, a fat boil behind one ear. He wears a black suit and white shirt buttoned to the collar, just as seven-year-old Dean Jr. does down the line. The girls just younger than Samuel, Ruth and Elizabeth, look like miniature sister wives, in floor-length cotton dresses and long braids. Even four-year-old Sarah and five-year-old Janeen wear long white dresses. Only Benjamin, the toddler, is clothed like a child, in knee-length black shorts and a short-sleeved white pull-over. He fidgets, but holds his face firm, lips pressed with comical intensity, as though he fears some noise will burst forth. He is her favorite, Benjamin. She catches his eye and smiles, and he returns the briefest furtive grin.

The prophet arrives at last, entering hunched and slow on the arm of his burly son. He aims a gray, murmuring smile toward them. One milky eye wanders. He is a walnut of a man—tiny and parched and failing and skeletal—and his nearness to death only adds to his authority. They assemble, and Uncle Elden stands in front, holding his knotty, trembling hands.

Ruth and Loretta flank Dean, and the prophet rasps about exaltation and salvation and obedience to the Lord's sacred principle of plural marriage. He speaks in a soft monotone, pausing often as if to rest. "It is there, brothers and sisters," he says, "in Genesis. Right from the beginning. Lamech and Esau and . . . Moses and Jacob. All living . . . in the Principle."

The prophet continues, speaking of the forsaken commandments and the world's abuse of the true Saints. "The government of this United . . . States has persecuted this priesthood. The Mormon Church itself has per—" A fit of quiet coughing stops him. His son hands him a handkerchief, and when Uncle Elden takes it from his mouth a strand of saliva catches the light. "Has persecuted this priesthood," he whispers.

His voice affects Loretta like a drug, a lulling sense of the sacred that goes deeper than her brain and whispers that she is wrong, that this is divine after all. Uncle Elden talks about the "the raid of '53," when Satan sent the federal agents to arrest the men of Short Creek and carry away the women and children, and the constant threat of the next assault from the enemies of righteousness. "No righteous people . . . live without remembering the sacrifices of their fathers."

In her head, Loretta flies to her worldly future. There, she wears pants with wide bottoms, and colorful blouses with short sleeves—T-shirts, even—and her hair hangs long and loose, and she paints her eyes with mascara. Every whorish thing. She wishes she could show her future self to her father, watch him burn. Her Tussy future, pink and bold. This future could be anywhere else and she will have a car, one of the sleek ones in the magazines, maybe the pink Mustang in the Tussy ad, and she will listen to rock music and watch television, and there is no Dean or Ruth, of course, no Uncle Elden, but there is no Bradshaw, either, or any man. Or rather, there is a man, but he is no man she has ever known. He is a warm, anonymous shape, and he exerts no force.

Uncle Elden makes a rattling sound in his throat, and continues. Loretta thinks that she'll have to learn the names of cars and which ones she likes so in her future she'll be able to choose the best one, the car that will show the world that she is free, the car that will announce that she is this kind of person and not that kind of person. The prophet mentions the veil of heaven, and now they all engage in a charade in which Dean and Ruth stand on one side of a curtain held aloft by Loretta's parents, and Dean reaches through the veil for Loretta and pulls her through, pulls her to them, because this is how she will go to heaven, drawn there by Dean and Ruth.

Later, Dean comes to Loretta's room, the anonymous room that never quite warms up against the desert cold. He shuts the door, sits beside her on the bed, holds his knees in his hands. It comes off of him in waves, how badly he wants to move toward her. Thick veins crawl along the backs of his hands, and he squeezes his knees.

"I have promised your father, little sister," he says, in a quiet voice. "But oh, you are a sore temptation."

Her breathing stops. A gust fills her lungs. Loretta feels overtaken, though there is nothing surprising here. This has been plummeting toward her, an enormous meteor pulsing down from heaven, a giant, inevitable stone, and she has averted her eyes and pretended it was not there. This must be how life works, she thinks—the lull of boredom and reverence dulling your mind for catastrophe.

Somewhere in the night, two dogs burst into vicious barking and fall quiet.

"I do believe it would be best for us to wait," Dean says.

He speaks so carefully. As though he were trying to talk her out of something. She takes him in from the corner of her eye: black wool suit, faded along the cuffs and knees, and polished black brogues. A not-unpleasant odor of flesh and cloth. His beard, the combed stubble of brown and red and white, and the tiny chapped areas on his bony cheeks, like dots of rouge on a doll.

She reminds herself: It is not lawful. It counts only if you believe it, and she will not believe it.

"Do you not agree?" he asks.

He places his hand on hers, his nails split and cloudy. Squeezes gently. He is younger than her father, but more worn. Taller. Leaner. Stronger. She wonders where Ruth is now, and what Ruth is thinking. Whether Ruth believes he will honor his promise.

"We are called to raise a righteous seed unto the Lord," he says. "It is the most sacred principle."

She wishes she could laugh, because there is something insane in this language, but she might never laugh again. He leans and whispers damply in her ear, a single brittle hair in his mustache tickling her: "You are trembling, little sister."

He grasps her thigh above the knee and squeezes. His hand is massive. A line of sweat trickles from under Loretta's hair, streaks down her back.

"I am as well," he whispers.

His hand gains one inch on her thigh and squeezes again, and she knows now that ignoring the meteor has not made it go away, and that it is worse than she feared, this fate, this stone, because she feels a tingle—a small, repulsive flutter—between her legs. His hand nearly encloses her thigh, and he holds firmly, and though she finds him ugly and repellent, an oaf, she wants to squirm against that tingle, to press against it.

Dean exhales like a stamping horse and removes his hand.

"This is hard, little sister, so very hard," he says. "But we will wait."

He speaks as though he were denying her. As though he, through his righteousness and self-control, were saving them from her.

"You will see that it is better this way."

He stands, and does not bother to hide the sideways prong under his black wool pants. Her eyes sting, and weakness floods her, runs into her veins and bones and pores and hair.

"Welcome to our family, Loretta," he says. "We are walking in the Lord's true light."

He places his hand on her head, and stands there. Showing it. She blinks madly.

Dean takes her by the chin and says, "Your father has told me about your nighttime excursions."

He must feel her chin shuddering.

"Those will end now, of course."

She nods.

"I would like to hear you say it."

She tries three times to get the word out, that word, *yes,* and when she does everything collapses. Tears scald her face and she gasps and coughs. He strokes her head, hair damp at the roots. She hates to cry.

"Shh, little sister," he says. "It's all right."

He leaves, and she lies there shaking, curled on her side on the unfamiliar bed, on the quilt Ruth made from patches of old denim dotted with tiny rabbit ears of white yarn, and she lies there a long time, an eternity, staring at the wall, thinking, *Bradshaw was right, Bradshaw was right,* until she gathers herself, becomes herself again, and makes herself a promise that she will do more than simply get away.

EVEL KNIEVEL ADDRESSES
AN ADORING NATION

First thing we jumped was pretty much nothing, a little hillock of dirt out there in the flats around Butte, a weedy little lump. We were tooling along on the old man's Super Hawk, that four-stroke piece of shit with the brittle fork, when something or someone urged our hand toward the bump. We have thought long on this, America, and believe it is not too much to suggest the presence of the divine.

We flew. Fuckin'-A flew.

Figure between 1.8 and 2.3 seconds airborne—call it 2. Two seconds of flying. Two seconds of everything you thought life could not be. So amazing. So exhilarating. Also, so incredibly fucked up: you live and live and live, and it all comes down to a tiny flash, a speeding moment that is gone so fast you can't believe it. All you can ever do is remember it and want it back. Still, those two seconds, holy shit: the warm blood of our heart expanded and sped through us in a way it never did again, though we chased it ever since, chased and chased it, all over the planet, from that lowly little bump outside Butte to the massive sea of cunt and worship we swam in for so long.

We dumped the bike, of course. We were fifteen. Our parents

were sad and old and gone to other places, Grandpa coughing up black shit all day long, smelling like piss and whiskey, and Grandma ignoring everything, just pretending, pretending, pretending, and we loved to take out that bike of Grandpa's, God, it was beautiful then, though we think of it now as an utter piece of shit. We'd take it and ride it from the house up in the warren of roads below the mine and the toxic tailing pond where geese died every winter, where they flew to their deaths believing in a safe landing, and we'd roar back down, below the mountains and the statue of Jesus Christ blessing the whole Summit Valley and we would head out into the flats and just roar.

That day, we flew for two seconds, and we found our place—the place we will always leave for. That little dent in the atmosphere that is shaped like us. We landed on the front tire, all wrong, and the bike squirreled out and we dumped it, scraped hell out of a shoulder and a hip, and put a big hairy scuff on the tank. Grandpa saw it that night when he came home stinking from the M&M, and he kicked open the door to our room and starting going off, Bobby this and Bobby that. Bobby, Bobby—the name that never named us. When he took hold of our arm we grabbed him back, by the front of the shirt, like some movie hero of olden day, and shoved him into the wall, and saw the news on his face: we were not who he thought we were at all.

Ruth checks the forms while Samuel and Loretta organize the orders, hauling the heavy square buckets from the pallets and stacking them near the garage door, sacks slumped at the bases. It is early—they rise at five, and Ruth returns to Loretta's door in two minutes if she's not up—and their breath clouds in the frigid yellow light. It's a huge garage, big enough for two cars, with a concrete floor and unpainted drywall, and pallets full of wheat, barley, flour, oats, powdered milk.

Samuel heaves a third bucket of brown rice onto a stack, and heads back to the pallet as Loretta comes by with a sack of oats.

Ruth says, "One more milk there."

Samuel rolls his eyes at Loretta, says, "Another one?" under his breath. Ruth shoots him a stern look.

"It's for the nursing home in Cedar," she says. This is new, Loretta thinks, a customer that isn't a family with twenty kids, but a big client, a business. Another sign, no doubt, of the blessings that have come their way since they began living in the Principle.

"A nursing home?" she asks.

"A nursing home," Ruth says, then points her hand-whittled inch of pencil at a sack of oats. "That's supposed to be a twenty, not a ten."

Out of everything Loretta had expected and feared about this life, she had not foreseen the way Zion's Harvest Bulk Foods would dominate every day. It sets the clock of the household—preparing deliveries in the morning, organizing inventory in the afternoon, and leaving the strange, midday slack times when Ruth announces Silent Scripture Hour and assigns a book of the Bible or the Book of Mormon, the Pearl of Great Price or the Doctrine and Covenants. The littlest children sit quietly with the Book of Mormon coloring books, but even Elizabeth and Dean Jr.—nine and seven years old—are expected to spend the hour reading scripture, running their index fingers under the tiny text. "And if ye shall say there is no law, ye shall also say there is no sin." Loretta finds this the worst part of any day, the clearest reminder that no corner of her life is her own.

The new driver will arrive at seven. The last man quit in January, and Dean says he's too busy to make the deliveries and collect payments himself, but Loretta can't see how. He leaves in his big truck after breakfast, and returns right at dinner; Ruth says he's finding customers, glad-handing, building the business, doing everything important that goes unseen. Maybe it's working. Sales are up. Dean doubled the amount he donated to the United Order in December over November. Everyone needs their "year's supply," their backup against disaster or the last days, but everyone's supply is being constantly eroded by their huge, ravenous families. Nobody can keep up. The business had always prospered, but once Dean got signed up to accept food stamps, Zion's Harvest boomed.

A few weeks earlier, at dinner, when Dean mentioned that the driver had left, Loretta had volunteered to make the deliveries herself. Ruth frowned at her over the table. The children stopped eating.

"What?" Loretta asked, feeling that she had smacked into another taboo though she wasn't certain what it was. They were everywhere.

Dean paused, a paste of half-chewed food in his mouth.

"We need you here," he said at last.

They finish the stacks, Samuel and Loretta teaming up on the last of the sixty-pounders while Ruth scans her list. When she's satisfied, she tapes an invoice to each tower of food. Inside, the girls make oatmeal, the same bland gruel that opens every bland day, with only honey and powdered milk because Ruth says processed sugar is how Lucifer gives you cancer. She is obsessed with cancer and the things that she believes causes it: sugar, too much meat, sin. Dean is upstairs, praying and studying scripture. He is on the Council of Elders now, as he frequently mentions.

Today there are eight orders: the Jordan Seniors get wheat, rice, oats, powdered milk, brown sugar, the deluxe spice mix; the Johnsons get puffed-rice cereal, powdered milk, dried onion seasoning, and the soup sampler; the Hales get one of everything and two of some, what with Brother Hale's four wives and thirty-four children; the Millers are trying the meatless bulgur mix; the wardhouse will get the weekly complete batch that Ruth has labeled "Manna"—every item on the inventory. And then there are the smaller orders, the odds and ends.

Later today and tomorrow morning, they'll prepare the largest order yet: three Mannas for the county jail. A new annual contract. Sometimes Dean thanks the Lord for the contract when he prays.

Loretta, Samuel, and Ruth go in and eat that horse food. In her mind, Loretta flees to her future, where breakfast will be a delicious indulgence, a feast of fruits and jams and sugar, spoonfuls of cancery sweetness. Then they hear car wheels on gravel, the new driver, and they go into the garage and Ruth rolls up the door and Loretta looks outside and stops breathing because there he is, leaning against the truck, foot crossed at the ankle, thumb in his belt loop. That bursting, vicious smile. Those pale eyes. Bradshaw.

When Loretta was eleven, her mother gave her a journal for her birthday. That girl wrote, "I love the Lord more than anything, except for Momma and Dad, and maybe it's the same for all three of them, and after that my brothers and sisters, Tommy first." Tommy, the oldest, who left and never contacts the family anymore. Did she love the Lord that much? Or did she just know to say the words? "When I sing the hims at church I feel the spirit inside me. My favorite is Onward Christian Soljer and Til We Meet Again." She would hum the hymns to herself throughout the day, that girl would. Now she finds them gloomy.

Sometimes at night, unable to sleep, Loretta goes through her box of things. Everything that is hers—everything that is her—is tiny and fading. It is all she brought from home, apart from clothes and a set of art paper and charcoal pencils, a birthday gift from her father. Only once has she ever tried to draw something: half a cat, so misshapen that she gave up. The last thing she does when she inventories the items in the box—the photographs of her infant self and long-dead dog, the Christmas ornaments, the arrowheads—is read her diary, and the last entry in the diary, the last of seventeen for reasons she can no longer remember, is her listing of the qualities she wanted in "the man I mary: rigteous, kind, handsome, strong, good singer, hero, all to myself!!!!"

Bradshaw grins, cocks his jaw, says, "Hidy, folks. I'm Rex Baker. Guess I'm your new driver."

Loretta's legs ripple. Her mind fills with chaotic flutter. *Rex Baker?* Ruth nods, and calls the children to help, and they all come, even Benjamin, toddling underfoot. Ruth looks over the piles of food, doing calculations in her mind. Bradshaw shoots Loretta a wink. She feels as if she will collapse.

Taking down the tailgate on the truck, Bradshaw asks, "What's your-alls' names?"

Ruth says, "Don't worry about that, Mr. Baker."

"All right, okay, all right." He holds up his hands like he's under arrest. "Sorry, ma'am. Just trying to be sociable."

"That's fine."

"I got family down with the LeBarons, you know. Down Mexico. I'm friendly."

Ruth nods, rebuffs his attempt at conspiracy, but Loretta knows he won't stop trying. She knows what he's saying is false, at least if what he told her before is true, that he grew up in Cedar City, always near but never part of this world in Short Creek, let alone Ervil LeBaron's followers down in Mexico. They were the guns and Revelation gang, the truest of the true believers, hungry for apocalypse.

"I'm not some outsider," he says. Loretta has a sudden image of him standing outside a window, a lighted window on the darkest night, looking in. *Rex Baker.* She will have to remember to call him Baker.

It is her night. Dean comes in around eight while she pretends to read the Book of Mormon. His feet are bare and white, sleeves rolled to the biceps. She knows he has washed his feet and hands, soaped his forearms, and washed his face and neck. He smiles wearily at her, head bowed, and sinks into the rocking chair. His knees angle outward like elbows, and he takes his jaw in one hand and presses anxiously.

"The new man seems acceptable," he says in his slow baritone. "Managed the deliveries. Very acceptable."

"Oh?" she answers, pretending to be drawn back toward a scripture she is not yet finished absorbing. "Good."

"Yes, he's fine."

Since the night of their wedding, Dean has not touched her when he visits her room two nights a week. "We are partners now, you and I," he sometimes says. "Partners in all ways." He hasn't touched her or made any mention of his promise, or any suggestion about his desire. He has sat in the rocking chair and rubbed his knuckles methodically, moving from knuckle to knuckle, finger to finger, and talked about whatever is on his mind or made simple, vacant observations. Though he asks for her opinions, she says little, provides the kind of agreement he is seeking and hides inside herself. She can tell he is proud of his self-restraint and imagines it will be rewarded.

He stretches his legs and yawns.

"I'm afraid I have stumbled into some hardship with the Elders," he says. "A kind of a bind."

He waits. Loretta closes her book, asks, "What is it?"

"They are asking more from me than I feel is proper. They are asking more from me than I believe the Law of Consecration requires."

The Law of Consecration. Uncle Elden speaks of it constantly from the pulpit, as he does the Law of Chastity, which governs times of sexual relations, and the Law of Sarah, which allows wives the right to refuse sister wives. The Law of Consecration is fundamental to their view that they are different here, better here, more righteous here—everyone shares all of their wealth with the Elders, who divide and return it to families as needed. We are a community of God, Uncle Elden says, and not a community of man's desires.

"They are asking me to turn over everything from Zion's Harvest," Dean says, a thin note of complaint in his voice. "They are demanding to see my accounts."

Loretta stumbles in her mind: Isn't that the law of the community? Isn't Dean an elder of the community?

"I am now turning over twice the tithe I was before you and I were joined," he said. "I am struggling in my soul, little sister, to understand what more I am required to give."

"Aren't you to give all?"

"They say I am." He works at a back tooth with his tongue, and then says in a rising, rapid voice, "Is it only avarice that might make me ask why that is? Is there no point at which I have contributed my share, more than my share, far more than my share, even, and might keep the remainder without being accused of a lack of righteousness?"

He stops as though embarrassed to have revealed himself so. Loretta doesn't know what to say. She had not expected this. Dean's expanding prosperity—his marriage to her, the growth of Zion's

45

Harvest, his selection to the Council of Elders—had seemed, in and of itself, a time of great fortune for him. A windfall of esteem and authority. And yet he seems now, rubbing his temples and breathing deeply through his nose, like a man sunk in trouble and misunderstanding. He has been buying gold, she knows, because he distrusts paper money. He buys only one-ounce golden eagles, and he's particular about this, quoting Old Testament verses about not having "diverse weights" in your bag, about having a "perfect and just weight." He is not turning the gold over to the brethren. Not tithing it. He's keeping it.

"It seems like," she says slowly, "there *should* be a reward," and Dean sits up in his chair.

"It seems so to me as well," he says. "Very much so. It is not that I do not want to provide to the community, or share the wealth. It is not, I hope, out of mere vanity or love of filthy lucre that I wonder this. I have struggled in my soul, Loretta, and prayed long over this. I do not wish to have anything the Lord does not intend for me to have."

He leans forward in the rocking chair, plants his elbows on his knees. Narrows his eyes, lowers his voice, and looks at her with an intensity he saves for times of greatest spiritual import—those moments when he believes he is being heeded, at the pulpit or in prayer, and a look of such gravity comes over him, such self-seriousness, such consciousness of demeanor, that it betrays his greatest vulnerability: his sense of himself as a righteous man.

He says, "I believe the Lord wants me to retain some of the fruits of my prosperity for my family."

Loretta nods. Of course He does. The only question was how Dean would work his mind around it. She thinks of his office, with the locked drawers and file cabinets. She thinks of how he hides away the keys to the truck and the van and the station wagon, as if they were precious treasure. She thinks of how he doles out money to Loretta or the kids—not Ruth, Ruth is trusted—by going into his office and shutting the door, and returning with cash folded in his hand. She thinks of the thick dowel that had been lodged against the sliding window in her bedroom. Dean had cut the wood to size, and climbed a ladder to her second-story window and put it there, so even on the hottest days she cannot slide it open. She thinks of the gold. A bag of gold like in a fairy tale. She thinks of taking that gold away from him, and keeping it for herself.

"Would the Lord not want to bless me for this? To bless us?" Dean says.

"He would, Dean. Yes. He would want us all to be blessed."

Jason and his friend Boyd sift strychnine powder into the rolled barley, wearing gloves and paper masks. Like surgeons on TV, Jason thinks. The odors of dust and oil, wood and machine, hang thickly in the shed. Outside it is as hot as August, and the jackrabbits are spreading across the desert like insects. They've been out for weeks now, bounding and skimming through the sage, chasing, stopping, and popping one another with their forepaws like boxers, the females fighting off the males, the males insane with lust.

"Mad as hares," Jason's mom told him a few weeks earlier as they watched them zipping about the haystack by the dairy barn. "That's where that comes from."

Jason said, sarcastically, "That's where what comes from?" His parents were so ridiculous. He thought he was going to choke on it—his ridiculous parents, and their ridiculous church, and this ridiculous farm, and this ridiculous town.

"Rabbit murder," Jason says now as he hefts the final sack onto the trailer. "Raise this stupid animal, kill that stupid animal, milk the other stupid animal, poison this stupid animal."

He hacks a dusty loogie and spits it into the dirt, where it coils and darkens like a worm. He thinks the jacks are kind of cool.

"I love rabbit murder," Boyd says. He wants to argue about every single thing lately. "I wish I could murder rabbits all the time."

It is late Saturday afternoon. Jason had hoped to take the LeBaron to Twin Falls, maybe stay and see *Jaws,* but instead his father gave him this to do. Extra chores every weekend. His punishment for spending his mission money on eight-track tapes and hamburgers at the Oh-So-Good Inn and gas for dragging Main. It's been more than a month since his mom found the stack of eight-tracks in his closet—Bowie and BTO, Sweet and the Doobie Brothers—and then, one question leading to another, discovering that he had spent most of the money in his passbook account. Money he'd earned raising and selling livestock at the FFA sales at the county fair. He was supposed to be saving for his two-year mission, the mission to convert the heathens that all Mormon boys were assigned to at age nineteen. Jason already knew he was not going on a mission, but his parents didn't, not yet, and they flipped out when they found out about the money. Now every time he asks if he can go somewhere, his father assigns him a chore instead. Like poisoning jackrabbits.

"Those little fuckers are gonna get it good," Boyd says, grinning behind his mask.

Jason's father says they'll try the poison first, and if it doesn't work, they'll move on to other methods—traps, arsenic, hunting parties. "This works best," his father had said, "but it works better on everything else, too. Dogs. Birds. Pretty soon you're killing everything just to kill one thing."

Everyone is trying to keep the jacks out of gardens and crops, and no one is succeeding. Fences. Blood meal in the gardens. Heading out to the desert at night with flashlights and rifles: spotlighting. The rabbits just keep coming.

Boyd swings his heavy black bangs out of his eyes and says, "Bleed to death right out their little rabbity asses."

"Nice," Jason says. "Nature boy."

Boyd is half Shoshone, and he's gotten political. "I am waking up to my heritage," he sometimes says, in a mock-serious tone that does not mean he isn't serious. Every day, it seems, he is incensed about some new cause: the American Indian Movement, My Lai, Pine Ridge, the Watergate trials. Boyd wants to free Leonard Peltier. He rails about The Man, and the conspiracy to move the Negroes out of the inner city. Jason has never heard anything like it. His upbringing has been a warm, constant bath of family, faith, and the GOP. He loves to listen to Boyd, as baffling as it is. It makes him feel like an outlaw.

They hitch the trailer to the tractor. Jason drives out onto the county road, Boyd sitting on the wheel well, and down the quarter mile to Grandpa's place, the small brick square in the middle of a weedy lawn that peters out at the edges. A truck passes and honks. Jason turns in and follows the dirt road out into the fields. They bump along for fifteen minutes until they reach the southern border of the 2,345 Harder acres, where they begin to trace the outline of the family's land with poison.

Jason drives slowly while Boyd shakes out a trail of barley, marking the black soil like chalk on a baseball field. The tractor grinds and vibrates, stinking of burning oil. Only winter wheat is planted this early, but Grandpa said if they start now, maybe they can kill enough jacks to scare away the rest before everything starts growing. They stop at sunset and look out over the desert running west. The fat sun touches the serrated horizon, shadows veer toward them, and dark smudges scoot across the desert.

"Here, bunny, bunny, bunny," Boyd says.

By the time they return to Grandpa's, empty trailer banging, the night glows with spectral pale dust. Boyd is whistling Zeppelin— "Going to California," far out of tune—and Jason hears a sound he can't quite identify. A wheezing or hacking. And then he sees his grandfather on all fours on the lawn.

"Holy shit," Boyd says, and hops off the wheel well. As Jason kills the tractor motor, he hears his grandfather heaving, choking, and when he turns toward them, Jason is stunned at the fear on Grandpa's face: taut, white eyed. It roots him to his seat until Boyd barks: "Hey!"

They get Grandpa into his truck, propped between them, and Jason drives. Grandpa's breathing slows, becomes less frantic.

Boyd says, "You doing okay there, Mr. Harder?"

He nods.

"Can't," he whispers, "catch my breath."

"No kidding," Boyd says, and Jason says, "Don't be a smart-ass."

Grandpa chuckles. Coughs and coughs.

"Sorry," Boyd says, and he does actually sound sorry for once.

Grandpa whispers, "No, no. *Do* be a smart-ass." Chuckles and coughs.

They come to the edge of town. On a small rise to the right is the abandoned tuberculosis hospital, like a decrepit castle. Highway 10 becomes Main Street, and Jason barely slows as they pass the Bowl-A-Rama's neon sign, the bright island of fluorescence at the Oh-So-Good Inn, the Safeway and the Mormon church, the farm implement dealership and the state school for the deaf and blind. They turn east, drive four blocks, and stop at the small one-story brick hospital. Gooding Memorial.

They help him in and he is taken away, and they are left to sit in the plastic chairs under buzzing tubes of light. Jason feels like there must be many things for him to do or say, but he can't imagine what the first one should be.

Boyd says, "Don't call your folks or anything."

Jason has never seen his grandfather in a position of submission or need. Everywhere they go, his grandfather is greeted as a leader, a patriarch, a man to be depended on. A lot of people seem to think he's kinder than he is, but even this contributes to Jason's sense of his authority. He'd kick a dog in a second, scold someone else's child. Jason once saw him fire a hired man for taking jars of milk. Everyone knew he took milk. It was expected, even. But one day, Grandpa saw Bart bring an empty jug from his pickup truck, fill it from the tank in the barn, and carry it back out again. Grandpa cleared his throat and scratched angrily at the back of his hand. He walked over to Bart and barked, "What's my son owe ya?"

Jason felt bad for Bart, but not so bad as to erase his admiration for his grandfather. It was a mean thing to do, but it wasn't weak. That was a few months before the Evel Knievel jump. Jason had asked his parents for permission to go, and his mom had said no, had said, "Let's keep the Sabbath holy." His parents had come to think his interest in "worldly" things—in daredevils and rock music and novels about hobbits and the loose and supposedly willing girls of Wendell—was getting out of control. Infuriated, Jason thought, *When I leave, I will engage all manner of wickedness on Sundays.* But that's not what he said. What he said was "Okay." And then his grandfather had stepped in and shown him what you do when you want to do something. You do it.

That's when he started spending his mission money.

As far as Jason knew, Grandpa had never told anyone about the day they went to see Evel Knievel, and he never brought it up again—though if he gave Jason a wink during a family dinner, Jason felt their secret was being invoked. The only person Jason ever told was Boyd, and he regretted it. Before the jump, Boyd had been merely dismissive of Evel Knievel as a showboater and fool. After the canyon jump, he was merciless.

"Twenty-five bucks," he scoffed. "You should have just burned that money."

"It wasn't my money."

"It's just so hilarious. I about shit myself."

"As usual."

Jason was whispering, standing in the kitchen with the long green phone cord wrapped around his arm. His mom walked in, set a potted plant in the sink, and Jason moved around the half wall into the living room.

"Were you laughing pretty hard?" Boyd asked. "I bet you were laughing your ass off."

Jason had not been not laughing his ass off. He had felt what happened as a nauseating throb below the sternum. There had been an instant that day when he had come to a conclusion: Evel Knievel would clear the canyon. This faith thrived briefly, and it was as wrong as could be. Because Jason had a lifetime of practice in forcing meaning onto events—attaching morals to stories, locating God's hand in the smallest events—he decided this had identified something about him, something large and definitive and fundamental. A failure to see correctly.

Jason's parents arrive, and they stop at the edge of the waiting area—not even a room, just a space off a hallway, defined by a thin rug and two vinyl-covered couches. His father clears his throat. "So?"

"Not sure," Jason says. "They've got him in there doing something or other. They said someone would be out to let us know what's happening, but it's been about an hour."

His parents stand behind the couch, as though they might not be staying. Jason's father is tall and lean, but gone slumpy in the middle and always blushing. Jason's mother is shorter, pretty at a distance and plain up close: something practical and taciturn in her short brown hair and bobbed nose, her splintery hazel eyes.

They sit down, and Jason's mother peppers him with questions: How had they found him? How bad was his breathing? Did he say anything about what happened? Did the doctors act concerned?

"I'd like to lead us in a prayer," Jason's father says.

Jason's neck crawls with embarrassment, because of Boyd and because they are sitting here where anyone might just come walking up. But he bows his head and folds his arms.

"Our Father in Heaven," his father begins, in the bass drone that sounds as though each word were being tugged from a posthole. "We come before you this evening to ask that you look after our father and grandfather, to ask you to protect him in his time of need." Jason cuts a look to Boyd, smirking. "We ask that you will bless him with the strength to fight his infirmities, and we ask that you help us stay strong to provide him the help he may need, our Father who art in heaven, to do for him, at this time in his life, as he has done for so many in his own life. In the name of Jesus Christ, amen."

With every amen lately, Jason feels a small, hollow place where something else used to be. He's been coming unstuck from the church for months, questioning, doubting, and bored. Three hours of church on Sundays, Family Home Evening on Mondays, youth group on Wednesdays, prayer five million times a day. He has simply taken the measure of that life, of the people in the ward, and decided he doesn't want it. He wanted to be different, and he wanted other people to know he was different, and by the time he recognized this, he already was different.

He was baptized at age eight. He often thinks of that day—the gleaming font and the scratchy, laundered feel of the baptismal garment, a terry-cloth coverall. The font was a huge tub sunk in the floor in a small room at the wardhouse. Family and friends filled the folding chairs. After a prayer and scripture readings by the bishop, Jason went to the edge of the font, at the top of a set of tiled stairs that sank into the water. Dad waited below, waist deep, hands folded before him and the wrists of the garment dampened darkly. He was solemn, unsmiling, and yet Jason knew it was a joyful moment for him. As Jason stepped down, he had the sensation that people were rising above him—Mom in the front row, tears in her eyes, Aunt Bonnie and Jenna and their families, friends from the ward. Dad read the prayer slowly, then laid Jason back into the cool, chlorinated water. When he emerged, he felt like a sleek animal, a cheetah or a puma, fast and glistening. Stepping out, though, he felt the garment cling heavily, and he slopped back to the changing room, where the day resolved itself in the most ordinary sensations: dress shirt sticking to his humid skin, the damp smell of towels and worn socks, the sight of looped black coils of hair on his father's chest, the echoing sound of him tapping a comb on the sink.

Mom made hamburger pizza for dinner that night. She and Dad were happier about this than about anything Jason had ever done, it seemed—way happier than the time he brought home straight A's, or earned the Webelos award in Cub Scouts. Now he was a full member of the church. Accountable in the eternal ledger. That night, as she tucked Jason into bed, Mom talked about eternity, about the never-ending time to come. Though Dad was the patriarch, it was Mom—the convert—who talked to him the most about the faith and righteousness, the one who seemed to take it to heart in day-to-day life.

"From now on, son, your actions have consequences forever," she said, smoothing his stiff hair with her hand. "We can live together as a family for time and all eternity. Never be apart. But we must be righteous. You must be righteous. You will, won't you, son?"

Whatever it was that Jason was supposed to feel at this moment, he didn't. But because it was so clearly the thing to be done, he said, "I'll be righteous, Mom."

The doctor arrives, jocular and smiling in his square metal-framed glasses. He tells them it appears Grandpa has an advanced form of emphysema, and he'll need to stay at least another night.

"Keep an eye on things," the doctor says, nodding. "Try to get some pictures of his lungs."

Emphysema. Though he'd never smoked or worked in an asbestos mine.

"Sometimes it happens," the doctor says. "Not for any reason we can see."

Jason's parents want to stay at the hospital, so he heads to Boyd's for the night. He loves staying over there. There are no rules. Boyd's mom is gone most of the time, they make a mess and no one complains, and he doesn't have to worry about his parents coming in and deciding, mid-episode, that *Kojak* isn't "appropriate."

At Boyd's, they make two frozen pizzas and watch TV while Boyd's mom works her shift at the Lincoln Inn. Boyd sits cross-legged on his couch—he calls it Indian style, sarcastically. Where Jason is tall and ungainly, Boyd is thick and earthbound, head like a medicine ball, with a wide, flat nose and thick black hair, black eyes, and a shaggy smile that looked sheepish at first and then defiant. At school, the other kids always call him "Chief" or "Little Bear" or something, and he always responds, "Good one, George," or, "Hilarious once again, George." Only Jason knows that "George" is Custer, and that in Boyd's happiest fantasies he rejoins his Indian brothers and sisters and rides down hard on Gooding High School.

Boyd says, "Well, dude, yes or no?"

Yes or No?—their rhetorical game. God: yes or no? Everything is an argument for or against, from Corinne Jensen's tightly packed H.A.S.H. jeans to Evel Knievel's failure to clear the canyon.

"That sucks," he says. "Don't do that now."

Boyd shakes his head. "Now is the perfect time."

Jason stares into the TV screen. *Emergency!* The paramedics are trying to revive a firefighter who collapsed in a burning building. They are shocking him, trying to restart his heart.

"I say . . . this one's a yes," Boyd says.

Jason stares at him.

"It's so perfectly bad, man," Boyd says. "So neat. So precise. So *constructed*. A godless world would be chaotic. Nonsensical."

"This is sensical?"

On TV, the firefighter comes coughingly back to life.

"Perversely, perfectly nonsensical. A disease he doesn't deserve in any way. Dude never smoked, and now this."

"What a godless world would have," Jason says, "is no sense of right or wrong. Even if cause and effect were all lined up—right and wrong, that's the main thing. In a godless world, the evil would triumph, the good would be punished or enslaved or something, or get diseases they don't deserve. Like Mordor."

Boyd shakes his head. "You can work those fucking hobbits into *anything*."

They watch the final credits in silence, the paramedics frozen in tableaux of bravery, concern, celebration.

"I don't know," Boyd says. "God must like to fuck with people. Maybe He finds it funny. Maybe He's just bored and screwing with us. Think about it: *we're* bored. How much more bored must He be?"

A tampon commercial comes on with a bicentennial theme. A gymnast in a spotless leotard vaults beneath waving flags.

"Good God," Boyd says. "If we were really all that free, would we have to be reminded of it constantly? Do free people go around talking about their freedom all the time? Like, tampons—and freedom. Hamburgers—and freedom. Everything and freedom. Wouldn't a truly free people not really notice it, because they're so utterly, amazingly free?"

Boyd's mom comes home as they watch *Saturday Night Live*.

The screen casts a blue pall, and Boyd's mother, puffy faced and smoky voiced, begins watching it even as she sets down her purse, bending unsteadily at the waist, her skinny legs straight. Her starchy, flyaway hair, as brown as a rabbit's, barely covers her scalp, and she curses more than any other woman Jason knows. She flops into the recliner and watches, head drooping. She reeks of something sweet and alcoholic, mixed with cigarette smoke. On TV, Belushi and the others bob around in bee suits. Lines of static run through them, slant the scene momentarily sideways. Her face sinks forward, snaps up. She stands, sways, puts a hand on the recliner arm.

"Oof," she says. "Boys, I am *drunk*."

Boyd laughs, flat, without looking away from the TV. His mother wavers, stares. Jason feels darkly clandestine, graced by the world outside his world.

"Bees," she says.

May 21, 1975

SHORT CREEK, ARIZONA

The sheet cake sits on the dining room table. *Happy Birthday, Aunt Loretta* spelled out in raisins. The cake sits there and sits there and sits there, on the long wooden table with bench seats, as in a monastery or penitentiary. Just sits there in its sheet pan, unadorned, on a red-and-white-checked dish towel. Nobody makes a big deal about birthdays here. Every time Loretta walks past it, she wants to run out the door, find Bradshaw, and go.

In his letters, he keeps telling her to wait. He's getting some things together. A little money. Hang in there, baby. It'll happen soon.

He doesn't even know today is her birthday.

That morning, he picked up the orders, and Loretta slipped a note to him as she passed a sack of rice, and he slipped a note to her as they teamed up to haul a box of sundries to his truck. They do this nearly every day—winks, notes, the furtive brush of a finger.

This thing Loretta thought would be impossible has turned out to be simple, just as living this life has turned out to be simple. She remembers wondering how she would hide her true self from them, and then discovering how easy it was, because no one ever asked her anything about herself.

So when Dean comes tonight, it will be the same, only more so. It won't be her with him, it will be her shadow, and it won't be too bad, it will just be another thing she can get through by shrinking into herself. She is not squeamish about the body.

You are mine lorry and that is not something that any fake polyg marriage can change, baby, and we are going to be together I promise.

She thought about telling Bradshaw, in her letters, that today is her birthday. He does not know, she is sure. He is not a birthday-remembering person, though he likes an elaborate fuss for his own. He thinks it has already happened; he thinks it's been happening. *I love you so much lorry that it don't count what he does to you.* She has not corrected him, because it feels strangely too personal. Now she wishes she had mentioned it, because maybe he'd have done something by now, and they'd be gone.

Since that first night, Dean has been gentle and kind, patient, never mentioning how much he wants her, never coming near her in that way. And every morning and evening when she sees Bradshaw, his eyes gleam and jump, he scuttles and hustles at every task. His hungry look never leaves her. Every time she glances at Bradshaw he is already looking back, and she knows that if one of these men is a demon, it is him.

My lorry you have my word that we are going to make the old son of a B pay. I wake up ever day just to see you.

Ruth has made chicken tortilla casserole, with chunks of canned tomatoes that Samuel and Benjamin will sequester on their plates, and that Ruth will insist they eat. The casserole sits in a rectangular baking dish at the center of the table, beside a large bowl of green beans and a stack of wheat bread sliced from the loaf. Ice water in a pitcher and no butter for the bread.

Dean sits at the head of the table, with Ruth to his right and Loretta to his left, and the seven kids lined up from there. Bowing his head, Dean laces his hands and props them before himself on his elbows. They all fold their arms and bow. "Our Father in Heaven," he begins, and Loretta's mind wanders. He prays several times a day, loves to hear himself pray. Sometimes he will draw it out, add a theme or rebuke a child. *And we pray, dear Lord, that you grant Elizabeth the patience to become more obedient.* He finishes, and everyone whispers, "Amen," and the food begins to move around the table.

"I would like everyone to think of one thing to share with the family about Aunt Loretta tonight," Ruth says. "One thing that you feel she has brought to our family. One thing about her that you love."

Samuel mumbles into his plate, "She's nice," and Ruth nods vigorously. "She is very nice, Samuel," she says. Elizabeth says, "She loves the Lord?" and Ruth agrees again, though she looks at Loretta as she nods. Benjamin says, loudly, "She weads to me!" and everyone laughs. Loretta, too. When it falls silent, Dean clears his throat and says, "I believe Loretta has brought a sweetness of spirit into our home," and Ruth nods in agreement with this as well, mouth pursed.

Loretta has never adjusted to the silence of these children, their obedience, though she has seen the cause of it when they disobey Ruth. She whips them mercilessly with her large wooden spoon or pinches them in strategic ways. If Loretta had considered Ruth a hard woman, humorless, before the wedding, she has come to realize how little she really knew. Ruth is harder than humorless—believing life is meant to be a trial, and her task is to drive these children into heaven, to teach them to ignore pleasure in pursuit of salvation.

She has told Loretta as much. *You must shut down that part of yourself that would coddle a child in weakness. When you encourage worldly softness, you are putting their souls in peril. It is the hardest part of a godly love, to be stern with your children.* Ruth often refers to Loretta's future children. *Your children.* They exist already, these children, and their souls await their chance to come to earth. It is her job to bring them here. Ruth believes this and Dean believes this and Loretta's parents believe this and virtually everyone Loretta knows believes this. Loretta believes this. She tells herself she does not, but when she imagines her childless future—her glamorous days and nights of freedom—she imagines particular souls who will suffer for this, who will remain stranded, and she feels bad for them, a little, but also hoisted and enlarged—seeing herself the way Dean must see himself, as someone toward whom other wills must bend.

Out comes the sad, flat cake, with the birthday message in raisins and a single candle burning. The children sing "Happy Birthday." She had wondered whether they would, or whether Ruth would consider it a worldly extravagance. Janeen, the six-year-old, sings loudest, and she smiles widely at Loretta when the song is over, a big gap in her nubby-toothed smile. Loretta blushes, wanting to check the feeling rising up inside her, because it is love.

If anything, hearing Ruth's ideas about disciplining children has made Loretta want to coddle them more. She looks upon the children with intense tenderness; she feels their slights and injuries more powerfully than they do. She can't bring herself to trim little Ben's fingernails, because she once accidentally cut him to the quick and he cried and whimpered, warm and tight in her arms, for half an hour. She relishes doing the girls' hair, and seeing them smile when she tells them they look pretty. She teases Samuel, who blushes hotly, and at night, when she tries to imagine her future, when she thinks about what Bradshaw must be doing with all that money of Dean's that he is handling, when she remembers how much she hated Dean and realizes how that hate has slid into something like accommodation, how she has found a place inside herself for all of this, she becomes fearful at the idea of never seeing these children again, fearful that they may love her, too, and that it will hurt them when she leaves.

They eat the cake. It tastes terrible, odd and eggy.

"Sarah!" Ruth barks, for the youngest girl has laughed with a full mouth of cake, sending a small, wet hunk onto the front of her dress. The girl quickly and quietly tries to wipe it off before Ruth rises and comes and takes the napkin roughly from her hand, dips it in her water glass, and begins to dab at the stain.

Dean wipes his mouth, pets his beard, and leans back with a satisfied aspect. "Thank you, Mother," he says to Ruth, and scoots back his chair and rises. Suddenly it is there again in Loretta's mind: tonight. What must happen. She has prepared herself. Talked to herself. How bad can it be? How long can it take? She imagines it might take an hour, and that an hour is not so much. How many other hours has she endured? Yet she is weak with dread.

Ruth, Loretta, and the girls clean up. Dean and the boys work in the garage on tomorrow's deliveries. Soon it's bedtime, and she begins shepherding—it's bath night for Janeen and Sarah, and the older girls need help putting up their hair. Ruth moves constantly through the enormous house, from the kitchen where she rinses a glass to the living room where she straightens the children's scripture books on a shelf to the garage door where she asks Dean a question, up the long staircase and down the carpeted hall past the bedrooms to the bathroom at the end, where she scolds Sarah for taking too long in the bath.

Loretta goes to the boys' bedroom. Her favorite part of the day. Benjamin waits for her, his hair buzzed close to the scalp, his big, light-filled eyes, and his entire face—that ripe, chubby face—alert with anticipation. She sits on the lower bunk with her feet up and leans against the headrest and he settles into her lap in the plain white pajamas Ruth has sewn for him. He loves *The Poky Little Puppy*. It's one of the few books Ruth tolerates, because the puppy is punished. Benjamin snuggles into the crook of Loretta's arm, and she reads. About halfway into the story he lays his head against her chest. His chubby hand curls into a loose fist, resting on her belly. She can smell his hair and his skin, a familiar scent—grass, sweat, play, boy, and something more, something family. She finishes the book. The wayward puppy gets what he has coming—no dessert. She thinks Ben has fallen asleep, but he lifts his head and says, "Again," and she starts over. The puppy digs and disobeys. Ben adjusts, shifts against her. Loretta presses her cheek against his head. What a warm, fragile being. Bone and flesh. Belly and brain. With only these people, this family, to care for him.

She lies under the covers in her garments, afghan to her chin, and watches Dean unloop a suspender from one shoulder, then the other, and step carefully out of his black wool pants, not letting them drop to the floor. He removes his shirt and drapes it over the foot of the bed. His blush runs from the side of his face, brightening the shiny half-moon scar on his earlobe, and streaks down his neck and onto his chest, burrowing into the V-neck of his gauzy garments, the blessed garments that protect him from evil. His breathing is shallow and rapid. He is already erect, a dark bulb pressing outward against the thin cloth of the garment. He drops his hands in front of it as he walks to the side of the bed, and says, "I apologize if this seems vulgar," and slides under the covers, sits up on his elbow, and puts on his serious face, his church-speaking face. "And I am sorry, little sister, for the way I behaved with you on our first night. I feel as though a demon has overtaken me when it comes to you, beautiful Loretta, and it is in this battle, this torture of the flesh, that I have found some spiritual solace these past months, that I have found myself tested, and imagined that I had battled this flesh in earnest, and, like all such battle, had gained something in my soul from it. Except for that first night."

"It's all right," Loretta whispers. She had hoped he might be wordless and fast. That she might dream her way through it. But seeing him at the foot of her bed, his erection tenting, had surprised her: she was intrigued. Not aroused, not that—but curious about that pronging, and about the way it might be like or unlike Bradshaw's pronging, which she has felt only through his jeans, though he has pressed her for more. When she imagines her future and wonders how she will get there, she realizes that it may involve

Bradshaw and his penis, and she wonders if there will be others, and how she will feel about those others, if they might be pathways to other things or simply ends in themselves, and so she is curious now in the way she might be curious about the first time she saw anything. And part of her has always felt that all of this—romance, passion, love, sex, men, and women—was overwrought, overdone, oversold, whether in the worldly world or in the church world, both places treating it like some magic thing when it was just a body thing, an animal thing. She wants Dean to get started now and stop talking about God and temptation and the flesh, but he is doing it again, talking about the flesh, and Loretta wonders how he could think it makes any difference if they do it today or if they did it last week or if they do it tomorrow. How could it matter?

Dean is up on one elbow, looking down at her. She is flat on her back, arms at her sides, and he smiles at her in a way that she has to admit is tender, loving, genuine seeming, and under these covers the heat rolls off him like a milk cow on a cold day, steaming. He puts his hand between her legs and presses lightly as he leans to kiss her on the mouth. The hairs in his beard prickle her face. He kisses her once, twice, three times, and his erection, the source of all that heat, presses against her leg, and his fingers move inside the slit in her garments, and then slide up and down, up and down, and then he withdraws his hand and reaches for the small tub of petroleum jelly that Ruth had brought her, saying only, "Sometimes this helps," and now he's talking about "heavenly comfort" and how this is one of God's true blessings for the righteous. Loretta tries not to hear, to concentrate only on the body. She is making a task of this. A chore. Dean gently moves her legs apart, widening her, and he slips on top, still in his garment, his penis out of the slit now, she feels it bump and prod, and Dean reaches down, helping it seek, and she feels the bit of slick he has rubbed onto it, and it occurs to her how much larger Dean is than she is, how much taller and wider as a human animal, how much more of a monkey or a goat he is, how his feet hang nearly off the bed and how his chest, with the bony, flaring rib cage, is on her face now, how it is almost as if he were pressing her into silence with his chest, and he moves in, and it doesn't feel too bad, not as painful as she thought it might, just a tightness, a fullness, and Dean begins to move and gasp and lurch and pant—heaving himself at her like an animal, teeth and hair, skin and bones and hunger, and she doesn't like it, she doesn't like it at all. But she is in it, and she knows that when you are in it, whatever it is, there is no point in wishing otherwise, and so she tries to let her mind go somewhere but she can't make it go anywhere, this is all there is right now, and then it is done, Dean tenses and flexes all over, his face contorts grotesquely, as though it were being smeared around by an invisible hand. It didn't take anywhere close to an hour.

Afterward, Dean pulls back the sheet and looks down at her, at himself.

Loretta knows what he is doing, and says, "Mine broke when I was riding a horse."

Later, after Dean is snoring, she goes to the bathroom down the hall and takes the latest folded-up letter from Bradshaw and the bottle she had hidden, the bottle with the solution of vinegar and ammonia that Tonaya had told her about, back when they were sneaking out together, the thing that always works, Tonaya said. *Nothing can survive that shit.*

It burned her there, hurt her worse than Dean had done, and she tried to wash away the burning and could not. What if there was a baby she had washed away? How soon did it start? Sitting on the toilet, she unfolded the letter.

Lorry honey I cant wait for this part of things to be over, but I do want you to know it is working out good. Real good. Hang in there and we will be set. More than you can imagine. D trusts me more every day. My thoughts are about you. I love you lorry, and you need to just wait for me now, just give me time, and soon it will all be over and we can go wherever you want to.

She tears the letter into tiny pieces and drops them into the toilet between her legs. She wonders exactly what he is doing, but has enough of an idea: taking money from Dean. She hopes he's being careful, because Dean keeps exact track. He talks to her, on his nights with her up until now, of the Council of Elders and their demands, and of how much they want, and of how much he will give them, and of how large this difference is growing, how he will turn over $2,291.66 for January; $1,891.34 for February; $1,996.12 for March—*Not a cent more, little sister, I swear it*— because that is half of his earnings, and because he has decided that the Law of Consecration is being abused by the Elders. *That is half, little sister. How can you say that is not a generous tithe?* And yet she knows the Council of Elders does not deem it so.

She has not said anything to Bradshaw about the gold. Dean talks about it, tells her about it, boasts about the precision of one-ounce golden eagles—the fifty-dollar coins—and their solid, righteous weight. He tells her everything about them, except where they are. She wants to take it from him. She wants him not to have it, and she wants to be the reason.

She flushes the toilet. It wasn't so horrible. Nothing ever is.

EVEL KNIEVEL ADDRESSES
AN ADORING NATION

What you need is a way in. In every circumstance, in every situation: a way in. The way in is like the ramp, like the lever, like the cocked hammer of a pistol. It is the way you turn an ordinary thing into an extraordinary thing.

The way in is always the same. You can spend years misunderstanding this, thinking that you have to find the way in for each new scenario, when it's always the same: the way in is to act as if you're already in.

To believe it before it's true.

It's like getting laid, America. The best way to do it is to act as if you already know—despite whatever the broad herself may think—that it's inevitable, that's it's happening, that there's no going back. You know she's gonna do it before she does. You don't seduce. You make it clear that it is completely unnecessary to seduce. That the fucking to come is not in question.

So the years roll along, and we perform our amazing feats, our miracles, and pretty soon the Grand Canyon dream is not so crazy. Is not such wild talk. And then there's a New York promoter getting on board. A Jew bastard naturally. But he's on board, and he thinks he can make it happen, and he starts looking into it, and he finds out that the government—your government, America—will not allow such a thing because it owns the land on the canyon rims or some shit, and so the New York promoter, the flesh peddler, keeps after it, won't give up, and he finds another spot: the Snake River Canyon, right outside Twin Falls, Idaho. There's a farmer there who'll lease the land for the ramp and for the crowds. There'll be some permits to get, some locals to persuade, some dicks to suck, but the promoter is good at that, and pretty soon we're set to go.

The way in was money. He was gonna pay us $25,000 plus some of the gate. He had a plan to show the thing live in movie theaters, sell tickets all across the land. A man jumps a canyon! A mortal defies physics! And yet, that was not the way in. Money was the way in. Money—the notion of it, the idea of it, the magnetic force of it.

The promoter understood it and we understood it, and so we gathered in New York City, and he got a big cardboard check with a big fake number on it: $6 million. And he handed it to me, and from that moment on, it became truer than true, $6 million, in all the headlines and stories, and of course America would watch this, of course the country would turn its adoring gaze to us, obviously there was no way this could fail, because now this feat drank from the wells of death and money, and the wells of death and money are magic.

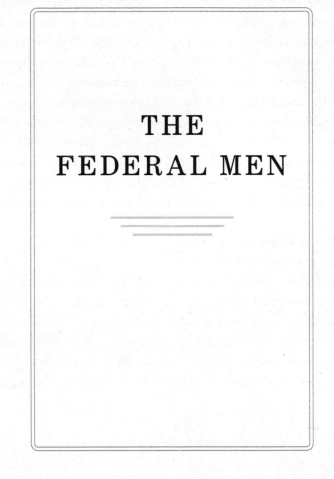

THE
FEDERAL MEN

July 26, 1953

SHORT CREEK, ARIZONA

Something booms in the night. Three times. Explosions, far away. The echoes drift. Is it the Lord? Is it the enemy? Ruth is too warm, and kicks off the blanket. The booms are like dream noise. Like heaven noise, hell noise.

"Good morning, little birds," Ruth's mother whispers. It is as dark as the closet with the door closed. "Come, come, little birds." Her mother is a shape of darkness inside other darkness, leaning over Ruth's younger sisters in their bed. And now she is moving toward Ruth, leaning over, a light hand on her shoulder. "Come quickly, Ruth. I need you to get Alma and Sarah dressed and come downstairs. *Quickly.*"

Her father's beard is like a tree. Or a forest. Dense and thick at the roots, it spreads and lightens at the tips, where the light slips in.

When his jaw moves and he talks to the Lord, his face is a dense grove of slender autumn trees, rolling along as the earth heaves.

The entire family is here. Her father and her mother and her father's other wives—Aunt Olive and Aunt Desdemona and Aunt Eliza. All thirteen of her brothers and sisters. Her heavenly family. Ruth is eleven, the oldest among her mother's four children. They crowd on the chairs and on the benches of the long table and on the floor. Ruth sits in a chair, an arm around Alma and an arm around Sarah, and Alma hugs her stuffed doll with the hand-drawn face, and then their mother comes upon them from behind and enfolds them all in an embrace. The room is warm with still bodies, and silent.

Her father is praying, and Ruth peeks at him, watching his beard tremble. "And if today is the day of your son's return, O Lord, if this is the day the righteous have awaited, our Father in Heaven, then we ask you to find us worthy, though we know we are not worthy, though we know we are sinners, we ask that you forgive us our sins and take us up, lift us up."

Is that what today is? Ruth presses her eyes closed. Somewhere outside of her, somewhere outside of this room, somewhere outside of the darkness that still covers this room, somewhere outside the visible world, she knows there is a force that opposes them. That opposes the righteous. But she does not understand what that force is. For days now, the grown-ups have been talking about the Federal Men. The Federal Men are being sent by the apostates, the false Mormons in Salt Lake, who are persecuting the true Saints here in Short Creek. But now her father is talking about something else: The last days. The reckoning. The Second Coming. She holds her eyes closed as tightly as possible. Fear tingles and squirms around her heart. She should never have been peeking during the prayer. Inside of her father's prayer she begins her own silent prayer, begging the Lord's forgiveness for opening her eyes during her father's prayer. She is disobedient. She is headstrong. The grown-ups always say so. *Forgive me, O Lord.* She wants to close her eyes so tightly that it makes up for their opening. *Forgive me, O Lord, and I will be your righteous servant eternally.* She feels it now throughout her body, a zing in the blood, a knowledge in the bones: it is the Second Coming. What if her family is raised up without her? What if she watches from below as they are saved, as she is swallowed up in the fire that will last a thousand years?

They walk to the schoolhouse, where other families wait, and where other families are still arriving. The grown-ups are dressed as if for church. The prophet stands in a circle of men, where her father also stands. Elden Johnson. Uncle Elden. He is shorter than the other men, but also taller, Ruth thinks. One eye is cloudy and one is clear. He wears his three-piece suit, his short white hair is neat, his mustache trim, and he smiles placidly. He speaks to God. God speaks to him.

Ruth's mother gives every older child someone to watch over. She is responsible for Sarah and Alma. "You watch them, little sister," her mother says. "You don't let them out of your sight." Every few minutes her stomach makes a noise that is audible to anyone nearby. She asks her mother, "What's going to happen?" and her mother says, "We don't know."

Outside the darkness lifts, slow and gray. Inside the schoolhouse, they are singing hymns. "Arise, O Glorious Zion." "Put Your Shoulder to the Wheel." They pray silently. The grown-ups talk somberly, greet one another as if at church, and though there is a somber cloak around the day, there is something strangely joyous as well, and this puzzles Ruth, or it makes her fearful, because she believes it means they are anticipating the Second Coming with joy, feeling sure of their own righteousness in a way she is not. An eternity without her family, she thinks. An eternity of her own reward.

A shout comes from outside, and then Brother Miller is scuffling into the schoolhouse. "They're coming down Partham Road," she hears him tell the prophet and the brethren who surround him. "Eight or nine cars." The Federal Men, she thinks. The Federal Men. She does not know what that means exactly. She knows what *federal* means, and she knows they are from the government, and she knows they are coming because the apostates are sending them or controlling them—but she has no idea what they might do, what she should fear. Outside, the sun is low and stretched, and Ruth wonders if it is already beginning, the Second Coming, if the sun is coming apart or moving away or approaching. Her stomach makes the noise and she feels as if her body were outside of her now. As if she were hiding inside of it, separate from it. One hot squirt of urine dampens her underwear, and she rubs her legs together to soak it into her clothing.

The families walk out into the street. They cluster and sing. The cars of the Federal Men creep slowly toward them, and Uncle Elden stands in front of the group, watches them come. Alma and Sarah stand at Ruth's sides, her hands on their shoulders. When the cars get close, Ruth sees that one of them has a sign on the door: ARIZONA STATE POLICE. She knows the difference between state and federal. She learned it just last month, in her civics class at the Hurricane school. She wonders why the state police are here if these are the Federal Men, and she wonders why everyone says "the Federal Men" if it's actually the state police. A man in a brown uniform with a star over his heart climbs from the car, hitches his belt upward against his belly, and begins to squawk through a bull-horn. Alma begins to cry. Ruth holds her closer, shushes her, but her eyes sting with tears, too.

The men line up, hands behind their backs, ready to be handcuffed. The prophet is speaking to the Saints, telling them to put their trust in the Lord. "See what the world calls brave men," he says to the Federal Men. "You are cowards to come down so upon us." He stands there in his three-piece suit, neat, trim, hands locked behind his back, the man who speaks to God. Ruth's father is near him, Ruth's father is looking at Ruth's mother, communicating some-thing urgent by eyesight, and then one of the Federal Men comes behind him and begins to move Ruth's father away, directing him by his locked hands as if guiding a boat with a tiller. His face clenches furiously. Ruth sees him close his eyes, close his whole face against it all, weaker than the thing that is crushing him, weaker than she has ever seen him.

They take all the fathers away. The mothers weep and plead, and the Federal Men hush them, and gently hold them back while they take all the fathers away. Someone is following the Federal Men as they take all the fathers away, shooting photographs with a large camera that hangs heavily around his neck. The man chews gum. Ruth watches him as he aims his camera at Sister Taft, her children huddled around her on the bench outside the school, the man with the camera moving, crouching, training his lens on Sister Taft and her children, flash popping, and as the last of the men is taken away, someone begins to wail sharply, a sound rising above a smaller sound, a lower sound, the sound of children crying all around her, crying quietly beneath the one piercing wail. Ruth's stomach never stops making the noise now. Something is alive inside her, and her outside feels dead. Her mother comes to her, face tight, and Ruth wonders if she knows, too, that this is the Second Coming, and her mother kneels before Ruth and wraps little Sarah in a hug, and that's when Ruth notices that the wailing has been coming from her little sister all along.

Then they take the mothers away. The children go into the school. The room is too small for all the children. They pack together. Ruth feels the heat of the children around her, but she does not look at them or talk to them or think about them. She stares at the shirt in front of her, at one fraying thread of a boy's shirt, and she keeps one hand on the shoulder of Sarah and one on the shoulder of Alma. Someone is smoking, a foul odor. Three of the Federal Men and two women who look like worldly schoolteachers are looking at the children and conferring with a man who is sitting at the teacher's desk. The man makes some marks, and the woman escorts a few children from the room, and they start again.

Did the fathers and mothers go up into heaven?

They take the children away in twos and threes. The brothers and sisters are crying. Ruth watches silently, and Sarah and Alma watch silently, and Ruth stares at the chalkboard, stares at the leftover sentence on the board, written in cursive: *Why does the man run?* Brothers argue and sisters argue, but they are taking the children away in twos and threes. *Why does the man run?* A remnant of a lesson. Ruth thinks there must be an answer. She thinks that if she stays very still, maybe this won't be happening. When the women and the Federal Men finally get to Ruth's family, they begin to take her brothers and sisters away.

"All right, then." One of the women is smiling, smiling at Ruth, and then smiling at Sarah, and then smiling at Alma, and then smiling again at Ruth. Sarah and Alma are trying to hide inside of Ruth. "Why don't you two come with me for a bit?" Ruth shakes her head, and wraps each arm more tightly around her sisters.

The Federal Man watches. The man with the camera is back, leaning against the wall. He chews gum. The Federal Man whispers something to him and he smiles.

Ruth can't figure this out. Did the fathers and mothers rise up to heaven? Did all of the children stay behind? *Why does the man run?*

The woman wears pointy glasses and her hair seems sculpted into a wavy bun. She smells of fancy lotion. "Come on now," she says, trying to carve the children away from Ruth's side with her hands, gently, gently, viciously. "It's okay. You two come with me." Ruth holds tight. She says, "No." The word is like a lump of food she needs to spit out. The woman doesn't stop. The Federal Man says, "You'll be all right, girls," and Ruth manages to spit out the lump more forcefully: "No!" She wonders if she can hold her sisters tightly enough.

The woman and the Federal Man stop, but do not retreat. The woman's hands are still touching Alma and Sarah, still resting on their shoulders, still poised to reach in and carve them away from Ruth.

"No," Ruth says, and then she says it again. "No."

She stares at them. These people. She prays for the Lord to stop them. To kill them. She asks for that, for the Lord to kill them. She asks that this not be the Second Coming. She says, very quietly, "No, no, no, no, no."

In the home of the man and the woman whose name she cannot remember, Ruth sits on a sofa with her sisters. They are together, at least. Ruth's mind keeps softening, drifting. Sarah and Alma sit beside her, legs straight before them, faces wrung white. Ruth wants to tell them to pull inside of themselves—she thinks of a turtle. She wants to tell Sarah and Alma to pull inside of themselves and just stay there. Ignore everything outside the shell. Just stay in there and wait. But the man and the woman whose name she cannot remember are sitting there, one in each chair, the chairs that match the sofa, the chairs and the sofa clean and new and fancy, like everything in the house. Carpet runs to the walls and tucks itself in like a made bed. There is cut glass on the cupboard doors, and teacups inside. The woman whose name Ruth cannot remember is saying something Ruth cannot keep track of, in tones that are sweet and pretty and false. Ruth cannot focus on her words, but now the woman seems to be waiting for something. They are together, at least. If only she could tell them, if only she could find a way to let them know: *Pull inside, sisters. Pull inside and wait.* The woman is kneeling down in front of the chair that matches the sofa, and Ruth thinks she is going to pray now, and Ruth thinks she should not pray with these people, that praying with these people would be a sin, probably, but then she realizes that the woman wants to give them a hug, then she realizes that one of her sisters is crying again. Which one is crying? Alma is crying. Ruth wants to tell her—*Pull inside and wait*—but she can't. The woman is kneeling there, and she is saying something softly, and her arms are open, and she smells like lotion, and Alma is crying, and Ruth wants to tell her but she can't, so she just says, "Go ahead," because it doesn't matter.

REUNION

August 23, 1975

GOODING, IDAHO

Boyd wrings the handlebar grip, dipping his shoulder, and the Kawasaki spits and flies toward a rocky ramp of lava. Jason found this spot—the tiny cliff that drops three feet onto a flat piece of desert—and now he watches as Boyd goes over the ledge, front wheel dropping. The whine halts abruptly. Boyd pitches headfirst over the handlebars, and the Kawasaki flips across the desert. For a second Jason thinks Boyd will be badly hurt. Even when Boyd hops up, holding his elbow and grinning madly, even then, Jason knows that he doesn't really want to do this. He wants to be away, alone.

The Kawasaki lies on its side in the duff grass, back wheel slowly spinning. Three jackrabbits inch up, sniffing, and hop off.

"I know what I did wrong," Boyd says, breathing heavily. "You gotta go faster and pull back harder."

It's not that Jason's scared. At least he doesn't think so. He's jumped other things—lots of them—and he's usually first to go.

But Boyd's wreck makes him nervous, a little, and that's enough, on top of this other thing, the fuzzed focus and half exhaustion that's been swamping him since Grandpa died.

"You look about half retarded right now," Boyd says. "Mouth all open."

Jason shrugs, and Boyd goes to get the bike. Boyd won't give him too much shit if he doesn't do it, Jason thinks. It's not the time for that, but as that thought enters Jason's mind he wonders: What is it the time for, exactly? His mother says it's time to reflect and remember the importance of family, the eternal verities, the celestial kingdom, et cetera. What is it the time for? Anecdotes and platitudes. Self-comforting nonsense. *It's better this way. He's out of his pain. He's with the Lord now. With Grandma. At peace.* Everyone has something to say. Everyone has a lesson to impart, an anecdote dragging a moral trailing a tidy little pat on the head. A grand, swamping tide of bullshit. Only Boyd had said the right thing: "Man, dude. That is fucked up."

Precisely right. Five days ago, Dad found Grandpa in his metal lawn chair, where he'd been spending each desert sunset and the cooling hour after, just sitting and breathing through his oxygen mask. It had been furiously hot, no rain for weeks, every parched inch of land one spark from inferno. Time to start the third cutting of hay. Jackrabbits swarmed, gnawing through barley and haystacks faster than anyone could poison or shoot them.

His father came into Jason's room that night. Which he never did. Jason was lying on his bed reading *The Hobbit,* bare feet hanging off the end of the mattress. Bilbo and the dwarves had just entered the forest of Mirkwood. A dark tangle of menace. Dad sat on the bed and stared at the wood-paneled wall, gray cheeks slack.

Outside, a wheel line repeated its watery *skirch*. Above them, trophies from livestock sales and Little League sat on shelves, tiny golden calves and batters, and images of Evel Knievel—in black and white, in color, crashing and landing—papered every wall.

"Your grandpa's gone," his father said, and Jason thought for a moment that he meant Grandpa had traveled somewhere, maybe Boise or Salt Lake. "I'm going to need you to be strong for your mother."

Dad sighed, and dropped his gaze to the floor. Jason waited for the moment to arrive—grief, heartbreak—but it simply did not. He felt tired. A little sad, a little hungry. He thought he spied a tearish gleam at the corner of Dad's eye and was glad for it. Jason had seen him show emotion only during testimony meeting, when he was displaying his deep and abiding faith for the ward. Jason wanted something to have the power to make him sad.

"Sorry, Dad," he said.

Dad turned, and his eyes were shiny but dry, the same glinty nuggets he trained on Jason when he screwed around during church or was late feeding calves.

Dad shook his head. "It was time," he said.

Time. What made it time? What made the time any better than, say, one day later? Or one day earlier? Why not another thirty-seven hours, or forty-two hours, or fifty-six hours and twenty-seven minutes and thirteen seconds? What made it so right that Grandpa didn't get another year, five years? Ten years? *It was time.* He felt surrounded by people who would swallow any goddamned thing and smile.

Boyd walks the motorcycle over. Jason won't do it. Not today. He feels relieved that he can put this off for another time. Out of everyone in the world, only Boyd understands him correctly, and this is how Jason knows that Boyd will not ride him about chickening out.

Boyd stops, his enormous head cocked and a gaze of evaluation trained on Jason.

He says, "Get on the bike, man. You can't be a pussy your whole life."

Here is how, according to the story Jason's mother told him on every birthday, he became the sole only child out of all the Mormon kids he knew:

Twenty-three hours of labor. A night and day and night of pain and desperation. Prayers and lamentations. A period of thirteen minutes when everyone in the delivery room believed he had died, followed by his birth, breach, with the umbilical cord wrapped snugly around his neck. Blue above and red below. Then, a revival. "A miracle. You're my miracle boy." But he was the last of the children, for reasons that were never fully clear—a complication, a risk to his mother's life. More children would have been unsafe. So he was the only one, and though he was surrounded by families of five, six, seven, eight, all these fertile righteous families, he could believe only that everyone was really just like him: the only one, the miracle of their own lives.

Jason lands the first jump, crashes the second. It is afternoon when he arrives home, elbow bleeding and shoulder aching, to find Aunt Bonnie and Uncle Ben have arrived from Pocatello, with their six kids in the converted airport van. Jason parks the bike in the shed and pokes around in the dusty heat, avoiding going in. The gloomy swelter of the shed forces itself on him, sends stinging trickles of sweat into his scrapes and cuts.

He comes out as a rusty gold Nova tears into the drive. Uncle Roy. Here from Boise. A Jack Mormon, never married, suspected of illicit pleasures like coffee and beer. Jason's favorite.

"Hey, kid," Roy hollers, elbow out the window as the car engine rattles and ticks into silence. "Staying out of trouble?"

"Not really."

"Cool, man."

He clambers out, slams the door, puts his hands on his hips, and surveys the place. Soft body on a big frame. His belly strains against a thinning terry-cloth shirt and his fraying bell-bottom jeans nearly cover his feet. Face thick and happy, with curly side-burns and an unruly nest of hair and a grin that makes you feel he knows where all the good times are hidden.

He comes over, rubs a hand in Jason's hair and hugs him hard, slaps his back, and holds him with one arm around the shoulder, tightly.

"Sucks about the old man," Roy says.

"Really sucks," Jason says.

"Just goddamn lousy," Roy says. Jason's eyes sting and tighten. Roy adds, "This next part's gonna be worse yet. Watching all the boo-hoo."

Roy pats his shoulder, releases him.

"Dean here?"

Dean. Uncle Dean. Supposedly, Jason met his uncle Dean once, when he was two or three, but all he knows is that Dean and his family live down in Arizona or Utah, with their million kids and strange ways. Old-school Mormons, fundamentalists. Just how old school he couldn't have said, but Dean lives down where the polygamists live. One of the places. They're up in British Columbia and down in Arizona and Mexico and even, a few of them, in Hagerman, just a few miles away in the Snake River Canyon. Little pockets of polygamists. They're an embarrassment to good, normal Mormons, and Jason's parents have made their own nervousness about Dean clear in their cautious avoidance of the subject. He is the signal omission from all their talk of family, family, family. The sacred family.

"I guess not," Jason says.

"You'd know it if he was."

"What? Why?"

Roy scrunches his features, as if he can't quite calculate the answer. "He'll be here soon enough. I don't want to spoil the surprise." He pats Jason aggressively on the shoulder. "Okay. Let's go greet the fam damily."

They go in. Hugs, kisses. Jason's cousins are mostly younger. While they're all saying shy hellos, Aunt Jenna and her five kids arrive in their station wagon from Salt Lake City. She has left her husband, Verl, behind. He'll come up in time for the funeral tomorrow. The house is suddenly so full you can't put a foot down. Cousins crowd into Jason's room, toss down sleeping bags. Jason's mother has put box fans in the windows, shoving waves of dank air, and laid out a buffet of cold cuts and salads on the kitchen counter, the start of the continuous meal that marks all family gatherings—the steady, informal eating, broken only by the moments of formalized eating. People stand around the counter, picking at the food, eating off trays, leaving the paper plates mostly untouched.

Suitcases and pillows pile up everywhere. Jason and his father set up cots in the living room and office. The day is blazing, near a hundred, and it's not cooling as the bright evening approaches. Conversations streak into a blur.

"Robbie says you had to hold out that heifer again."

"Is that sour cream in this?"

"I don't believe those boys could make a tackle to save their life."

"Yeah, she takes sick more than the rest."

"Just a little plain yogurt."

"Yep. Pinkeye."

"So she takes off her clothes and runs into the ocean."

"Glenns Ferry is gonna take 'em apart."

"Mom! Mooooom!"

"And while she's out there skinny-dipping, something starts to yank her under the water."

"You got Pong?"

"Roy! What are you telling those kids?"

"Mom!"

"Pong and four other ones. I got it for Christmas."

"It's just a movie, Becky."

"Sometimes one just is that way."

"You see old Ford's speech the other night?"

"Heavens. I wish we had someone better."

"Better than awful?"

A knocking rattles the screen door. Someone yells, "Come in," and an entire family clad in denim enters. Three boys in dark dungarees, light denim shirts, and suspenders. Four girls in prairie dresses of pale plain blue. Mother and father the same, like the largest in a set of nesting dolls. The chirping of grasshoppers is suddenly audible. The man holds his hat, squints into the room, as if he has just arrived from 1875 and is waiting for his eyes to adjust.

His beard makes a neat berm along his jaw, and his bony Adam's apple gives him the cast of an Ichabod or an Abe.

"I gather we missed the announcement," he says to the room.

He has the unmistakable Harder lank and pall.

Dad reddens and comes to the door, says, "My word, Dean, how would we ever know how to reach you?"

It is past eight P.M. Through the screen door, behind the Ingalls Wilders, the sky darkens from pink to purple and orange. Dad and Dean stand at cross angles. Dad nods vacantly at nothing, and Dean's family clusters as if for warmth. Dean's wife looks cornered, as Mom blitzes in with the aunts.

"Heaven's sake, you must all be starving," she says. "Come get something to eat."

Dean frowningly hugs his sisters and Jason's mom, but his wife gives them grim smiles to convey that she will not be hugging anyone. Dean says, "Thank you, but I think we'll just go over to the house and get settled."

The house. Grandpa's house. Dad stops nodding, and Mom starts, very slowly. From the far edge of the room, Roy calls, "Don't go pocketing the silverware," and Dad says, "Roy," but Dean's expression doesn't change. He just says, as he herds his kids out, "Hullo, little brother."

August 26, 1975

SHORT CREEK, ARIZONA

Loretta wakes into baffling stillness. Somewhere outside a car accelerates. Bird trill flutters through the window. Has she ever heard a bird before, inside this house? The family squelches all incoming signals, and now that the clamor has departed, the silence is delicate and pure and enormous. A dog barks, a hundred miles away.

She stays in bed, though the sun is up. No one knocks. No one calls her to breakfast or asks her to help with the children or points to a bucket with a floating sponge or kisses her on the top of the head or asks her to get more honey from the pantry. No one tugs at her skirt or tap-tap-taps her on the arm, as Ruth has ordered the children to do when they want a grown-up's attention, and no one cries when they fall down after jumping off the shed roof or gets their pants caught on the barbed-wire fence or are told, sternly, that they cannot keep the stray cat they lured home only to have

Ruth chase it away, whipping stones at it in short, expert strokes. It will not be her night tonight. She will not have to do that, though she ordinarily would, would prepare for it all day, reminding herself it's just a gesture of the body. She will not have to hear Dean's questions about whether she has noticed any queasiness in the mornings.

All of that doesn't happen, and something else. She does not leave. She does not plan to leave. She could not dream of a better chance. She could not dream of a door more open. But she is not going, and she knows she is not going.

Before now, the idea that Dean had parents of his own, that he grew up with brothers and sisters, had not entered Loretta's mind. Then he received a phone call from a friend in the Reorganized LDS Church in Hagerman, Idaho, who'd seen an obituary for Dean's father in the *Times-News*. Dean's name had not been included among the survivors. The friend thought perhaps his family had failed to notify him.

"It is just the kind of betrayal I would have expected from Louis," Dean said that night, after the children were asleep, as he and Ruth and Loretta discussed what would happen now. Dean would have something coming up there, surely. Land, money. He would have an inheritance to claim.

"Even if I have to force it," he said.

"It's only what's right, Father," Ruth said. "You can never be wrong when you stand up for what's right."

Dean smiled at her. She did this for him, Loretta saw: confirmed him in his positions. Dean sometimes came to Loretta for the same thing, asking her without directly asking her to support him in his interpretations of scripture, in his decisions about disciplining the children, in the products he would add or remove from the Zion's

Harvest inventory, in his recent battles with the Council of Elders. He was not seeking permission or anything like it; Dean knew what he thought was right. And yet there was something in him that needed support and confirmation.

Dean drank hot Postum with dehydrated milk. Ruth nibbled raisins one at a time, aggressively. She did most of the talking, but Dean gave the final word. Every so often, Dean would look at Loretta, as though remembering to include her. Loretta was hungry, but not hungry enough to eat whatever was available here; before, back with her parents, there had always been a bounty of junk food, sugar cereal and potato chips and store cookies, and now Loretta sometimes feels as if she were starving. When the children complain of hunger, Ruth suggests to them that they chew on kernels of raw wheat, and they do, chewing and chewing until it forms a gum, but Loretta wants nothing to do with Ruth's food, with raw wheat and carob and one-at-a-time raisins.

"Maybe this can be your way," Ruth said. "Maybe the Lord is bringing you an opportunity to overcome your obstacles. With the council and such."

Dean had left the Council of Elders. There had been talk of disfellowship. Excommunication.

Ruth said, "How about this, Father? You and me and the children go to Idaho for the funeral, and Aunt Loretta stays behind here. Minds the house. Takes orders. We can see what the situation is like there. Consider. There's no need for us to introduce anything just yet that requires extra explanation."

Dean and Ruth cast cool, appraising looks at Loretta, and Loretta felt as if she were more their child than their spouse. They were wondering, she could see, whether they could trust her.

"You make good sense, Mother," Dean said at last. "As usual."

It is not quite seven thirty. Loretta remembers a time she would have considered this early. She can't remember the last time she just wallowed around in bed. Every day, she drags herself out, against her will and ahead of the sun.

Why is she not going?

She can make each of the competing arguments to herself: Go now. Go alone. Go with Bradshaw. Wait and plot and gather "provisions," as Bradshaw calls it in his letters, and leave with Bradshaw. Or without him. Or. Or. Or. Her mind circles the options constantly, but now she realizes that she isn't waiting for one of those options to clarify—she's waiting for something else. Another choice. Another way. But all that thinking has nothing to do with why she's not leaving. She simply feels it. She is not going.

She does not relish this life in any sense. She despises it, feels it like a web holding her in place. But she knows it. It is all she knows. And what she tells herself she wants—freedom, a worldly life, music, magazine life, slacks, and makeup—of that world, she knows absolutely nothing. She thinks of the Tussy ad. "Win a Mustang to Match Your Lipstick!" The brazen girl on the hood of the pink, pink car, so colorful and bold and distant. An eternity away from here.

She will not think of herself as afraid.

Seven forty-five. Bradshaw arrives each morning at eight. He knows nothing of what's gone on here. Dean trusts him. There is an idea in the air—a hint, an undecided notion—that they could all just leave here, escape the problems with the brotherhood, and that Bradshaw could help run the business here while they are away. When Bradshaw understands what is happening, he will want to go. He will want to go, go, go.

Dean told Loretta his story with a neatness she distrusted—a mosaic of cause and effect dragged into the service of the ideas Dean wanted to convey about himself. That he had been raised in a misshapen faith, in a perverted version of the truth, and that he had found his way to the light.

He grew up in the mainstream church in southern Idaho, the oldest of five. His father held leadership roles in the local ward—a bishop or a member of the bishopric, a high councillor, the stake president—and the family was stalwart, at the wardhouse on Sundays and at the farmers co-op on Mondays and at the livestock auctions on Fridays at the fairgrounds. Though the church and its demands were great, Dean found himself at a young age wanting more rigor. More fire. In prayer, during the sacrament, while reading scripture, he would feel liquefied in the forge of the Lord, and when he emerged, he would see that his fellows were the same earthen lumps. They had not entered the fire. When he accompanied his father to the auctions or the cafés, and he watched him laugh and glad-hand with the worldly men, the farmers telling crude jokes or smoking cigarettes, he resented his father for not turning his back on these men and their ways.

He came to know some of the Reorganized LDS members down in Hagerman. The RLDS was a small sect that had broken away from the mainstream church more than a hundred years ago. Little pockets of the church stayed true, tiny congregations here and there around the country. There was something clandestine about them that fed Dean's desires. They were polygamists, and as Dean studied the origins of the faith, he began to see that the principle of plural marriage kept returning—godly men building lineages of righteousness. As he read the writings of Joseph Smith and Brigham Young, as he read the Old Testament with new eyes, he began to understand that there was a wide range of Mormon believers out there, a variety of little shoots and branches off the main body of the faith, and that one of these might contain the truth that the mainstream church had forsaken, and that the Principle stood at the center of this truth.

He was twenty-three, working the farm with his father while Louis served his mission, when federal agents raided the Saints in Short Creek. The officers tore children from the arms of their mothers and held righteous men at gunpoint, wicked and prideful, while the newspaper whores took photographs. *A clarion to awaken the righteous,* Dean had whispered to Loretta, telling her this story late into the night. *Your aunt Ruth was one of those children.*

His devotion grew until the Hagerman congregation could not contain it. Five years later, at the end of the harvest, he traveled to Short Creek. He returned home just once after that, a month later, when he held counsel with his father and his brother, poring over scripture and urging them to reject the mainstream church and join the brethren in Short Creek. When they told him they would not, he knew they were filled not simply with wickedness but with the most dangerous belief on earth—that their wickedness was righteousness.

She waits for the sound of Bradshaw's truck in the drive. She is in her nightdress, the thick cotton over the temple garments—

the silky two-piece underwear with the markings at the nipples and the belly, the garments she was given upon her marriage and which she is to wear at all times. It occurs to her that she could take them off.

She answers when the knock comes, and when she sees him again, like this, unguarded and not pretending, he is too much. Hungry grin, twittery eyes of ice, almost turquoise. One hand high on the doorjamb, one on his hip, one foot forward and one back, his Wranglers long at the boot heel and the arms of his pearl-button shirt cut short and fraying, and his hat, bill curled tightly and worn through at the front edge, bearing the words "Sandy Excavation" in lariat script.

"Darlin'," he says. "Sweet Lori," he says, and he is upon her.

He kisses her face off. He kisses her like he's trying to eat something. Her lips go raw, her jaw aches. He puts his hands everywhere. She likes it but she doesn't. It feels half like he's trying to hurt her. She holds his back, recalls how tightened with muscle it is, compared to Dean's thick, spongy flesh. She starts to push him away, and says, "Stop, stop, slow down," and it takes her a long time to wake him from the fever, and when he finally does he looks at her in pain and disbelief, groans and rolls to the corner of the couch, and wails. "Lori," he says, begging. "Lori."

Whether she wants it or not seems like the wrong question. Bradshaw is handsomer than Dean, funnier, younger, better in every way, and she would rather do this with him than with Dean. But it is not a choice between Bradshaw and Dean. It is a choice between now or later. Between Bradshaw or Dean or something else entirely. She could do it. Easily. She could do almost anything now. You hide inside yourself, and whatever happens out there still happens, but you're less there, you're enough not there that you can keep talking to yourself, telling yourself whatever you've decided to tell yourself, until it's done.

She says, "Not like this, baby. I want it to be right. To be us, somewhere else, living our own life. Not here. Not in Dean's house."

Bradshaw groans and holds his head in his hands as though he has been struck in the face. Loretta could not care less about the moment or the place. But she understands that this is a thing he would expect her to care about.

She could just give in. That would make Bradshaw happy. It might even make her happy. But none of that matters—not her desire, not his desire, not this man or that man, not being married or being free, not whether she wants to or not.

It is only about the choosing. Nothing else. The choosing, and that it be hers.

Later, when he's got his smile back, he tells her, "Well, hon, I'm sorry but there ain't any money."

Dean called in everything before he left town, got all the accounts in order. He had been settling up with Bradshaw once a week, and taking Bradshaw's word about a couple of "late payments," and generally had allowed Bradshaw to create pockets of uncertainty in the cash flow. But that was over now, and Bradshaw had to give over all the money he had squirreled away off the top of the payments to Zion's Harvest.

"Didn't have no choice. But this thing of Dean's is exploding. Sales off the freaking charts. When things settle down again, it'll be nothing to skim off . . . I don't know. . . ." He acts like he's calculating in his head. "A lot, baby. A shitload."

A love of money is the root of all evil. It is easier for a camel to pass through the eye of a needle than for a rich man to enter the kingdom of heaven. Your gold and your silver have rusted, and their rust will be a witness against you. Loretta has heard these words all her life, and she has always wondered: How could you not love money? Is it even possible?

He's not even trying to talk her into it now. He wants to wait for the money, too.

EVEL KNIEVEL ADDRESSES
AN ADORING NATION

The taverns. Oh, the taverns. The Muddy Bumper in Reno. The Silver Pony in Baker. The Mint in every Podunk Montana town. The little-town bars. The dusty afternoon light, thrust through the bar dark in thick planks. The freak-show glow of the egg jar, pickling in amber, and the sharp bite of a seventh cigarette. The Rockin R in Bozeman. John's Alley in Moscow. The Dry Dock in Moses Lake. The little-town taverns, unannounced. Walk in, await an audience, watch the night grow. Buy rounds, unscrew the top of the cane, drain the Wild Turkey. Wink at the best-looking gal first chance you get. The Sports Page in Pocatello. The Bawdy Dog in Orem. The Baby Bar in Spokane. The Stockmen's in Elko. People pressed around us so tight we felt their heat, their life, pouring into us. We walk in, and wait for the eyes to turn, for the looks to begin, for the approach and the surprise—their thrill when we sit with them, share ourselves, their glorying in us—and the delivery of the best kind of love, the only kind of love: wild, momentary, complete.

September 1, 1975

GOODING, IDAHO

J ason's dad sits in the high cab of the tractor, pulling the baler
as it spins the cut hay into its mouth and spits out a trail of
tightly twined rectangles. Jason and Boyd swap between bucking
bales onto the flatbed and driving the truck. They should finish by
nightfall. Finish for the day, finish for the season, finish forever.
That's what Jason is thinking, that this will be his last day of this,
ever, and that now that school is starting, his senior year, everything will be the last of its kind, the final one. Next year, he'll be
eighteen, a high school graduate, and gone. The thought gets him
through it all: the throb in his temples, his pasty mouth, the ache in
his shoulders.

The day is spangled, wincingly bright—white-gold fields, a haze
of dust. They have been haying behind Grandpa's place, by the
falling-down gray shack and the old tractor grown through with
weeds. They stop for lunch. Jason and Boyd eat in the truck cab,

drenched in sweat and daubed with hay dust, while Dad clears weeds from the teeth of the baler.

They eat quietly until, across the field, they see Dean emerge from the back door of the house and lope to the shed. Everyone else left not long after the funeral, but Dean and his family stayed, without explanation. Now a pickup truck and a horse trailer packed with boxes are parked in the drive.

"Are they moving here?" Boyd asks.

"I don't know."

"They look like they're in some pioneer movie."

Jason feels an odd impulse to defend them. The ugly tether of family.

"What are they, like, square dancers?" Boyd asks.

"Probably."

"Do they spin wool into thread? Can they churn butter?"

"I'm sure they can churn amazing butter."

Jason's parents have been deeply uninformative about the situation. His father has been particularly terse and dismissive, pretending he's surprised anyone might be interested in what Dean is doing. Across the field, Dean emerges from the shed and strides to the horse trailer. Ruth comes out from the back door, and begins pulling down what seems like one hundred pairs of overalls from the clothesline, two kids romping at her feet like puppies.

"Spectacular butter," Jason says. "You'd want to rub yourself all over with this butter."

It is so hot it no longer feels hot. Jason's mouth is furred, no matter how much warm water he chugs from the thermos. He sinks drowsily into the soft, springy seats, closes his eyes, wonders how quickly they will make it through the final windrows. Four more hours? Five?

Done forever.

Boyd spits out the window. "I don't get why you don't know if they're moving here," he says. "What's the big secret?"

Boyd can't understand Jason's family, Jason knows, because they almost never tell one another anything, while he and his mother tell each other every embarrassing thing. Jason doesn't know what to say about Dean. He can feel already how having them here is going to reflect on him, on his family—how it will create a new zone of caution between him and others.

"They're just old-fashioned," he says. "They live down there on the Utah-Arizona line. It's like they're half Amish."

"Down there with the polygamists?"

"I'm not sure."

Dad comes to the truck, boots crunching the shorn hay stalks. He takes off his hat and squints at them, sweat sheened, the tips of his nose and ears a deep red.

"All right, boys, let's get back to it," he says.

"Hey, Mr. Harder," Boyd says. "Is your brother moving here or what?"

Dad pulls on his gloves, gets them snug.

"We're still figuring that out," he says.

Grandpa has been dead for two weeks now, the funeral come and gone, and everything still feels tilted on its side. For as long as Jason can remember, this has been the order of things: him, his parents, and Grandpa down the road. His grandmother died when Jason was four, and he doesn't remember her at all. The current arrangement—the family, as he understood it to exist—had taken on a feeling of permanence.

And then there is the pressing strangeness of Dean and Ruth and their kids. Dean calls Ruth "Mother" in a stern voice, they dress like pioneers, and an air of self-imposed privation hangs around them. None of them says much, always waiting for Dean to talk. They don't watch television or go to movies or dances, and they eat weird food. For one of the family dinners before everyone left, Ruth made meat-free hamburgers out of bulgur. Everyone picked at them unhappily while Ruth talked about the benefits of eating less meat and sugar. It was the quietest meal of the week, as people nibbled the crumbly patties and held their tongues.

Afterward, Roy had driven Jason into town for cheeseburgers, tater tots, and suicides at the Oh-So, where they laughed themselves to tears over Ruth's food.

"*Ho-ly shit*. Those poor kids," Roy had said, sinking a tot into a tub of pink fry sauce. "Someone ought to set them free. Nobody should be forced to eat like that."

"Why do they?"

"Why do they do anything? Don't ask me." He seemed happily unconcerned. "I used to tell my friends that Dean had crooked calf disease. You know what that is? When their feet are turned under and twisted all around? Nothing you can do for 'em. It's just unfixable. Dean's like that—just *deformed*. From the ground up. His feet are all fucked up."

Jason is tempted to say he hates them, but why would he hate them? He feels a stinging blade of hatred in the side, like a stitch in the abdomen from running—a resentment that they magnify everything he dislikes about his family and church and town, the limited horizons, the boring reverence, the feeling that the people who were considered wise were in fact stupid. And the truth of it, the real thing: the fear that they are him. That he is them. These freaks.

In the days before the funeral, Dad, Dean, and Roy spent a lot of time huddled together, speaking in low voices, pointing, and shaking their heads. Sometimes Bonnie and Jenna would join in. They were sorting through the inheritance—Grandpa had left each of the five siblings a share of the land. Dad already had 250 acres and the dairy, which he'd bought years earlier. The brothers were going to buy out the sisters, but some unknown tension remained unresolved.

The night before the funeral, Jason walked into the kitchen to find the brothers around the table. Mom stood at the sink, her back to them. She seemed smaller than usual in the waning glow from the overhead light. They all tower over her, the Harder men— even Jason is a head taller—but she never seems short, exactly; she has a way of bringing your eyes down to her, a directness that could make a high priest squirm. She was washing jars in steaming water; the women were going to can green beans and tomatoes the next day.

Dad was saying, "But I *bought* it, Dean. How's that supposed to count against me here?" Dean stared at a point between his long, thickly knuckled hands, splayed on the table before him. The skin around his eyes had tightened whitely. Roy winked at Jason.

Jason opened the fridge and scouted, waiting for them to resume talking. He grabbed a Tupperware bowl, opened it, and looked at a lump of leftover ground beef. The hamburger looked like volcanic rock, a solid created from a liquid's lack of geometric logic. At his back, a fingernail ticked on the laminate tabletop. He imagined a tiny mountain climber rappelling down Hamburger Mountain into a greasy white crevasse. Dad said, "Jason, you're letting out all the cold air."

"It's not like there's only so much cold air," Jason said. "Like there's only a certain amount of cold, and you've got to keep it trapped in there, like bees."

He could be so stupid. Jason thought he was going to choke on it.

Roy laughed. "He's making a certain kind of sense, Louis."

"Thank you, son," Dad said, ignoring Roy. "Now clear out of here and let us talk."

"Talk. Please."

Mom turned, holding a gleaming, soapy jar. "I don't know where all this mouth is coming from," she said. "But that's enough."

Jason closed the fridge door and sauntered out, steaming. He couldn't believe they were fighting over this place. Who would ever want to be here?

They move into the last field, the fifty acres between Grandpa's house and Shoestring Road. Some of these final windrows are barely even there. This is where the jacks had hit a few weeks earlier, gnawing half the hay into bare patches and paths swirling through the field like the scribbling of a giant.

Dad stops the combine and climbs out. Shakes his head. A sudden rustling at the edge of the field startles Jason. A single jackrabbit springs into the air, long ears back, bounding into the desert in ten-foot leaps. Boyd points an imaginary gun and says, "Boom."

Later that afternoon, when they're halfway through the field, the end in sight, Dean comes striding through the stubble, raising a low cloud. Jason sits in the sweltering, oil-rank cab of the combine, engine roaring in an obliterating drone. Dad follows in the truck, while Boyd bucks bales onto the flatbed. Everyone stops and watches Dean. He doesn't wave, and they don't, either, and when he reaches them, a few strained, silent seconds pass.

Finally, Dean says something, and Dad shrugs and gestures toward the rumbling cab, or toward Jason. He's come to help, it seems, though they are all but done. Jason turns off the engine, and Dad calls, "Whyn't you let your uncle Dean up there for a minute?"

Dean climbs in and nods, says, "Jason." His denim shirt is buttoned to the neck, darkened with sweat at the collar, and he wears a green John Deere cap with a stiff bill. He smells sour and fundamental, like homemade soap and tent canvas. He looks around, at the pedals and the gearshift and back at the pedals. The sun illuminates the calcified grime on the cab windows. He turns the key and the engine bursts into life.

"Gotta watch that clutch," Jason shouts.

"I don't require any instruction from you."

Dean might be teasing. He presses the clutch, forces the gearshift into first, and eases his foot down on the gas. The gearshift begins to grind and vibrate and his foot slips off. The engine chugs and dies.

"Well, Judas Priest," Dean says.

He twists the key, presses the clutch, and tries again. This time the baler lurches forward, coughs, and dies. Jason feels testy, impatient; they are so close to done. Dean stamps his foot and mutters.

He tries again. It chugs and dies.

"You know . . ." Jason says.

Dean points toward Jason sideways, without looking up, like a prophet banishing a demon. "Do not!" he spits.

Dad and Boyd watch from the ground, shading their eyes. Dad calls, "Maybe you ought to let Jason show you."

"Louis!" Dean shouts, and Jason hears the tone of an older brother. "I do not need instructions from a boy in how to operate a simple piece of machinery. I think if you maintained your equipment properly, we wouldn't be having this problem. This clutch is slipping all over the place."

Jason looks out and catches Boyd's eye. He smiles.

"That *is* a bear of a clutch, Mr. Harder," Boyd says.

Dean stares at Boyd, breathing slowly and deeply. Then he reaches for the key again and turns it, slowly lifting his foot from the clutch. This time, he fails to give it enough gas, and it sputters out weakly.

Dean spins in the seat and climbs down and stalks off across the field toward Grandpa's.

Dad calls after him, "Dean! Heaven's sake," but Dean keeps marching into the sun until he's a shadow again, and they go back to work.

They finish haying, and Jason takes the minibike out to the barley fields to move the irrigation pipes. Finished haying forever, he thinks, and soon, once this barley is cut, he'll be through with that forever, too—through moving pipe, through choking on hay dust, through picking rock, through milking cows, *through*. He is thinking about buying an eight-track player for the LeBaron, like the one he saw in Roy's Nova. It hung under the dash, a squat mechanical face with silver knobs for eyes and an inch of plastic case sticking out like a tongue. "New Zappa," Roy had said, turning it up. Jason had no idea what he meant by that. Was it a code? A language? The music was strange and plinky, moving in uneven time. Roy tapped the steering wheel, and sang along, horrendously: "'*Watch out where the huskies go, and don't you eat that yellow snow.*'"

Jason wrings the gas, pushes the bike to top speed—thirty-three miles an hour. It is nearly sundown, a burning indigo along the black edge of the horizon. When he asked Roy how much the eight-track player cost, Roy answered, "Think your old man will let you have one?" Jason shrugged, and Roy said, "Sixty bucks or so." Sprinklers on hand lines go *chk-chk-chk* in the barley, beside the parched, stubbled hay fields. Jason's got sixty bucks. There's still $134 in his savings account. He could put the player in the LeBaron and his parents probably wouldn't even notice.

He rides through a cloud of cooled air, comes over the rise, and approaches Grandpa's house, and standing in the yard is a girl or young woman, her back to Jason, a smooth drape of long brown hair squared upon the white of her blouse and her ankle-length dress. He has no idea who she is. She is pinning a shirt by the shoulders to the laundry line, one of Dean's white shirts, and Jason wonders if all these people do is hang laundry, and then he is past her. A worm of nervous excitement moves through his guts, though there can be no good reason. What could he see? Nothing. Hair, a dress, the back of a head. A bending motion, like nodding barley. Nothing. And yet he feels it—girl nervousness, the anxiety of the suitor.

They eat a late dinner. Dad glumly answers Mom's peppy questions, about the harvest, the yield, the jackrabbits. He nods as she tells him all about her plans for Jason, now that his senior year is beginning—scholarships and grants, college opportunities. She has somehow gotten it into her head that he will study agriculture, become the educated farmer, though he has lately thought he will study architecture, for no reason other than the impressive sound of it. She considers how he will work his mission around his college. Mom finally stops talking, and Dad sighs, staring at the lump of cheesy hamburger casserole on his plate. It is odd that he has not gulped it down and spooned up more. The plain, heavy silence infects Jason with an unfocused urge. He will definitely buy an eight-track player for the LeBaron. And maybe that New Zappa, too. Who cares if they catch him?

"I guess Dean and Ruth have gotten set up over there," Dad says at last.

"For good?" Jason asks.

Dad shrugs. "For now."

Mom puts her hand on his forearm.

"We'll make the best of it," she says.

"That's right," he says, but he sounds exhausted.

Mom smiles forcefully at Dad—her way of drawing him out of his gloom, of insisting happily that he not disappear into his own mind. He avoids her eyes. He coughs once, hard, to clear his throat, and says, "They've got a young girl over there with them. Ruth's niece, Dean said."

Mom stops chewing. And blinking. She stares at Dad, and he looks back, and they seem to forget Jason. It would not be too much to say they look terrified. Soon everyone they know will know this, too. Everyone in church. Everyone in town. Everyone.

Mom says, "No, Lou."

Very carefully and very slowly, he says, "Dean says she's Ruth's niece, and she has nowhere else to go."

Nobody speaks for several seconds.

"And I don't know any different," he says, looking stubbornly at the center of the table.

Jason feels like he might throw up. Like just vomiting, there on the table, among the three of them and this new development, might be what's called for.

"You don't?" he says. "Really?"

Dad exhales sharply, the sound like a sack of grain dropped on its end, and says nothing more.

September 7, 1975

GOODING, IDAHO

Dean says they have to, so they have to. And so, when the time comes, when the old clock in this musty house makes a single weak reverberating bong, Loretta swings her legs off the bed and stands, brushes her hands down the front of her dress, and takes a deep breath through her nose. She does not know those people, she reminds herself. Doesn't know them and shouldn't care about them. And yet she is flushed with self-consciousness, a constant rose of warmth wrapping her neck and ears and temples now that she is out here, in the world.

She goes downstairs. Ruth herds the kids. They are dressed as if for church, though they will not be attending services here, Dean has informed them. They will be having their own services, led by Dean. He reminds them all, often, how vigilant they must be against the dangers and temptations of the world, where Satan rules. Despite herself, Loretta expected to find demons everywhere; so far, she's been disappointed by how much this place is like home:

the desert here is not as pretty, more like a weed patch with dying grasses and tick-filled sagebrush, but in most ways what she has seen of Gooding and the countryside has been a lot like Short Creek. Farms and fences, barking dogs. Horse trailers on blocks beside mobile homes, spread over with rust. Pole sheds with small weedy junkyards out back. A kind of galaxy circling the town—the farther away you get from the center, the farther apart the houses are, until you get out to Harder land, out to the biggest farms and ranches, and beyond them, all the human structures start coming together again, as Gooding turns into Wendell, the next town over.

The differences, though. There are no other people like them here. No groups of five, eight, eleven children walking along the roadside. No women in long chaste dresses and long braided hair. No young boys in wool pants and long-sleeved shirts.

Dean says he's praying about what to do. About whether they might find a new home here, on his family's land. In his father's house. He tells the family he's praying about this, and he tells Loretta—in these first days since he came to retrieve her—that he's praying about this, but Bradshaw told her that he was already making plans to move the business to Idaho. Dean has even asked Bradshaw if he would help run it.

"He wants to pay me to come up there. Isn't that something?" Bradshaw said, delighted. "Doesn't the Lord work in mysterious ways?"

A demon. She feels sure of it now. How else could this be happening? How else could it be that her husband is bringing Bradshaw into the family? Dean's God, she feels more and more, is a fake. Dean's God is simply Dean's mind. But the world behind the world is real. Something must operate behind everything—guiding, shaping, directing. She cannot imagine otherwise, and Bradshaw comes from that place.

Dean arrives in the living room dressed in his black suit, his beard darkened and damp. He has lectured them about his brother Louis and his family, who are well meaning but misguided, and whom they should embrace and mistrust in equal measure. The children are aligned perfectly, militarily, descending by age: Samuel, Ruth, Elizabeth, Dean Jr., Janeen, Sarah, Benjamin. And Ruth at their head, like a sergeant. Loretta stands behind them all.

"I expect you all to be on your best behavior," Dean says. "Good manners at the table. Polite to your aunt and uncle. Do not make your mother and me ashamed. Don't make me go to the belt."

Dean goes to the belt about once a day. The backs of Samuel's legs, Loretta knows, are chapped with calluses, which he earns for his stubborn, silent rebellions—refusals to complete chores, to finish his bulgur meat loaf. Dean nags him relentlessly, reminding him that he is the eldest, and he is falling short.

"You understand that we have to be less than honest regarding your aunt Loretta," he says. "We have no choice in this. We are no longer in Short Creek, among the righteous. We are no longer among those who understand the righteousness of the Principle. Satan is in control out here."

"At Uncle Lou's?" Samuel asks, and Dean gives him a silent look.

"Everywhere. The world over. Your uncle is not an evil man. But neither is he a righteous one. And Satan is ever watchful for opportunities to tempt and persecute the righteous."

Loretta knows that Dean considers himself a perfectly righteous man, though he would never admit it out loud. A perfectly righteous man would not be so vain. How do you come to feel that way about yourself? How do you ever feel so fully synchronized with the purpose of the universe? There must be a beauty in that feeling. Sometimes she thinks of the world as Dean versus Bradshaw. And other times she thinks of the world as Dean plus Bradshaw, different expressions of the same confidence.

"Okay, then," Dean says, and Ruth opens the front door and the children exit in single file, through the screen door and onto the front step, the red paint walked off in the middle, and onto the path worn into the lawn. Then Loretta goes, then Dean, then Ruth, and the children wait for Dean to take the lead. They walk out onto the gravel shoulder of the narrow county road and begin walking the quarter mile toward Uncle Lou and Aunt Becky's. The heat of the past month is cooling, but still Loretta feels too warm in her long dress and wool stockings, a hint of dampness already inside her lace-up shoes, at the tight neck of her dress. They begin walking up the small rise that separates the two homes, the harvested hay fields to their left, and the cow-filled pasture on their right, and a pickup roars over the top, a dirt-caked Ford F-150 with a cracked windshield. The plump, red-faced man inside turns to watch them as he passes, looking mystified and pleased, here on this ordinary road that he must drive all the time without the magic of any surprise.

When Dean came to The Crick to get her and their belongings, to fill the horse trailer with the boxes that Bradshaw helped them load, bantering with Dean, making him laugh and shake his head, when he came for her and had her by his side as he prowled through the house, choosing what would be needed and what could be left behind for now, he had taken her into his office while he compiled certain papers and locked others into his steel filing cabinet. He had opened the bottom drawer of the cabinet and removed a strongbox that he opened with another small key, and then had shown it to her with wide eyes, with shared amazement: a pile of gold coins, shined carefully, an incoherent pile of one-ounce golden eagles, thousands of dollars' worth of gold. He had removed eight coins, and relocked the box, and placed it back in the cabinet.

"You're leaving that here?" Loretta had asked.

"For now," Dean said. "For now."

He looked at her gravely, lips pressed and brown eyes brightened. She could sense in him an assessing mood, an evaluative moment— the kind of seriousness that might come over him in prayer or spiritual leadership, his sense of himself expanding even as he adopted a veil of humility.

"What?" she asked.

"If I show you something," he said, "you must promise me to hold it as a sacred secret."

"I promise, Dean."

He withdrew a leather pouch tied with a cord, sagging as if it held a misshapen grapefruit, and held it toward her, fist tight around the top, his chapped red knuckles as big as walnuts and one black crack running across his thumbnail.

"Take it," he said. "Feel it."

She reached out, and he said, "Use both hands," and he set the pouch in her cupped palms, and said, "Don't drop it, little sister," smiling, thrilled, looking as he did sometimes in bed, beforehand, ready to climb on, his brown eyes backlit with intensity. She felt the contents of the bag settle and shift as he gave it to her, and it nearly forced her hands to the floor, so great was the distance between its weight and her expectation of its weight.

"What is it?"

"It is gold, little sister."

He was whispering, inches from her face. She had never felt so intimately connected with him. She set the pouch on the floor and opened the top.

He whispered, "It is gold from the California gold rush. Some of the first ever discovered—by Saints. By Saints, little sister."

She opened the top of the pouch tremblingly. Inside, the lumps were dark and brownish, but for a few tiny gleaming curves, where the lumps of ore caught the light.

"Discovered by Saints, Loretta, though you will never hear it spoken of by the Gentiles. They say a man named John Sutter discovered the gold, in a place called Coloma in California. They named it Sutter's Mill. You can read all about him in the histories. In the schoolbooks of the Gentiles, his story is well told."

Loretta reached in and took up a single nugget. It felt almost soft between her finger and thumb, as if she might mash it.

"But you will never hear the Gentiles talk of the Saints in Sutter's Mill, and how the Saints settled California, how the Saints discovered the gold. You will never hear the Gentiles tell the truth about that, little sister, because what if they did? What if they had to accept the righteous history of the nation? That it was the Saints—the ones everyone repudiated, the ones everyone scorned and scorns still, the Saints, abandoned by their own church, ostracized by all—it was the Saints leading from the very first, Loretta. Setting the example."

Loretta had stopped noticing anything but the small lump of gold. Gold. She hadn't conceived of it like this before—as a substance of the earth, a rock. Dean reached out and took it from her, and placed it back in the pouch as he continued talking about it, telling her it was sacred gold, Mormon gold, and that this *particu-*

lar gold had been held in the hands of the true Saints for more than a hundred years. Saints had left Utah and gone to California, and gold had come back to Salt Lake and bolstered the new Zion under Brigham Young.

"And where did you get it?" Loretta asked.

Dean merely shook his head. Never mind. He tightened the pouch and placed it back in the bottom cabinet drawer and locked it.

They left the room and he locked his office door behind them. He explained that they were entering a world full of dangers, of persecution, of enemies. He told her for the ten-millionth time about the Short Creek raid, the agents pouring into the homes of the righteous, driving out mothers and children, locking up their fathers.

"That was not so long ago, little sister," he says. "Your aunt Ruth was among those children. That is still the world that we live in."

Those two days had been awful—Dean climbing onto her every half hour, it seemed, until she was so sore she asked him to stop, until she feared that nothing could stop her from getting pregnant now, not with this flood of his seed, and when she used the solution it burned so badly she bit her thumb and cried.

But she took careful note of the ring of keys that Dean carried. Careful mental note of which keys, among the thick ball of them, opened four locks: front door, office door, cabinet, strongbox.

They arrive at the house in single file, crossing the dirt driveway and aiming straight for the side door. Both of these houses, this one and Dean's father's home, are squat, square brick affairs, with front doors and side doors facing their dirt drives, each door fronted by a cube of concrete. Uncle Louis's place has a shed out back, and a cinder-block milking barn across the driveway, and cow pasture all around. Behind the barn are haystacks and a low row of calf pens. Loretta finds the smell—fresh manure and cut hay—comfortingly familiar.

Dean raps on the screen door, and Aunt Becky sings, "Come in, come in," and in they come, clustering on the bright yellow linoleum, not leaving Loretta enough room to let the door shut behind her, and so she stands there, framed, as Aunt Becky dries her hands on a towel and fusses, never stops looking about, offering a hand, patting, smiling, moving, nervous. At the counter stands a tall, knobby boy with a rubbed brush of reddish hair, leaning with half a buttered roll in his hand. When Loretta glances at him he looks away quickly. She feels him tracking her in his peripheral vision, shooting quick visual sorties her way, and his appraisal lights up her nerves. She is familiar with this kind of attention, but usually not from boys. The boys in Short Creek tend to leave, or be kicked out, by the time they're in their middle teens. Loretta feels both younger and a thousand years older than this worldly kid in blue jeans and T-shirt, though she knows that he is older, that he is Jason, that he is seventeen, that he is technically her nephew if you drew it up on the family tree—but that he considers her unrelated. Or not very related, anyway.

The children crowd farther in and she lets the screen door close behind her. On the boy's T-shirt is an image of a large red tongue hanging from a set of bright red lips, a lush sexual image, and under it the words "Hot Rocks." She feels herself blush behind the ears.

The boy says, "Welcome to Idaho," says it directly to her, but it is Dean who answers, "Don't forget I grew up here."

Uncle Louis sits at the head of the table, offers Dean the seat at his right hand. Aunt Becky's seat stays open at his left, while she and Ruth shuttle the dishes to the table: roast chickens, mashed potatoes, green beans, hot rolls, jugs of milk. Loretta sits among the children, across the long table from Jason, the two of them volleying looks. He seems to be watching her even when he is not watching her. He is not handsome, particularly—gangly, hips wider than shoulders, a scruff of curly reddish hair cut close, with those big Harder ears and small Harder eyes hidden behind his bulb of a freckled nose. But she finds him awkwardly beautiful, like a calf or colt. He acts like a shy boy, and she finds herself feeling like a shy girl, and it shocks her—it assaults her how simple and nice it is, how childlike, how innocent to be shy and embarrassed and nervous, and how normal that is, how utterly typical it is everywhere and for everyone except her.

Uncle Louis smiles and looks around, waiting for people to settle. He and Dean avoid each other's eyes, touch the silverware, scratch at their jaws, watch their folded hands in their laps. Louis glances past Jason, but his gaze snags on the T-shirt. That mouth. That tongue. He doubles back and stares.

"Son," he says quietly. "Go put on something appropriate."

Jason moves his head twice as if preparing to speak, tucking it back both times, and looking into his lap. Aunt Becky reaches with a plate of rolls over his shoulder, sets it with a thump on the table, and pats Jason on the shoulder.

"Let's go," she says.

He ducks, mopey, pushes back, and clunks out of the room.

Loretta wants to go with him. To see what his room is like. To see the kinds of clothing he might choose among, the sorts of blankets on his beds, whether he hangs anything on the walls. What does it look like, his worldly life?

Ruth and Aunt Becky talk. Dean and Uncle Louis stare at their food, watching it move from plate to mouth. Jason has put on another T-shirt. On it, a ghostly figure holds a lantern over words and symbols Loretta does not understand: Led Zeppelin. At one point, Jason asks her whether she knows that Evel Knievel is jumping thirteen buses today in London, at Wembley Stadium, his first jump since the Snake River.

Loretta smiles and says, "Who is Evel Knievel?"

Jason gazes at her dumbly. Dean watches him. Ruth watches him. He wears his infatuation like a star-spangled cape.

"It's on the *Wide World of Sports* later," he says.

Dean shakes his head. "We do not watch television."

The food goes around and around. The children are quiet, sometimes the young ones giggle, stopping at Ruth's abrupt looks. Dean complains about the jackrabbits. Louis says, "I'm not sure how much more there is to be done about them," and Dean says, "I am."

Becky interrupts to ask whether Loretta will be enrolling in high school. Dean, Ruth, and Loretta all stop chewing at once.

"Classes start tomorrow," Aunt Becky says.

Dean clears his throat, says, "She finished her school already. Tested out. Loretta is one sharp young lady."

"What about seminary?" Aunt Becky asks.

Seminary. The early-morning church class. Loretta would definitely be going to seminary if she were just a regular Mormon girl, a niece living with family. What about seminary?

Dean and Ruth look at each other. You can sense them gauging, measuring.

Dean clears his throat. "I guess we hadn't thought of that."

"She could always ride in with Jason," Dad says.

Jason alerts like a bird dog. He is so cute, this boy. And he likes her so much.

EVEL KNIEVEL ADDRESSES
AN ADORING NATION

Most crashes are blur and smash, a sensory blast that's far too fast
to register. There's just before, followed by an obliterating sensation,
a destruction that somehow does not destroy, and then the adding-
up after, the backward tracking, the figuring out, the mending.

But this one, America. *Shit.* This one made every bit of itself
known. We felt it all.

After the canyon thing, we had no choice. When the world tries to
crush you, your only choice is to crush back. So: Wembley Stadium.
Thirteen buses. *Wide World of Sports.* Jolly old England.

Hell must be a whole lot like England. Everything somewhat
normal. Somewhat regular. Then you're talking to someone and
they say *I saw you on the telly,* or *You could take the lorry,* or *Are
you 'avin' a go?* whatever it is they say, and it's just enough to tilt
you on your fucking ear, and then it's just one strange thing after
another, driving on the wrong side, kings and queens, everything's
a pudding. We arrived two weeks before the jump, left Linda and
the kids at home—the kids, Jesus Christ, you're not supposed to

say this, but the goddamn kids were just killing us then—and we set that town on fire.

We felt somehow angry at the English.

We felt that the English were not appreciative enough of all we had done for them. Everything America has given them. The rotten-toothed, ratty little fuckers.

"You should just say thank you whenever you see an American," we told our limey publicist, Harry O, while he took our picture loading that pretty Smith & Wesson .38, surrounded by cash on the bed at the Tower Hotel. "You should just say thank you for keeping us from being fucking Germany."

"Are you 'avin' a go?" he asked us. *'Avin' a go.*

"Learn your history," we said.

For fun, we pointed that beaut right at him. Right into the lens.

"You," he said, "don't know your history from your arse."

You will never understand, America, how difficult it was for us not to pull the trigger that afternoon, how heroic the challenge to our being, our honor, our noble whatever the fuck. But we let it go, we let him go, we let him live. That photo ran in every newspaper over there for weeks.

So, yes, this is after the fuckup at the canyon, the screwing those "engineers" gave us. They worked on that Skycycle for two years, tightened every bolt, honed every spark plug, did all the math, and then fucked up the parachute bay? The parachute bay?

It's embarrassing, is what it is. We put our good name out there. Put our life up, is all, put it up for sacrifice, for the entertainment of the people. We climbed into that thing, ready to sacrifice all, like a modern gladiator, like Jesus Christ, and those dumb fucks with the wrenches, drinking and eating steak all over southern Idaho on our dime and our name and our grace, screw it up, and no one knows who they are, no one writes newspaper articles about what a sham it all was, a fake, no one spins a million lies in the *Los Angeles Times* or *Rolling Stone* about them.

There was only one thing to do. Go bigger.

It was not as hard as you might think.

At Wembley, every moment of the crash announces itself. Every altered atom in our body, each as it altered, a cracking network of breakage running through us, and every instant palpable.

We land on our right shoulder, pulverizing the humerus and clavicle and driving one large crack through the scapula and two vertebrae, and then all the way down the right side of us by degree, crushing and chipping and fracturing, ribs, sternum, pelvis, femur, tibia, fibula, rolling over onto our back and sliding, sliding across the ramp and then the earth, chipping the spinous process here, the transverse process there, finely cracking the facet joints and the vertebral body but somehow not breaching the spinal canal, America, the magic of the thing, our majesty and life, protected. We roll, grinding across the asphalt covered with turf that buckles and bundles under us, and the breakage spreads to the other side of us, and the bike, that heavy fucker, the Harley XR750, lands on us, breaking our legs in seven places, our old friends fibula, tibia, femur, and when we grind to a stop, we feel like a receptacle of glittering, broken glass, like a deerskin bag full of coins.

At first, the massive pain remains silent. Somewhere out there are ninety thousand people, making noise or making no noise, and then the face of the TV handsome looms in over us, and he thinks we are dead, that's clear, and whatever else has happened here: Fuck that. Fuck him and his thinking we are dead, *because we are not dead.*

We make him hold us up, the TV handsome, we make him hold us up before that massive crowd, and we press it all over him, the breakage, the blood in our breath, the blood tasting of iron and Wild Turkey, and when we stand before that crowd, they fall silent, all ninety thousand of them like congregants in a cathedral, and we speak.

Strange. We can, even now, recall the exact progression of injury from that crash. The tracery of breakage. The order of disassembly. We can recall standing there, being held there, by the TV handsome and someone else, and we can recall the way the sun was dipping down below the top of the stadium, making a series of expanding and contracting orbs of yellow and red against our spotty vision.

But we cannot remember, nor can we believe, what we said that day.

When we came to in the hospital, there were Linda and the kids. We wondered whether they'd been to the Tower yet, whether they'd seen the room. We wondered what evidence there might have been left in that room. We could not recall the final state of things, just the parade of the days before: the English "birds" as quick as the American ones, the Wild Turkey bottles, the golf clubs on the balcony, the new red Lamborghini parked out front. All that before, then the jump, and now this: family, fatherhood.

Life is stupid, America. But not at all bad.

This is what they say we said:

"Ladies and gentlemen of this wonderful country. I have to tell you that you are the last people in the world who will see me jump. Because I will never, ever, ever jump again. I'm through."

SEMINARY

September 8–12, 1975

Monday

On the first morning of his senior year, Jason pulls up to his grandfather's house in the LeBaron, crackling slowly on the gravel, and honks. It is 6:45 A.M., cool and lilac-gray. Jason's stomach pulses, a nervous fist clenching in time with his clash of emotions. All night he planned what to say to Loretta. He will ask her a brash, direct question, a question one of the jocks at school, the popular thugs, would ask. Because he has no idea how to talk to girls, and the popular thugs clearly do, and what the popular thugs do is flirt aggressively. Take liberties. Poke, poke, poke. He will ask her a question as if she were just an ordinary teenager: "Aren't you pissed that Dean's making you go to seminary?"

Gauge her response. Get a read.

He spent last night poring over his Evel Knievel scrapbook, the cutout quotes from newspapers and magazines, trolling for bravado and inspiration. "You come to a point in your life when you really don't care what people think about you, you just care what you think about yourself." "If you fall during your life, it doesn't matter. You're never a failure as long as you try to get up." He built a reservoir of confidence that has leaked away. Loretta needs saving, saving from Dean and all of it, and he feels that it has been arranged for him to save her.

If he could just be the right guy.

As soon as he sees her coming out of the side door, though—dressed like a normal girl, more or less, in jeans and a long-sleeved blouse, hair pulled into a ponytail, features fine and smooth and tensed and lovely—Jason begins cursing himself, knowing that he is not the right guy.

She climbs in. Says hello very, very quietly. Looks off across the desert, showing him the pale pillar of her neck. He backs out of the driveway.

"Excited for your first day of seminary?" he warbles lamely.

"I don't know," she says, not turning from the window.

She is less perfectly beautiful this morning. A little drawn and sleepy eyed. Jason notices a strange sloping bulge on the bridge of her delicate nose. Which is fine with him. She is a lot better looking than he is, and anything that closes the gap will be helpful.

They ride without speaking for seven minutes. It is much harder than he guessed it would be, sitting alone with her and trying to think of things to say. Then, as the abandoned TB hospital on the edge of town comes into sight, she releases a deep breath—a lush, weary sound—and says, "I hope it's not too weird."

"It won't be," Jason says.

He is so wrong. It is too, too weird. They arrive at the church as sunrise blares through the tops of the trees, burnishing rooftops, power lines, and steeples. They park and walk in behind two freshman boys and a girl. The freshmen don't say a thing, don't look at them. Jason and Loretta follow them in and down the hallway of cool tile into the seminary classroom. Three rows of folding chairs face a blackboard and a little mini-pulpit on a table. Brother Kershaw stands there, reading from a workbook and chewing a pencil, belly straining outward above skinny legs. On the blackboard, three words are whitely chalked: *Remorse, Repentance, Restitution.*

"Brother Harder," Kershaw says. "Good to see you looking bright eyed and bushy tailed."

And then he looks to Loretta and his jovial energy lurches to a stop. Jason flushes anew, introduces Loretta as Ruth's niece, who is visiting for a while or maybe longer, and sees the blood is hot in her face, too. Loretta takes the seat in the far back corner by herself, and Jason sits in front of her, not next to anyone, and they each avoid the eyes of the others. There are fifteen other kids there; half the seats are full. A cloud of assumptions fills the room. Loretta sits quietly, filling a notebook page with an expanding spore of tiny squares. Kershaw calls on her just once, after reading a passage from the Pearl of Great Price:

"'Wherefore teach it unto your children, that all men, everywhere, must repent, or they can in nowise inherit the kingdom of God, for no unclean thing can dwell there, or dwell in his presence.' Why must all men repent?" Kershaw asks. "Loretta?"

She says, in a hushed, glorious voice, "I don't know."

Afterward, she takes the LeBaron back home. Jason catches a ride to school with Ben Jenkins and Jed Story. The two talk football. Ben's a fullback and linebacker, and Jed plays wide receiver, and they look like variations on a theme: wide-legged jeans, short-sleeved terry-cloth shirts, helmety haircuts parted down the middle and feathered. They tune in the rock station from Twin Falls, Z103 FM, blasting "Ballroom Blitz."

Jason is happy to be left out of their conversation. But as they pull into the high school parking lot, Ben says, "Hey, Harder," with the sneer that lets him know he's in for it.

"What?"

"Your cousin's hot."

Jed snorts.

"She's not my cousin."

"What is she?"

"My aunt's niece."

Jed says, "I think that makes her your cousin."

"You can't fuck her, anyway," Ben says.

Jed cackles. A brush fire breaks out in Jason's upper intestine. A knife blade pierces his side. Jed slaps his open palm on the dashboard. "You'd make a retarded baby."

"One of *us* could fuck her, though," Ben says, waggling his thumb between himself and Jed. "Maybe you could set that up."

A vial of acid bursts in Jason's stomach. Ben and Jed laugh and laugh, gasping and clutching themselves in glee.

"Knock it off," Jason says, puny.

"Fine," Ben says. "Make a retarded baby."

Jason walks into school alone. He goes to first-period biology and doesn't talk to anyone. He goes to second-period trig, where his only words are an awkward and ignored hello to Corinne Jensen, the former girl of his dreams. He goes to third and fourth periods and doesn't talk to anyone.

He imagines the cloud of knowledge from seminary following him, spreading into every corner of the school. At lunch, Boyd asks him how things are going with the pioneers.

"Hunky-dory," Jason says.

"They say there's a new girl."

"A new girl?" Jason returns this with a hard, sarcastic spin. "What does that mean?"

"Hey, this is me," Boyd says. "You know what it means. And you know what everyone is saying it means."

"She's my aunt's niece," Jason says.

Boyd gazes at him. Jason studies the tater tot casserole on his lunch tray: it is a creamy prehistoric ocean, mushroomy and thick, with tawny islands of potato for the swimmers, the strivers, to cling to while they rest and regain their strength. Jason imagines he is on one of those islands, and Loretta is on another one. And everybody else—family, school, church, town, state, nation, world—is the gray, gloopy sea.

Boyd says, "Dude," and shakes his head.

"It's weird," Jason says. "I think she doesn't belong with them."

"People from the twentieth century don't belong with them."

Tuesday

Loretta feels lit from within. Neon. Like no one can stop looking at her, aglow in the dark, like she is made of fine glass tubes, easily shattered. Since she walked into that church, every moment since, even at home in her bed, she feels watched and judged and known.

She hates it more than she hates Ruth's bulgur meat loaf. She hates it more than she hates sleeping with Dean. She hates it because it has tainted the best thing in her life—her future, the magical time that is supposed to arrive when she enters the outside world, the world of pink Mustangs and matching Tussy lipstick—by announcing the truth about the way she will be in that outside world.

Ruth says she can't quit. Not yet. They have not figured out their relationship to this community. If Bradshaw were up here, Loretta would leave with him, go anywhere, sleep under bridges, under sagebrush, eat jackrabbits, eat grass, eat dirt, eat bugs. She is brave enough, if only she had someone to share it with, she knows she could be brave enough. But Bradshaw is in Short Creek, running the business, while Dean scouts for customers up here.

Jason picks her up in the morning, all corny and nervous. He reminds her of the children—alternately endearing and aggravating.

"Hello again," he says.

"Good morning."

She does not like how much he likes this. Three minutes expire. On the glove box is a word in script: *LeBaron*. She thinks of Ervil LeBaron, the polygamist leader down in Mexico with thirteen wives who broke with the Short Creek brethren. Mr. Blood Atonement—the guy had his own brother killed. Dean once told her, *Ervil's methods are extreme, but his beliefs are sound.*

She yawns. She could go right back to sleep. In her future, Loretta will never rise before the sun and grog through the gray hours. She will not do chores or make biscuits. She will not live so close to cattle that it is all she can smell, all the time, the shit of cattle.

Jason says, "How'd you like your first day of seminary?"

"Another joy sent by the Lord," she says. Caught by surprise, he snorts moistly, then looks away, ears scarlet. She feels one ounce better.

At seminary, she sits in the back corner. She averts her gaze from the eyes of others—on the floor, over their shoulders, at their feet—and no one speaks to her, not even Brother Kershaw, and she can tell by the insistence with which they try to show her they aren't noticing her that it's all they are doing, noticing her.

She thought that among the Mormons here there would be some bit of kinship. Some similarity. But these kids are utterly worldly. The girls wear jeans high on their hips, snugged up their cloven rears, and their hair parts into cascading waves. They all wear makeup, and even the homely girls dress like whores. And the boys are like monkeys, in their bell-bottoms and T-shirts, all except for the three who are farm boys, in Wranglers and boots and purple FFA jackets, the closest thing to Short Creek style she has seen here. These three boys are clearly the lowest caste. Jason and a few of the others are somewhere above them, and the top caste consists of the two largest monkeys, the two with the biggest bodies, the square-jawed, acne-scarred football player boys. Ben and Jed cut looks at her constantly, and elbow each other, and show their interest more plainly than the rest.

It is Dean's night. She finds it more unbearable than usual. He smells like a sour washcloth, and the mole on his neck is grotesque and wrinkled, and his face is contorted into a twisted grimace that lacks all self-consciousness, all reserve, and she knows she will never be able to be someone who has not experienced this. He is marking her.

Afterward, she says, "I was wondering, since we're not going to church here, if it makes sense for me to be going to seminary. I mean, will it make sense to *them*?"

Dean seems stumped. He lies on his back in his garments. The prickly black hair that covers his body presses against the sheer white material in swirls and eddies. He rubs his eyes with the heels of his hands, starts to speak, rubs them again.

"Huh," he says. "Well, little sister, you may be right there. You may be."

He falls silent. He drums his fingers on his chest, gazes at the ceiling. Something washes over him afterward, some lassitude. Loretta wonders whether he'll come at her again. He's frustrated that she isn't yet pregnant, because he believes himself so fertile. His fertility is an expression of his righteousness. She has kept her methods a secret, and yet she understands that it is starting to be taken in the household as a failure, a failure of righteousness and belief and commitment, a failure for which blame will be located and assigned.

"Maybe I should stop going," she says, grazing his beard with her fingertips.

"Maybe," he says. "We'll see."

Wednesday

Waiting in the LeBaron for Loretta, Jason spots a jackrabbit perched on a rock at the back of the yard, spindly ears high. His duff color blends with the morning twilight. He's barely visible, and he doesn't move as Loretta scuttles out and slides in.

"Look at that guy," he says. "Just watching us. He's not even scared."

"Dean says we've got to do something drastic."

"We were using carrots before."

"What—feeding them?"

"Yeah. You cut them up, soak them in strychnine, and then lay out a line of them along the edge of the field. You've got to start with some nonpoison ones first. Works pretty good. We were hauling eight or ten a day out of there for a while."

She doesn't answer.

He says, "We tried some other poisons, too. In barley."

"Dean says you can't shoot 'em or poison 'em fast enough."

They're actually talking. *Okay, Jason,* he thinks. *Keep it going.*
He says, "Yeah, that's what my grandpa said, too."

"He wants to have a drive."

A drive. A bunny bash. Herd the rabbits into a circle of men,
who club them to death. Regular people had stopped doing them.
The *New York Times* had written up the last one, over in Mud
Flats, and run a photo of a bloody-shirted father-and-son bashing
team. It became a big deal, and everyone got defensive. The gas
stations sold bumper stickers with a cartoon image of a hippie hugging a bunny, set inside a gun sight. The local papers ran editorials
about big-city animal lovers, and the letters were full of righteous
indignation about liberals, hippies, environmentalists, the media.
Jason had never seen a drive, and he didn't care about jackrabbits.
Sometimes he and Boyd would take .22s out and try to shoot them
in the desert, though the rabbits mostly bounded away untouched.
But if there is anything he doesn't want right now, it's more weird
attention at the farm.

"Great," he says, sarcastically. "That'll be super cool."

"I don't know," she says. "They're just a bunch of stupid rodents.
Gotta get rid of 'em somehow. Dean says they ate up about half the
crops."

A revelation sprints across Jason's mind, illuminated by her de-
fensiveness: She would be having sex with Dean, of course. She
would be—What? Every other night? On some kind of schedule?—
welcoming Dean into her room. His creepy uncle would climb on
and get to it, grunting and farting, probably, and covered with
moles and bristly hairs. *Holy goddamn shit.* Jason thinks he will
puke. She would hate Dean, of course. She must. Jason could think
of her only that way. But even so, she would find herself aligned
with him against others.

Loretta reaches over and turns on the radio. Jason notices her knuckles are large and red for such trim, tapered fingers. Like she pops them too much. He welcomes every unflattering detail. The radio is set at his dad's AM country station, KART. They listen to that awful music—"Grandma's Feather Bed," "Rhinestone Cowboy," the hideous sound track to his life—all the way to town, while she hums along.

At lunch, Jason doesn't say anything to Boyd about Loretta, and Boyd doesn't ask. Boyd says he's thinking about seeing if his mom would let him borrow her car to drive to South Dakota for a demonstration in support of Jonathan Raincounter.

"Dude's getting hosed," Boyd says.

"Who's he again?"

"Man, you have got to pay some goddamn attention."

Boyd reminds him: Jonathan Raincounter was an Oglala Sioux, unjustly imprisoned for shooting two FBI agents. Most people Jason knows take a different view of the case than Boyd; most people he knows see the case—Indians shooting FBI agents!—as one more sign that they have entered the last days, that the sinful world is tinder dry and ready to burn with apocalyptic fire, that the approach to the Second Coming of Jesus Christ is nigh, and that the righteous will soon be heaved upward by the Lord, for that reason and many others, including the following:

Nudity and sex talk in movies
Filthy rock and roll
Women's lib
The Equal Rights Amendment

Tight blue jeans
Rampant sexual perversion and immorality
Unshaven men with long hair
Roe v. Wade
The fall of Saigon
Jackrabbits eating farmers out of house and home
Queers and hippies marching in the streets of the cities
Liberals attacking the family
The end of the gold standard
Drugs
Oil shock
Creeping federalism
Communists

It is the entire context for Jason's people. Their atmosphere. They are the Lord's chosen, saved for the last days, when wickedness will overrun the planet until Christ returns and cleanses the earth for a millennium—a thousand years of fire—followed by the three-tiered afterlife, in descending order of glory. It is coming, it is nearer every day, it is all around them.

What Jason always wonders is: If we're living in the last days, why are we living like this? School, work, church, chores, bills, striving, arguments, chastity, oil changes, milking cows, cutting hay? He wants to live like time is running out. Like the hippies at the Snake River Canyon. Like Evel Knievel. Like driving to South Dakota to raise forbidden hell. Like falling in love with his uncle's second wife. Like precious time is really, actually running out instead of plodding along forever.

"What do you think you can you do about it?" Jason asks.

"Not a thing."

"Then why go?"

"Fun. Adventure. Freedom. Just to be on the right side of things for once." He waves his fork around, a gesture that encompasses not just the cafeteria, with its folding tables in the space between the auditorium seating and the stage, but their entire universe. "This *place*. The fucking Indian jokes. The retarded politics. I mean, people here still like Nixon, man."

Jason's parents still like Nixon. A couple of popular thugs walk past in their letterman's jackets, red felt with black leather sleeves. One of them says, "What are you staring at, Tonto?"

Boyd says, "Nothing, George," and flips them off.

Then he says, "I need to *go*. I need to get out of here. At least practice getting out of here."

"Maybe I could go with you."

Boyd laughs. "That would be hilarious. Boy Scout gone wrong. Break your parents' hearts."

"Screw off."

"Plus," Boyd says. "The thing about South Dakota. I think I might find my dad there."

"What makes you think that?"

Boyd shrugs.

"Karma. Kismet. Whatever it is. Indian intuition." He chews, watching his plate. "Day's gonna come when we get back what's ours. I find my dad, and we start working in tandem on this— whoa. You Europeans aren't going to know what hit you."

"Come on. You're about as much an Indian as I am."

Boyd stops. He stares at the table, bugs his eyes in frustration.

"You know, dumbass," he says. "Everybody thinks the problem, the race thing, is the guy who hollers some shitty thing, calls you an Injun, burns a cross, whatever."

"That guy's not the problem?"

"That guy is *a* problem. But *the* problem is guys like you. *The* problem is guys who want to tell you there's no problem. Guys who want to tell you to just calm down."

"Calm down."

Boyd is the only Indian Jason knows, and though there are a couple of Mexican kids in school, he really knows only white people, and he cannot imagine why Boyd doesn't simply let all this go. Jason would say all people are created equal and that by writing a three-page paper on *To Kill a Mockingbird,* he has done his part.

"The problem," Boyd says, "is dumbasses like you."

And then he lets it drop. He turns his irritation to his mother, who he is convinced is not telling him the truth about his father.

All Boyd knows about his father is that he is an Indian. Years earlier, his mom told him his dad was Shoshone, but once he really started asking questions, she said maybe he had just been *from* Shoshone, the town and not the tribe. All she knew, he'd been living around Boise about seventeen years earlier, a real charmer, tall with white, white teeth and scarred-up hands. "She says last she heard he was working ranches and rodeos in Montana and Wyoming, but that was ten years ago. He could be anywhere, she says. Even dead—she wouldn't be surprised."

"You probably ought to just let it go."

"Easy for you to say. You've got a father."

"You can have him. He's all yours."

"Easy for you to say."

Thursday

In the car again, on the way back to church, Jason says, "I was sure sorry to hear about your parents."

Loretta is confused: heard what about them? She thinks it through—what the story is, who's been told what.

"Hear what about them?" she asks.

"I thought I heard your folks had some . . . health problems. Or passed away?"

"You did?"

"Maybe I'm remembering wrong."

"They're still hanging around. I think."

"Oh. Good."

She looks over at him. Roseate patches bloom on his cheeks and ears, complementing that auburn scruff of hair. His nerves tremble through the whole car. She imagines they are two ordinary teenagers. Shy and nervous and young. Children. He turns to her, and flushes even more deeply to find her looking at him. To be liked in this way, to be buzzed by such naïve, clean interest, feels pure. She thinks he will be a handsome man, this boy, when he loses his flush and downy cheeks, when he hardens a bit, but she cannot imagine him ever being less than simple and readable, and this morning that feels like the best quality a person could have.

"What?" he asks.

"Nothing," she says.

He pauses. "I guess I somehow got the idea that your folks had died, and that was why you live with Dean and Ruth."

Instantly, it's back—the irritation, the self-consciousness. She tells him the story, the lie, tersely, bites it off. Her father's business had failed in Cedar City, and her mother's Crohn's disease left her in bed most days, and there was just no money in the house.

"Mom and Dad just needed a little relief," she says. "That's all that was."

"Weird," he says.

"What's weird about it?"

"Nothing. I mean—nothing."

He drives, clearly struggling to come up with something to say. Telling the lie about her parents reminded her of the truth about her parents—that they gave her to Dean. Gave her to Dean, and when she stopped speaking to them, in church on Sundays or in passing around Short Creek—they stopped, too. Like they didn't care about her any more than she cared about them. Which made her care.

Jason finally says, "Ready for another thrilling morning of Brother Kershaw's moral tales and lessons?"

"I don't know."

And then he sort of gulps, or gathers himself, and blurts, "Are you pissed off at Dean for making you go?"

Out the window, she watches the landscape blurring past: lava rock, sagebrush, fence posts, haystacks, fallow, harvested fields. Fat drops of rain strike the windshield like pellets. The question feels more important than it is. The rain begins splattering loudly, a gust rustles the trees clustering a farmhouse, and she says, "Yeah."

What will he say to that?

"Yeah, I hate it, too. I actually told my parents I wasn't going to go anymore. Until they dragged you into it."

She teases him, as Bradshaw might: "What an outlaw."

That night Dean stands at the back of the yard and looks into the fields while Loretta plays tag with the children, sprinting around the lilac bush that sits beside the laundry line.

"Little sister!" Dean barks urgently. "Run into the office and get my pistol from the bottom drawer of the desk. It's behind the lockbox."

A crowd of jackrabbits is dancing in the fields—leaping, turning, flying, it seems like dozens of them, dark smears on the darkening land. Loretta doesn't move at first; Dean has never asked her to go into his desk, into any of his things. He has always been so secretive about them.

"Hurry, Loretta!"

She runs inside, past Ruth at the sink, and into the small room at the top of the basement stairs where Dean has jammed his desk. She opens the bottom drawer, and there, behind a sheaf of papers in folders, is a canvas bag, top bunched downward, and a metal box, and behind them, at the back of the drawer, is Dean's revolver.

Loretta reaches into the drawer, grabs the bag, and lifts it. Just an inch or so. It is heavy. Heavier than it looks. Heavy enough to be just one thing. She looks in and sees coins—maybe thirty or forty of the fifty-dollar golden eagles—but not the nuggets. Not the Sutter Creek gold. Hadn't he told her he was leaving it in Short Creek?

"Loretta!"

Her blood tingles, her mind circles. She carries the pistol and the worn, heavy box of bullets out to Dean. He stands there shooting until dark, reloading four times, while Loretta pretends to watch from behind him, trying all the while to shut down the racing of her body, and she doesn't realize that Dean is missing every shot, that he doesn't hit a single creature, until he lets out a strangled bark of frustration and hurls the gun into the blackening desert.

Friday

Over breakfast, Jason's mother questions him about Loretta. What has she said about living with Dean? Has she mentioned whether they're planning to stay? Or what they're up to over there? Will they be going back to Short Creek anytime soon?

The interrogation follows four days of silence from his parents about Dean and Grandpa's place. The one time Jason tried to ask about it, his father brusquely replied, "I don't know what they're up to over there, son," and when Jason had started to say something more, his dad interrupted angrily, "What did I just say, Jason?"

"So now we're talking about it?" Jason says to his mother.

Her pressed lips go white. Her forbearance face. She turns her back to him, stands at the sink, and lets the water run full blast. She hisses, "Your uncle is making a *spectacle* of himself!"

Jason almost says, *You're the one that has me taking her to seminary.* But he doesn't.

On the way to pick up Loretta, Jason tries to figure out what to put into the new Sanyo eight-track deck slung under the dashboard. He settles on Sweet. "Fox on the Run." Perfect, he thinks, and yet within one minute she asks him if they can listen to something else, and tunes in the country station. "Rhinestone Cowboy" is playing, and Jason groans. "I cannot listen to this music."

She reaches out and turns up the volume, and belts out, "'There'll be a load of compromisin' / On the road to my horizon . . .'"

"Noooooo," he cries, snapping off the dial. She laughs, alert and alive for the first time all week. It comes off her like a charge, and Jason reads it as something shared between them. Love's little seedling.

"I don't think I can stand one more minute of Brother Kershaw," he says.

"So let's not go."

So simple. So amazing.

"Go where instead?" he asks.

"I don't know. You tell me."

He knows just where. "I'll take you to Twin Falls," he says. "Show you Evel Knievel's ramp."

She shrugs. Says okay. She is the most beautiful human being Jason has ever seen, lit up with her love for him. Right? The greening, luscious seedling of love? Her hair is pulled back, her wet brown eyes glow as they scan the desert. She needs saving, and it has been arranged for him to save her, but how? It must be what she wants, too, though this thought is buried so deep in Jason's assumptions that he doesn't actually think it. It is simply what occurs, it is simply what men do: rescue women. Superman, Spider-Man,

Batman—rescue women. John Wayne rescues women and so does Clint Eastwood. On TV, the guys on *Emergency!* and *Baretta* and *Kojak* and *The Rockford Files* all rescue women. It's their job.

For the half hour it takes to drive to Twin Falls, Jason tells her about Evel Knievel. He describes his jumps, details the bones he has broken and at which stadiums, the numbers of buses and cars he has surmounted, his outfits, his retirements and his coming-out-of-retirements. Jason tells her of his own ramp building and driveway jumps—though he does not mention his posters or Stunt Cycle action figure. When they reach Twin Falls and cross the Perrine Bridge into town, the sun is up but the canyon remains doused in shadow. They pull off at the overlook and Jason points out the ramp, a sloped hill of dirt a quarter mile away on the canyon rim.

Loretta stares. "That's it?"

"That's it."

"You drove me out here to show me a pile of dirt?"

"Well. I drove you out here to get out of seminary."

She giggles. Is this good? He thinks it is, though he is disappointed at her inability to see the grandeur of the ramp. He pulls back onto the highway, heads back toward Gooding. He begins to tell her about the day he came to see the canyon jump with Grandpa. He mentions the lie, and how much he had loved the lie, and how happy he had been to have this secret from his parents, and how fun it had been to actually be there, to see him, to watch all the crazy people, and how even though the jump had failed, disappointing him to the bone, he had actually liked it, too, in some way. When they had pulled Evel Knievel out of that canyon with a crane, and he waved at everybody with that same grim, purposeful look he had before he jumped, it was like he wasn't even embarrassed.

"It was just, I don't know, still cool," he says. "I don't know why."

"I do. Maybe. I mean, he tried something amazing."

"Yes!" Jason says. "That's right. He tried something amazing."

Jason tries to give her a significant look. A look of deeper communication. She looks back, possibly puzzled. Jason thinks of Evel Knievel crashing in England, bones crushed to dust, insisting on standing to address the crowd. He thinks, *Okay. Go.*

He says, "Are you okay living there with Dean and Ruth? I mean, happy and everything?"

"I guess so."

"You know what people think it is?"

She doesn't answer. He tries again.

"Is it what people think it is?"

"No," she says, so quietly Jason can barely hear it. His mind allows itself to believe her, because she wouldn't lie to him now that they have Evel Knievel between them. She says something he can't hear.

"What?" he asks.

"What it is, is nobody's business."

She stares straight ahead, chin tucked in, refusing to turn. Jason shrinks. Gazes at the highway with his hands on the wheel.

"It's family business," she says.

Jason tells Boyd about it later, finally tells him about all of it.

"Dude," he says. "What'd you think she was going to say?"

EVEL KNIEVEL ADDRESSES
AN ADORING NATION

We just sat there in that truck, tinted windows, cab full of Buddy's goddamn cigarillo smoke, and waited for that miserable fuck to come out of the concert hall. That "writer." The one who wrote that book we will not name. We had a bat, one of those new metal softball numbers, and Buddy had his billy club, police-issue ironwood. It was like looking at the ramp from the end of the runway, our insides an electric gelatin, like we were being turned from something dull and dumb into something grand, and we knew that feeling well enough to know that we had to focus on it, feel it, try to seize it though it would not be seized, because we were heading into the air now, into the divine space, and we would only be there for a few seconds, for glimpses and flashes, and then we'd be down again, and maybe the landing would be hard and maybe it would be soft, but it would be a landing nevertheless.

He comes out. Just look at that fucker. Pale denim bell-bottoms, boots like some California faggot, nice and clean with shiny leather and little heels, faggoty boots, and a shirt made out of that fuzzy shit like a towel, and his hair all Farrah Fawcett, and bronze sunglasses, and a little smile on his pudgy face, a tiny confident smirk, and we were relieved to discover that upon seeing him we did not lose any of our desire for the moment, that we were energized, inspired, set upon a righteous path. In his book, he wrote all manner of lies about us—about us, about our mother—and now, here, he would pay. Pay for each individual slander, and then for his larger trespass against us: the taking and perversion of our story, the holy scripture of our life.

He didn't even run. Just fell down and let us do it. His soft body felt like a sack of wheat under our blows. The bones in his forearms gave way as we struck him with our bat. The Tennessee Thumper. Aluminum as shit.

People have told some lies about this—have called us a coward for taking Buddy to hold him down. We were not afraid of him. We wanted him held down to make it worse when we hit him. So he couldn't curl up, cover his head, protect himself in any way. This was so much worse. So very much worse, and that was his punishment. We chose it carefully, and were prepared for him to die, America. Vengeance is mine, sayeth the Lord, and we sayeth that, too.

He screamed like a girl, Mr. Book Writer did. Screamed just like you'd think with those faggoty boots and that hair.

By then, we had grown and grown. We had become so large, so multitudinous, that we sometimes felt as if we were exceeding the boundaries of our physical form.

They made a movie. All they had to call it was *Evel Knievel*. It sold itself. George Hamilton made the thing. Wrote it and starred in it. When he came to ask us for permission, came to our hotel room in the Sands to ask us to sign the deal and take the check, we made him read the script, start to finish. At first he wouldn't do it, but we took out that shiny new Luger and pointed it at him and said, "Read it, motherfucker," and he read it, and he trembled, and we signed.

It was a mistake. We make them, occasionally. On film, George Hamilton looked soft and weak, and somehow he made the scripture sound like shit:

"Ladies and gentlemen, you have no idea how good it makes me feel to be here today. It is truly an honor to risk my life for you. An honor. Before I jump this motorcycle over these nineteen cars—and I want you to know there's not a Volkswagen or a Datsun in the row—before I sail cleanly over that last truck, I want to tell you that last night a kid came up to me and he said, 'Mr. Knievel, are you crazy? That jump you're going to make is impossible, but I already have my tickets because I want to see you splatter.' That's right, that's what he said. And I told that boy last night that nothing is impossible."

As if we could be imitated. As if you could pretend to be us.

We spent our time in jail for the beating and we smiled our way through it. We called in limousines to take us to our work-release jobs—to the shit-shoveling, broom-holding, tray-filling labor they tried to punish us with—and so we called our people and had them line up sixteen limousines outside the Los Angeles County jail, and all these guys got a ride, showed up for the shit shovel in a limousine, thanks to yours truly, and they did not forget it, these guys, they worshipped us, just like everyone else. And when the jailers complained, and the judge hauled us in, and told us he had half a mind to restore our full sentence—first-degree assault, he called it, a two-year hitch—we simply smiled and apologized and told him, "Why, Your Honor, I merely wanted to return to these men some of the dignity they may have lost within the walls of incarceration, not to make light of the punishment, Your Honor, but to return to these men some sense of their own natural grandeur, their own native royalty, so they might see themselves as something other than low, something more than criminal, and return to society with the hopes and dreams that might make them all better men," but still, they said no more limousines, no more press conferences at the jail's back door, and we said, Okay, sure, thank you, Your Honor.

It was hard. It was humbling and hard, America, and don't you forget it. We swallowed that down, and we swallowed everything else in those days. The toy people pulled their deals, and that was the hardest, because we were rolling in the toy money then—the wind-up racer, the action figures, the bicycles with the Evel Knievel nameplates, the Evel Knievel cane. On and on and on, little idols of the god in every house, and every one of them sending us the purest American love there is: the dollar. But now we were losing that love. Our agent told us to lie low for a while, let it blow over, but no: we called a press conference and apologized to the judge—wink!—for turning his courtroom into a joke, if that's what he thought we had done, and pledged to take it more seriously from then on.

Winked at the press boys, and they howled. Like broads, the newspaper boys. Give 'em a wink and a story and they'll drop right to the floor.

Got home after all this and what did we find? On the gate—

that marvelous fucking gate, the scrollwork, that beautiful Butte artistry—was a little handwritten sign: SEE THE SON OF EVIL KNIEVEL JUMP. TWENTY-FIVE CENTS.

Eleven years old, he was. Little fucker. Couldn't even spell the old man's name right.

DRIVE

October 4, 1975

GOODING, IDAHO

Loretta is awake, lying on the makeshift pallet behind the blankets tacked up in the basement, light filtering through the shelved jars of peaches and tomatoes, when Ruth taps down the stairs and calls, "Good morning, Sister." She waits for Loretta to answer before going back upstairs. Loretta sits up. Her insides coil and uncoil. She has been awake for hours.

She brushes her teeth at the deep washbasin and washes her face and hands with the blackened bar of industrial soap, and puts on her dress. She can't stop thinking about Bradshaw up there, at the table already, probably, grinning and grinning. *Here.* Here to help with the rabbit drive. Here to help set up Zion's Harvest in its new home. Here in the constantly watching world. He will sit there, the truth of him and her showing in her face.

She comes into the kitchen, and there he is, cheeks stuffed, eyes upon her. The sight of him fills her with sick thrill. Outside, framed in the window above the sink, Dean argues loudly with a man standing in front of a TV news van—KMVT-11, "Your Local News Leader." Other pickups and vans have parked in the driveway as well, and groups of men are moving around out there. Strangers. Dean has said this will be a way of establishing themselves in the community. A way of distinguishing himself from his brother.

"Like a welcome-home party," he said.

Jason clomps across the yard in his rubber boots, and goes into the tank room of the milking barn. Behind a swinging door, he sees his dad at work between the chutes, aiming the sharp, hissing stream of a hose at a shit-splattered udder. The suck and gasp of the machinery obliterates all other sound, and milky air fills his sinuses. At the sink, behind the gleaming silver tank, he fills the bottles, attaches the large red nipples, and loads the wire carrier. Heading for the calf pen, dull with weariness, he looks at the edges of his boots, crusted with bits of grassy manure and half-digested bits of hay, and thinks of the day when he will sleep as late as he wants to and wake to sweet-smelling air.

It sucks, the milking, but it sucks less than seminary. Today is Saturday, but Jason has returned to morning chores full-time ever since the day he and Loretta skipped seminary. That night, Ruth called his mom and said they didn't think Loretta would be going anymore, because the other kids made her feel out of place. "I'll bet they did," Jason's mom said drily when relating the conversation over dinner, and no one else commented. Jason finds it infuriating that no one else seems to think about Loretta. About what they need to do for her. All his mom and dad can consider is their embarrassment.

So he'd stopped going to seminary. A minor insurrection, but one that his parents fought every day, in indirect ways. He could feel them eyeing him, wary, trying to get a read on the best way to overcome this and set him back on the path. When he had first told his parents he wouldn't go to seminary anymore, his father had stopped and blinked, as if he hadn't understood the words, and then he said, "That's ridiculous."

Still, now, day after day, even this morning as he upends the bottles in the wire holders, watching the calves slurp hungrily at the thick red nipples, Jason clings to this: *Still think it's ridiculous, Dad?* Over there, Dean is getting ready to have his bunny bash. The rabbit drive. Talk about ridiculous. Talk about ridicule. It's been in all the papers, on the TV news. The Humane Society has raised hell about it. Ridiculous.

Jason is retrieving the empty bottles when his father comes crunching up in his canvas jacket and red-and-black Scotch cap. He is unshaven, and the gray on his hollow cheeks makes him look weak. Sick, even. Something in him has crumbled lately, and Jason holds this against him.

"Need to replace those nipples yet?" Dad asks.

"Nope."

"You keeping that white-faced bully out of the others' milk?"

"Yep."

Jason can feel his father struggling for a way in, and he is glad not to help. From the far back of the milking barn, across the pasture and the patch of rocky desert, he sees trucks and motorcycles gathering in the driveway of Grandpa's house. Dean's house. The yard light is on, and Dean and a few other men are unloading rolls of orange temporary fencing from the back of a half-ton truck. A few hundred yards down the road, on the other side of the house, two VW vans sit along the shoulder, and people mill about in the barrow pit. Jason knows from the morning paper that some bunny huggers from Sun Valley have planned a protest.

Jason says, "You going over?"

"Naw. I'll pass."

"I'm going."

Dad nods. Takes off his hat and scratches furiously at his scalp. "There's no way this can do anybody any good."

Jason starts gathering the rest of the empties.

"You can come to think that doing what you want to do and ignoring everybody else is the right thing to do," his dad says. "The honorable thing. Because everybody else is dumb or dishonest or mistaken or something. That's what your uncle thinks—that everyone is just wrong about everything, and the only thing to do is ignore them. Maybe it is, sometimes. But usually the honorable thing to do is think about others. To consider others, and the way your actions might affect them."

"Affect us, you mean."

"I mean everybody. Us, too, but everybody. People all over the country are going to know about this. And when those reporters start writing about it, they might get more interested in your uncle and what's going on over there. And then . . ."

"Then what?"

"Then the story gets all that much better." He coughs. "Worse."

The sun is all the way up now, air warming. They both know that whatever is happening with the story at Dean's is already happening. It's burning like a fire. Since Dean taped up Ruth's handwritten signs on flag stationery at the co-op—JACKRABBIT DRIVE! YOU BRING A CLUB, WE'LL SUPPLY THE FOOD!—it has energized the town. Crop prices are lousy, the football team is losing, and people have fixed upon the bash. Kids talk about it at school. Some of the popular thugs are for it. Some object on the grounds that it is redneck and uncool. Certain farmers—the angry ones, the political ones—wrote letters to the editor of the *Gooding County Leader,* anticipating the criticism that would follow the event. "If New Yorkers don't want us to harvest these pests, maybe they'd like to take them home to Central Park."

"*And,*" Dad says, "this thing—it's not just that it looks barbaric. It is barbaric. Just awful. You hate to see anyone enjoy something so bloody."

He puts his hand on Jason's shoulder and squeezes.

"Probably the least effective way to get rid of jackrabbits is to stand in the desert with a club and try to beat them all to death," he says. "It's just dumb."

Jason ignores him and walks back toward the barn. He doesn't want to bash any bunnies himself. But he's absolutely going.

Loretta and Samuel set up the Zion's Harvest table, while Dean and Bradshaw load fencing into a pickup. She has to remember to call him Baker. Zion's Harvest is a big part of this day. "Two birds with one stone," Dean said. It was Ruth's idea; if they're moving up here, they'll need the business to grow fast, she reasoned; the rabbit drive is the best marketing opportunity they'll have. She has a mind for that, Ruth does—for imagining what others need and how you might speak to it. Loretta and Samuel tape the butcherpaper sign to the front of the table, sitting at an angle to the driveway so everyone who drives or walks in will see it: ZION'S HARVEST BULK FOODS.

Ruth is alert to something in the air. Something with Bradshaw.

Loretta felt it at breakfast—attention flowing from Bradshaw toward her, and Ruth's awareness of it. Loretta feels them both watching her this morning. And she feels self-conscious about the drive, about the people who will be here, about the watching that will come with that. The noticing.

"Bring out some of them buckets," she says to Samuel.

He's moody, hanging his head because he's not with the men.

"Go on," she says. "And bring some flyers, too."

At breakfast, Bradshaw had been scooping up huge mouthfuls of scrambled eggs. She noticed a dullness in her response to him that she'd never felt before. After months of Ruth's horsey breakfasts, Loretta found herself more attracted to the steaming plate of eggs than to Bradshaw, sitting there sock footed and sleepy eyed. Loretta had looked eagerly to Ruth and asked, "Eggs?" Ruth approached with a bowl of oatmeal and dropped it in front of her. "Mush," she said.

People drift into the driveway, clumping in groups and talking, cups steaming. Dean's hired the auctioneer's food truck to serve hot drinks and lunches. Everyone carries a baseball bat, or a length of pipe, or a two-by-four.

Bradshaw comes to the Zion's Harvest table.

"Hidy, there, Lori," he says, pretending to look at the clipboard where customers can sign up for the newsletter. "Holy Christ, I'm about to leap over this table."

Loretta can see Ruth in the corner of her eye, pausing at the laundry line.

"Keep your powder dry," she says. She pays meticulous attention to the sign, to making sure it is straight along the table.

"My powder," Bradshaw says, "is about to blow."

He adjusts his cap. Rubs his face. Takes a deep breath. Exhales.

His face is strained and splotchy, and even across the table she can smell him—armpit and work clothes and a hint of the chasings of the night.

"I hope you're ready, girl," he says. "Because I am ready."

He is not a demon or an angel or anything of the sort. She sees what he is, because he is surrounded by others just like him—bandy-legged men in fringe-heeled Wranglers and curl-toed boots, caps with their bills tight, some with chew-can rings in the back pocket, spitting, scuffing their heels, boring and dumb. He waits for her to respond to him, and something mean seeps into his look when she doesn't.

"You *are* ready," he says. "You are."

Boyd shows up with his mom's aluminum softball bat, the Tennessee Thumper, tapping it in the palm of his hand as Jason opens the door. He bounces on the balls of his feet like a prizefighter, the frayed bells of his jeans splashing softly around his ankles.

"Time to get some bunnies!" he says, as Jason emerges and they start walking over.

"I'm not getting any bunnies," Jason says. "I'm a complete spectator."

"You are such a pussy," Boyd says happily. "You need to kill something."

"That's stupid."

"Such a pussy."

Boyd is as happy as Jason has seen him in weeks. He's been bitchy and bleak since his mother refused to let him drive off to South Dakota for the American Indian Movement protest. Jason hadn't understood it—hadn't understood, even remotely, Boyd's expectation that his mother would let him go—but Boyd took it as a grievous offense. "This fucking place," Boyd said, disgusted. "This fucking town. This fucking school. This fucking point and time in the history of the fucking world."

He and Boyd trudge through the days like prison inmates in a chow line. Jason picks him up for school every morning, they bitch and listen to *Houses of the Holy,* go to classes and meet again at lunch to bitch some more, return to afternoon classes, and meet again after school to bitch some more. Teachers, parents, cops, laws, principals, bishops, uncles, aunts, cousins, girls, cars, store clerks, waitresses, television stars, the bicentennial. Dean and Loretta. This could not be their lives. They could not breathe. Boyd kept saying he was going to the AIM protests anyway. There or somewhere.

"Just go," Boyd said. "One of these nights, just—gone. And not for two nights, either."

As they approach Dean's, Boyd begins swinging his bat before him like a sword.

"Feel my wrath, bunnies!" he calls. "I am the avenging angel! Re-*pent* your evil ways!"

They walk down the county road. Ahead, Jason sees trucks and cars parked in a line that spills out from the driveway. The animal rights protesters are clustered in the barrow pit across the road. Farther ahead sits a TV van from Twin Falls, and between them stands a stocky, thick-haired man with a microphone interviewing a woman in a patchwork dress and loose, long hair. Jason feels the creep of embarrassment—the prickling crawl up the back of his neck, the flush, the sense that an appraising look is aimed from every direction.

He looks for Loretta but doesn't see her. The food truck is set up behind the house, beside a picnic table laid with plates of dough-nuts and a thermos of hot chocolate. There's a table with a sign advertising bulk foods, and Samuel—Dean's oldest—stands behind it, speaking to no one. It is warming up, frost melting off the windows and the metal fencing. You could almost take off your jacket. Men clump in knots of three and four, holding baseball bats, two-by-fours, and nine irons. Out in the desert behind the house—far back, on the other side of the barley field—a group of men stretches out lines of orange temporary fencing, making a chute. Once a fire is set on the far side of the bunchgrass stands, the men on motor-cycles will drive the jacks toward the chute, and the chute will lead the jacks into the circle of men and boys. Afterward, suppos-edly, the jack meat will go to jails and groups that feed the poor.

Boyd spots a man he knows from his mom's softball team and they banter about who will kill more rabbits. The man holds a small wooden club, a fish-killing club, and he demonstrates how quickly he'll strike.

"That big ol' bat's gonna wear you out, boy," he says, air-whacking rabbits at a furious pace. "Look at me go. You'll never keep up."

"You won't even knock 'em out with that little thing," Boyd says, holding the bat before him. "These rabbits are going to know they got hit by me."

Jason goes for a doughnut. He snags an old-fashioned from the paper plate, and the first bite falls apart like dirt in his mouth. He looks at Grandpa's house. He's been inside just twice since he died. Now Jason wants to run in and find it just the way it used to be—same couches and furniture, same drapes, same neat and or-derly kitchen with the smell of yesterday's bread or today's roast, the big boxy TV in the corner with the doily and the glass figurines on top, the cool dusty smell. He wants to find that vanished place and sleep in it.

Loretta's head appears in the kitchen window. She gazes impassively for a moment, sees Jason, waves quickly, and ducks out of the window. Jason forces down a mouthful of doughnut. Dean materializes beside him, his stiff back and beard in Jason's peripheral vision. Dean holds a Styrofoam cup, and nods hello. Jason wonders if Loretta has told him about their conversation—that he asked her about the arrangements here. Dean looks at Jason for an uncomfortable few seconds.

"Need a club?" he asks finally.

"I don't think so."

"Just gonna use your fists?"

Dean betrays none of the signs of someone who's joking. "Maybe you can help the ladies with the food, then," he says when Jason doesn't answer. "Where's your father today?"

"He's home."

Dean nods.

"Figures."

They set the desert aflame about two hundred yards away, a wavering orange hyphen on the land. Loretta walks out with Ruth, and they stand in a half-circle of watchers, nested behind the half-circle of clubbers. The men and the boys. Standing apart, separated from the line of other watchers, is Jason, hands stuffed in his pockets. She sees that his friend, the chunky, kind-of-handsome Indian guy, has joined the circle of clubbers, around twenty-five of them, who start whooping and hollering when the fire is lit. Bradshaw is the loudest, and he swings his club—the weapon he made himself, hammering nails into a four-by-four. He shakes his hips lewdly and dances, and Loretta knows he's performing for her. A couple of guys start beating the ground with bats, raising low clouds of dust.

Rabbits emerge on the desert ahead, erratic black shapes cohering into a mass. Three men on motorcycles sweep back and forth, working the flanks of the herd like cowboys in a cattle drive. Untended, the flames reach a thick stand of sage and burst into the air. Dean, standing at the center of the circle, shouts, "Who's on that fire? Who's got that fire?" Nobody answers, but it won't burn far in the damp and cold. The jacks develop a chaotic bristling unity, a dark carpet rolling and tumbling across the desert.

Loretta doesn't want to see this. She looks at Ruth, Ruth with her countenance set firmly, and Ruth turns back, almost softens, almost allows a sense of unease to slip into her demeanor, then shrugs. The jacks race closer, within a hundred yards, then seventy-five, flowing through the sagebrush like a burst river. Loretta sees the Indian kid turn to Jason, act out a maniacal laugh. Jason stands back, apart, she thinks, alone among them all, and that takes a kind of courage. In front of the pack of rabbits are the fastest few, darting this way or that but trapped by the rolling mass behind them. As they near, they bring a drumming, as if from a herd of distant horses, and then the first of them enters the wide-open mouth of the fencing.

"Get ready!" Dean calls, and the men pound the ground with clubs and bats, and it seems to be happening too fast now, rabbits leaping and weaving, rolling over any fellow creature that slows or loses a step, and then the most beautiful sight: rabbits breaking from the pack and soaring, majestic ten-foot spans, twenty-foot spans, across the moving mass beneath them, and the rabbits now twenty yards away, ten yards, and each leaping creature seems hung in the air, slowing as everything below them gains speed.

"My word," a voice says, and Loretta registers that it is Ruth, blanched and stunned, and when she turns back the men are bent to it, heaving their weapons downward again and again, filling the air with the sound of wet cracking and thudding blows. A few jacks straggle through, fugitives, panic eyed and zigzagging, though many more fall at the feet of the men. A mist of blood rises. An ammoniac stench. The terror of the doomed creatures imprints itself on Loretta's mind. One rabbit slips through, dragging a leg and shrieking. Almost childlike. A copper taste floods Loretta's mouth as the lone rabbit shrieks and drags itself toward the watchers and away from the bashers, the men pounding down and down, the rabbits before them a fleshy mound, black with damp and dust. Every few seconds a freshet of blood spurts into the air, like a blown sprinkler valve.

Ruth breaks suddenly forward, leans over, and takes up a hunk of lava rock. She raises it in two hands above her head and hurls it downward, and the shrieking stops.

Looking at the circle of men exhausting themselves dumbly, blindly, exhilarated with the sport of it, leading their children into it, hand in bloody hand—looking at their farmer clothing, their overalls and snap-button shirts strained thin in the back, their *hoo-rah*s and *yee-haw*s, looking with a disdain that builds with every blow— Jason feels a severance. A finality.

He is not of this. Not of them.

When Ruth smashed the rabbit with the broken leg, turning the creature into a silent mass of thick blood and gleaming organs, Jason went distant in his mind, and somehow it stopped touching him, until it was silent and the pounding was over. Slowly, the men leave the circle. In the pile of carcasses, an occasional jerk shudders through. A frantic scuffling. Just another incomplete maiming. Dean steps to the front of the group, blood sprayed on his shirt in a way that makes Jason think of speckles flying from a roller dipped in too much paint, and adopts the demeanor of the patriarch.

"We owe you men a debt of gratitude," he says. His face bears a scrim of dust with a black smear above his left eye. He folds his arms and bows his head.

"Our Father in Heaven," he says, and Jason hears that when Dean prays, he sounds just like Jason's father, "we come to you today with our hearts full of gratitude for the assistance you have given us in protecting our crops and our land. We thank you, oh Lord, for giving us the strength and will to accomplish this task, unpleasant though it may be . . ."

He prays on, thanking the Lord for the food provided for breakfast and lunch, and for health and families and the abundance of their lives, and for the Gospel—which makes Jason think about what Dean means by the Gospel, and how that differs from what his parents believe about the Gospel, and from what the Catholics and Methodists and Lutherans believe about the Gospel—and for sending his only begotten Son to redeem all mankind.

Jason looks around. Most of the men are bowing their heads, hands folded. Boyd is looking around, too. Their eyes meet, and Boyd smiles. The sweet spot on his baseball bat is smeared black and matted with spiny hair. Jason feels shock, a padded distance from the moment. He turns his head and finds Loretta staring at the ground, skin paled across the bridge of her nose, beside Ruth, whose eyes are closed.

After the prayer, the men load the carcasses into gunnysacks and pile them onto a flatbed truck. Boyd and Jason walk back toward Dean's house with most of the others, Boyd giddily exultant and Jason silent. It is sunny and cool, and the bitter smell of burning ditch grass comes across the desert, distinct from the scorched, sweet scent of the sagebrush fire. The shouting from the roadside has mostly died down, and the TV van has left. It is almost lunchtime. A small crowd of subdued bashers gathers in Dean's yard around the cook wagon, which is serving hot dogs, hamburgers, and chili.

"Them little buggers is fast, I tell ya."

"Faster'n shit. You can't try to hit one."

"No, sir. You just have to hit into the bunch."

"I don't know how many of those little dudes I got—I bet thirty or forty."

"You probably got twice as many as you think."

"Kinda fun, really."

"Good cause, anyway."

Boyd goes to the cook wagon, and Jason walks to the edge of the yard and looks out to where they just were. A couple of trucks and a few men are finishing the work out there. Smoke from the burned-out fire drifts thinly. Then Loretta is beside him. Something tugs her face downward. She seems tiny inside her dress, and she is looking at him so intently that he pulls away before catching himself.

"My word," she whispers.

"I know it," he says.

He is close enough to reach for her. To touch her. They stand side by side, facing the desert. Loretta sniffs. She says, "I have to get away from here."

The clouds in Jason's mind clear, a gear springs into place. It would be easy. It is so possible. His grandfather floats out of the space-world of death, his voice in the truck as they rode home that exhilarating Evel Knievel Sabbath, as he told Jason about leaving home at seventeen to enlist in the army: "Had a fire in my britches, just to get somewhere. Anyplace else."

Seventeen—Jason's own age.

He isn't trapped. They aren't trapped at all.

"Where do you want to go?" he asks.

She looks at the desert without seeming to see it. Ruth calls, "Loretta," in a voice without music, and the moment scampers away.

Loretta turns and glides toward the house. Where does she want to go? In her future, she anticipates all manner of experiences and freedoms, wears any kind of fresh clothing, eats candy and beef all day long, drives a pink car, and wears Tussy lipstick. But where is it? What place?

She stops at a picnic table to gather paper plates and cups. Bradshaw walks by, does a little sidestep shuffle for her. Dust muddies the blood on his hands, forearms, shirt, and pants—the filthiest patch covers his groin and thighs. He shoots her a wink.

In her peripheral vision, Loretta can feel the shape of Ruth, watching from somewhere. Bradshaw moves by, but then Jason comes up, gangly and shy, flushing. *Go away,* she wants to say, because it's too much, and Ruth is right there, watching, and why is she watching?

Jason picks up a ketchup-smeared plate and says, in a blatantly obvious way that he seems to think is covert, "Where do you want to go?"

Bradshaw's braying laugh cuts through the noise. Ruth's face seems locked in place, inside the kitchen window. Loretta moves to another picnic table. Focuses on gathering paper plates. Jason isn't moving. He's watching her. He has decided something, and it makes her nervous. *GO AWAY.* Whatever it was she saw in him during the bunny drive—a stubborn distance, a defiance—now seems merely obtuse. Juvenile. *GO AWAY.* Ruth comes striding across the lawn, holding a plastic garbage bag. Loretta can feel Jason's radiant hurt; it must be apparent to everyone. Ruth stops before Loretta, snaps the bag open before her. Loretta dumps in her trash, and Ruth turns to Jason, repeats the motion, and Jason tosses the one plate he's holding into the bag.

Ruth shakes the bag to settle it. "Okay," she says, pointedly.

Jason—*stop it, stop it now, just go*—looks stubbornly at Loretta and says, "See you later."

Loretta does not answer.

Ruth says, "Tell your mother we'll have you all over real soon."

"For rabbit?" Jason says.

Loretta loves and hates that equally.

"They fry up fine," Ruth says.

Jason walks home—leaves Boyd and goes. His life has been too empty, and now it is too full. Impossible to absorb. Are they doing something now, he and Loretta? Is this real?

At home, he watches a football game on TV without paying attention. The news comes on, and he watches the KMVT report about the bunny bash. There's footage of Dean arguing with the reporter, but what they show of the bash is distant and unrecognizable. It looks like a football game, a big scrambling mass. Mom hollers questions from the kitchen.

"Ruth said she's going to invite us over for dinner," Jason says.

"Let's not hold our breath," she says.

At dinner, Dad doesn't mention the bash until he's started on seconds, and he doesn't bother to look up from his plate.

"Everywhere I went today, people were asking me about that circus," he says. He jabs his fork in the direction of Dean's place. "Didn't take him a couple months to turn the whole place into a joke."

"Lou," Mom says. "That was over there."

"That place is this place," he says. "We're all in the same place."

He chews rapidly, forking in bites as though he were punishing the roast beef. Angry scarlet spackles his hairline. Without looking up, he asks Jason, "What about you? What'd you think of it?"

"It was terrible," he says. "It was— gross."

He remembers the rabbit that came through broken, and Ruth, and the stone.

"Told you you wouldn't like it," Dad says crisply, dropping his fork on his empty plate with a clang.

Jason burns. His self-righteousness. His useless certainty. It is all one piece. It is all together, what happens here and what happens there. That place is this place is that place.

Where do you want to go?

EVEL KNIEVEL ADDRESSES
AN ADORING NATION

The heels of our boots never sounded right in that thing. That should have been a warning. The X-2 Skycycle—red, white, and blue, our name spangled all over the bastard, our own personal rocket ship, and when you stepped in and your boot struck the metal floor it echoed like a piece of tin. Cram your ass in, the thing creaks and groans. This, you think, is the vessel to carry us to glory?

So much time and effort and fuckery precedes the moment. Any moment. Each one is so frail, so pushed along the tracks by everything that came before, everything you promised, everything you feared. We started talking canyon jump before we ever jumped a thing. It was in us, this faith. First it was the Grand Canyon we would jump, and then it became the Snake River, and then time pushed us down those tracks and pushed the canyon jump from a thing said to a thing said often to a pledge and then a promise. Time warped it. Turned it real. The steel and the rivets and the steam engine and the leases and the newspaper boys and the things we said, the things we said fueling it, the things we said and the rocket and the parachute and the marching band and the things we said, the prayer in them, the calling forth of them, the things we said entering the air as sound and sign, gathering atoms and molecules and simple fucking weight, America, gathering power, gathering heft, gathering mass, until they become true things, free-standing and undeniable, made into a vessel to carry us forward, a bullet—a train a bullet a star-spangled rocket ship a whatever the fuck, a universal torque impervious to physics and the boundaries of glory.

That was where we sat that afternoon. On the tip of that bullet. September 8, 1974. We walked through those throngs, touched those people, and saw all that we had done to them. We rose to the ramp on a throne, and they roared. We thought of Caesar and Kennedy, of Alexander the Great. We thought of ascension. We believed in the bullet of the moment, the pressure of the instant, the nobility that must live in us, that must, because we saw all it had grown into, what we said, we saw all that what we said had become, and they saw it, too, these people, and they came to worship.

And then we put our foot into the cockpit, and felt the heel of our boot drum on the tinny bottom of the Skycycle.

And we knew.

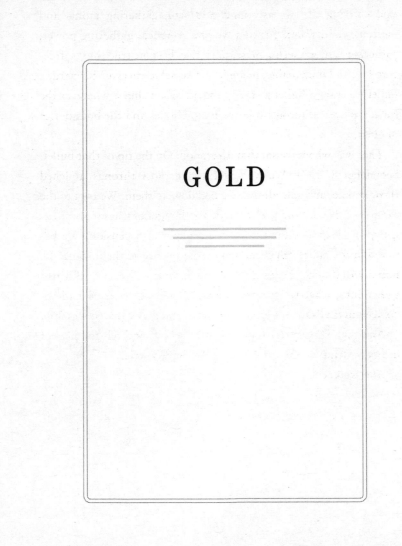

GOLD

October 18, 1975

Boyd

Never in a million years, Boyd thinks, would anyone have guessed Harder could pull this off. An hour ago, even, as he waited at home, one duffel bag packed, praying his mom didn't come home early from the Lincoln Inn, even then, Boyd never imagined they would really leave. Never imagined that Harder—good boy and Eagle Scout, who whispered when he cussed and flinched when you fake-punched him—would dredge up the balls for it.

But here they are. Going, going, gone. They are crossing midnight as they pass slowly through Wendell in the big LeBaron, and Jason sticks to the speed limit as they pass under the sign in the middle of town—THE HUB OF THE MAGIC VALLEY—past hotel, grocery store, bar, grain elevator, and onto I-84.

Jason drives, Loretta rides shotgun, Boyd's in back. Honestly,

Boyd doesn't see what the big deal is. Skinny brown-haired chick. Bet she can bake like a grandma already. He's thrilled to be going, but baffled at Harder, his oldest friend and still a mystery: baffled that he's done this and why. Running away from his rich life. Jason took this car from his parents, though it was sort of his car, he drove it all the time, the 1970 Chrysler Imperial LeBaron. Pea green with a black top, it slides over the road on soft shocks and pulls hard around corners. A land ship. The stitched seats are wide and deep, and the speedometer spreads across the dashboard, needle moored at the top so it swings upside down through the miles per hour. The all-or-nothing heater blasts noisily, and the new eight-track player hangs under the dash. They clear Wendell with a silence building in the cab, a tension inside of that silence because none of them knows how to be together. Jason begins to speed up as he approaches I-84, engine straining, and the upside-down needle ticks past fifty, past sixty, and the LeBaron settles into its speed now, they enter the freeway, and it feels to Boyd as if they have left the earth and are flying.

Loretta says, "Who wants pie?"

Runaways, Boyd thinks. That's what they'll call us. How soon? Will his mother discover he's gone before morning? Will the radio put out bulletins? Will the newspaper run their photos? *Runaways.* It's hard to see through this toward any kind of ending, but for now, he has become something he was not before, and it will always be cool.

"Shit yeah, I want pie," he says.

Jason is quiet at the wheel. He drives and drives. Boyd thinks, *Don't pussy out on us, Harder.* Loretta leans forward and withdraws a foil-covered pie from the bag between her feet, and fusses with it on her lap for a second, and then hands back a piece of pie with a bloody mass spilling out the sides.

"Rhubarb," she says, smiling at him crookedly, squintingly, mischievous.

"Ugh. Okay."

"Don't do me any favors," she says, turning back to the pie. "Jason?"

Boyd says, "Rhubarb's one of those things—like, who do you think first decided to put that in a pie? It's like smoking. Who did that first? And then, after doing it just once, why'd they keep doing it? I mean, I understand what happens if you smoke fifty times and get used to it or something, and then you like it or can't stop or something? But that first guy who smoked? Why'd he keep smoking?"

"I'll have some pie, thanks," Jason says.

"And that first guy who made rhubarb pie? Why'd he keep making it?" Boyd says.

The pie feels heavy in Boyd's hand, like a dead thing. Loretta hands a wedge on a napkin to Jason, a wet bud of tongue peeking from the corner of her mouth.

"Ruth's rhubarb pie," she says triumphantly. "She's going to be so pissed."

Jason takes a bite and groans. Loretta reaches across and wipes a gelatinous smear from his chin, as if he were a toddler. Boyd takes a bite himself, and his mouth contracts: it is as sour as a lemon.

"Holy shit," he mumbles, as he rolls down the window. He spits the mouthful into the rushing winter air, and a gelatinous mess schlumps along the side of the car. "Is that pie a joke?"

Loretta doesn't answer. She holds a third piece of pie in her hands and looks at it, lost in thought. Then she says, dreamily, "That's how she makes it."

She rolls down the window and gives the pie an underhand toss into the icy night. Brisk air rushes in, and Boyd throws his out, too. Jason hands his piece to Loretta, and she tosses it out as well, then picks up the pie tin from the LeBaron's floor and holds it in both hands, like she's gripping a steering wheel. She turns sideways and sticks the pie out the window with both hands, preparing to lob it into the night.

"Do it," Boyd says. "Yes."

She waits, waits, and an exit sign emerges on the road ahead: TWIN FALLS 1. She lobs the pie gently into the air—an expert move, Boyd thinks, the move of someone who understands the physics of throwing something at a road sign from a moving vehicle. It clangs thinly, leaving a Doppler wobble in their wake. Boyd whoops like a cowboy, and Loretta grins thinly as she settles back in. And what is Jason doing up there, so quiet? Is he regretting this? Being scared?

He better not fuck this up.

They turn off at Twin, drive across the bridge. Thin patches of cloud stretch across the stars. It is not much past one, but even the lights ahead can't erase the feeling of an emptied world. Boyd waits for Jason to say something about Evel Knievel, about the ramp over there on the canyon rim, silhouetted, but he miraculously doesn't. Loretta turns the radio knob, staticky AM blaring and fading, and stops on a preacher, calling to them from out of the darkness in a gentle Southern baritone.

"'I looked when He opened the sixth seal, and behold, there was a great earthquake; and the sun became black as sackcloth of hair, and the moon became like blood.'"

Boyd groans and says, "Change it!"

"'And the kings of the earth, the great men, the rich men, the commanders, the mighty men, every slave and every free man, hid themselves in the caves and in the rocks of the mountains, and said to the mountains and rocks, "Fall on us and hide us from the face of Him who sits on the throne and from the wrath of the Lamb! For the great day of His wrath has come, and who is able to stand?"'"

"I am!" Boyd says, and Loretta turns off the radio. Jason sticks in Kiss's *Hotter Than Hell,* and Loretta smiles at him while she lowers the volume and unfolds a map. "Go through to Highway 93," she tells Jason. She's the one who charted their course: down through Nevada to Short Creek, where she has some things to pick up. Then they'll figure out what's next. Jason says Ohio, to see Evel Knievel's next jump; Loretta says the ocean, because she's never seen the ocean; and Boyd says Pine Ridge; but none of them seems convinced that there really is any next.

"God-*damn*," Boyd says. "We are actually doing it. We're on the road. We're free. Totally, totally free, you guys. Check it out. Feel it. Pay attention. This is what it feels like. Feel it. It feels good, right? It feels great."

Loretta yawns. Jason says, "Should we stop somewhere?"

She says, "Elko? I was thinking Elko."

"Hell, no," Boyd says. "We've got to go, go, go."

"I might just close my eyes for a second," Loretta says.

"Go, go, go, go, go," Boyd says, and pounds the back of the seat with his hands.

They pass through Twin Falls, come out on a highway where the night becomes a velvet crush weakening the headlights as they plumb south toward Nevada. They pass a deer once before they even know it, just standing on the side of the road, eyes red in the flash of the LeBaron's lights.

Loretta sits up, rubs her eyes, and says, "Let's play a game."

"Like Monopoly?" Boyd says.

"Like, we each say one thing about ourselves. Take turns and go around. One thing at a time. It'll help us get to know each other. Just one quick thing. About whatever you want. I'll go first. I'm married to Dean. Get that right out of the way. We got married last year. My folks set it up. I didn't want to."

"Whoa, whoa, whoa," Boyd says, pretending to be amazed, but also genuinely amazed. "What? Like, *what*?"

"Knock it off," she says, smiling back at him. "It's not a legal marriage. Enough about it. Now you, Jason."

"Can't we talk about this some more?" Jason says.

She slugs him on the shoulder.

"Go."

"I'm two merit badges from Eagle Scout. Probably not going to make it."

"Boyd?" Loretta asks.

"I," he says, "am a supersonic jet pilot. I am a master contortionist and a student of the dark arts. I know the secrets of the Bermuda Triangle. I've seen *Jaws* four times."

"*One* thing," Loretta says, amused. "Okay, now me. I like country music."

Jason says, "I like rock music."

Boyd says, "I like Zeppelin, Foghat, Bad Company, Cream, Kiss, Pink Floyd, the Rolling St—"

"One thing."

"Oh. *One* thing."

"Okay," she says. "I was born in Sedona, Arizona."

"I was born in Gooding, Idaho," Jason says.

"I was born in Emmett, Idaho," Boyd says.

"I can't stand church."

"Me, neither."

"What's church?"

"Okay, then: I don't even believe in God," she says. "I think."

Boyd finds this incredibly sexy. He says, "I'm half Indian. Which just about every kid around here claims but with me it's true. You can tell by looking. This nose? This nose is a Nez Percé nose. Or maybe Shoshone. Don't know my dad. He's Native, but Mom doesn't even know what tribe. It's like she made it with some guy from Europe, but didn't bother to find out if he was from France or Italy. His name is Francis Daubert. Frank."

"One, Boyd." Loretta turned to him, smiling.

"Oh. Forgot."

"I want to live in Texas," she says.

"Why Texas?" Jason asks.

"No questions. Or maybe Montana."

"Okay. I've gone to church every Sunday, more or less, my whole life," Jason says.

"I want to live anywhere but Gooding. I hate it there. *Hate* it there. Dumbshit capital of America. Can't wait to get out—oh, wait, I don't have to wait to get out. I am out. Hooray."

The stories add up, sort of. Jason talks *Lord of the Rings* and steadfast Samwise Gamgee. Raising calves for the livestock sale. Going to see Evel Knievel, of course. Boyd tells of picking up his mom one time when she passed out at the Mirage. Loretta talks about an argument with Ruth over her refusal to learn how to knit and sew—how Ruth began leaving knitting needles and hanks of yarn in her bedroom. She says she would rather go to jail than live in that family. "Though I love those kids," she says.

The game ends. Loretta and Boyd argue about the bunny bash. Loretta hated it—the blood, the violence, the brutality, the sport of it—and Boyd defends it, says they're just rodents and need to be killed, and it's no better to leave out poison and sneak away than it is to stand there and take care of it with your own hands.

"It *is* different," Loretta insists. "If you poison them, you're not doing it because you *enjoy* it. There's something wrong with enjoying that much death and blood. It's creepy."

She turns in her seat and points a mock-accusatory finger at Boyd.

"You're creepy."

Boyd cannot help but notice. Saying it seems to make her very happy.

Jason

It has all gone wrong so quickly. How long have they been on the road? Two hours? Jason's watch says it's nearly two A.M., and ahead is the moon glow of a casino, an island in a parking lot of nacreous light, and Loretta has announced that she would like to drive.

Jason is slow to answer, and she says, "Please? *Please,* Jason?" and Boyd says, "Jesus, Harder." Jason's whole idea of this is vanishing. Has been ever since the bunny bash, really. She's the one who said she wanted to go first. Later, she was the one who reached out to him—coming to him in the early morning, as he fed the calves, to plan their escape. She was the one who set their route to Short Creek, because she needed to get something she has not mentioned, and she was the one who said they should go through Nevada at night, because Nevada at night is like a wasteland and Utah is full of cops. What does it mean, he thinks, that Loretta knows what Nevada is like at night and how many cops there are in Utah?

She is the one flirting with Boyd. She is the one who has not looked at him with any kind of special look, any sign whatsoever. She is the one who said, *Let's go to Elko on the way,* and when Jason said, *Elko?* she is the one who said, *Come on. It'll be fun.*

They are barely into Nevada now, in Jackpot. Jason pulls the LeBaron into the far reaches of the parking lot. The sign reads CACTUS PETE'S, a giant neon cactus against the sky.

"Yippee," Loretta says. She's practically bouncing in her seat. Boyd says, "Don't kill us, Lori," and Jason thinks: *Lori? Lori?* He says, "Be careful. It's my parents' car," and whatever it is that's wrong about that seems immediately clear, but Loretta is the one who says, "Are you sure it's still theirs?" and laughs and slaps her palms on the dash.

It's all wrong. All turned around. And, if Jason is honest with himself, it has been ever since she saw him in that Rolling Stones shirt, with that fat, lascivious tongue. Since she said, "I have to get away from here." Since she figured out how, in the days after that pronouncement, to communicate with him and plan their escape.

It has all been her. He keeps telling himself that he is her rescuer—because that is who he is supposed to be, that is how the story goes—and yet it has always been her.

In the days after the bunny bash, Jason had conspired with every circumstance to find a way to Loretta. Two days later, he had stopped by their place after school, under the pretense of borrowing a fence puller of Grandpa's. But Uncle Dean was in the yard and he simply got it from the shed. No sign of Loretta. The following day Jason brought it back. Ruth answered the door and told him to put it back in the shed, without inviting him in. Each time, before he arrived he would itch with nerves, wondering what he would do if he saw Loretta, and afterward he felt bereft. He called their house three times that following week, and every time, Ruth answered. "Harders." Like she was angry at the name. Jason simply hung up.

Meanwhile, just as events called for him to be a man of action, he became a mooning girl. Lying in bed, awaiting sleep, he imagined scenarios in which he and Loretta ran off together, giddy in love. He pictured them at the ocean, kicking at the waves or chasing a kite. He imagined them at a Grand Canyon overlook, arms around each other as they gaped into that humongous hole, or at Niagara Falls, holding hands in the mist. These were places he had seen in magazines or on television. He never imagined them anywhere he'd actually been—never at the new mall in Twin Falls or at a football game at the high school. He concocted fantasies in which he struck back at Dean—punched him, or cracked him across the back with a two-by-four, or held him at gunpoint while he and Loretta backed slowly out of the house. But mostly he just thought of Loretta and him together, living in a city apartment like the Newharts, all sliding glass and evening light. He imagined her coming to him, draping her arms around his shoulders, pressing her nose into his neck. Chaste scenarios, impossible and lifeless. And whenever he faced the fact that he didn't know her at all, he filled her in with his imagination, and her character became marked by one and only one outstanding quality: a blind, unwavering attraction to him.

He didn't see her for days. He began to wonder if he had misunderstood what they had said to each other that bloody afternoon. Weren't they talking about doing something? Something for real? He thought they were. He waited and plotted, and blew everything up in his mind, filled himself with ludicrous notions and expectations. He felt that now, finally, he understood what people talked about, what they sang about—this wrenching, consuming ache. Wasn't it grand? Every lousy song on the radio was for him. For them. *"How sweet it is to be loved by you." "Lovin' you is easy 'cause you're beautiful." "Love will keep us together."*
Eight days after the bunny bash, Jason arose at five thirty,

walked through the stiff silence of the house to the mudroom, stepped into his boots and work coat, and walked out into the ice-metal cold foretelling the winter to come, across the dirt yard to the front room of the barn, where he dipped each of the eight large, hard plastic bottles into the tank and topped them with the red rubber nipples. The whoosh and spray of the barn carried on behind the filthy swinging door with the yellowing window. Dad standing behind it. Jason carried the heavy rack out to the calf pens, and upended them in the wire holders, and stood waiting, watching the little piebald slurp and drool on jittery legs, listening to a truck somewhere across the desert shift whiningly into gear, noticing a hiss and rustle behind the shed. The misted sun tried to rise from the horizon. Jason heard another hiss from the direction of the shed, followed by the staccato bray of a calf. And another hiss.

Then, as he turned toward the sound, his name.

"Jason."

Peeking out from the side of the shed, Loretta's face was tensed and red in the cold air, and her hair was tied back, covered by a gray wool hat, thick and hand knit, that made her face seem frail and small—chapped, rose cheeks, nub chin. Nervous eyes wide and gleaming. A ranch coat, denim and wool lined, and no dress. She wore the slightly baggy, square-looking jeans she'd worn to seminary. She smiled, and he tried to smile back. Here they were. Here they were. He looked around, walked over. An arrhythmic spasm crossed Jason's face, and he wondered what he looked like to her. She seemed to be waiting for something, so Jason said, "What are you doing here?"

"I've been trying to talk to you forever," she said.

"I've been trying to talk to *you* forever."

"I've called. I've come over."

"*I've* called. *I've* come over."

Her brow pinched, and she frowned a smile, as if she thought Jason was messing with her.

"Okay, never mind." She took a breath. Her tone was the tone of a schoolteacher laying out the rules. Someone burying fluttery doubts under a plan. "We need to talk. Am I wrong about that? That we need to talk?"

"No, we do."

"I mean, I thought we had a little something, a little agreement or something, and if we don't, then fine, but I thought we did." She didn't seem nervous, really, just set loose. "You asked me, right? You asked me where I wanted to go, and then I couldn't talk to you, I couldn't find you, because everything is so screwed up at my house, and maybe at your house, too. I called, and you never answered. I came over here with preserves, and ran into your mom. I came over Saturday and pretended to return a rake—again, no you. I was starting to think I had imagined the whole thing. And that was terrible, because I got so excited about everything."

She paused for him to say something, but not for long.

"I didn't imagine the whole thing, did I?" she asked.

"I don't think so."

"You don't think so. You mean you're not sure? You mean— what? You don't think so?"

"No, you didn't imagine it."

She peered at him intensely. None of this—this talk assault, this forward speed—was part of his picture of her.

"Does Dean know you're here?" he said.

She bugged her eyes.

"Are you insane? Like I'd tell Dean I came over here to plot my getaway?"

A noise burst, like gravel being scuffed, and Jason nearly leaped. She smiled and said, "Easy, bronco."

This was not right. She was not supposed to be the cool one.

"Okay, so. You remember what we talked about?" she asked. "At the rabbit thing?"

"Yes."

"You remember what you asked me?"

Was this it? Were they leaving now? He was scared. He had been such a good boy, for so long, and he didn't know how to be different.

"Where do you want to go?" he said, quoting himself.

"Right."

"Yes," he said. "I remember."

The calves brayed and trotted around their pens. Dad would be expecting him to return with the empties soon.

"I know where I want to go," she said.

She had it all worked out. She knew everything.

Loretta is a fast, fast driver. Sometimes she takes her eyes off the road, and the LeBaron drifts, and Jason has to speak up before she notices, and then she laughs.

She is talking about Elko. She says she'll get them a room and pay with a check she stole from Dean. She'll take care of it. It's all so wrong. Jason emptied his bank account and brought all his mission money—$71.53—but she doesn't need even that.

"Dean has checks?" Jason asks, because he knows that Dean distrusts banks.

"For business. For emergencies," she says happily. "This seems like an emergency."

Good Lord, she is beautiful.

"Wait," Boyd says. "Why would they take a check from Dean from you?"

"You can talk just about anybody into anything," she says. "If you really try."

Loretta

She said Elko because why not Elko? She said Elko because she wanted to do every free thing, now that she was free. She said Elko because Bradshaw had told her stories about Elko. She said Elko because she wanted to see what the boys—these boys, these eager children—would say to her if she said Elko, and what they said was interesting.

"Isn't that out of the way?" Jason asked.

Boyd said, "Holy shit, Harder, you are a super fun guy."

Dawn breaks as they draw near Elko. Down between the mountains they come, winding and flattening toward the neon constellation ahead. Boyd snores gaspingly. For the past couple of hours of deep night, Loretta has felt the exhilaration of those first hours dampen. She is overtaken by gloom, by this moment and its failure to be transcendent. She had come tonight thinking what a nice boy Jason was, what a simple, clean thing, and that he and she were a team, whatever that meant, and she had thought maybe it meant something. Perhaps it would grow, this clean, fresh thing. But soon enough she saw Jason's irritation with Boyd, saw his confusion and jealousy, and realized he was simply another part, as was Boyd, of the wide world that looked at her and wanted to turn her into something of theirs.

It is past three in the morning when she guides the big sloppy car into the parking lot at the Stockmen's, the pit of light in the center of town. A bank of windows, a neon bull's head, and a huge sign in red glowing like the entrance to hell on top of it all: STOCKMEN'S HOTEL.

Jason says, "I don't know," and Loretta wants to hit him.

She parks the car and says, "Wait here," and sets off. As she walks across the parking lot she feels it again—the lift, the joy, the hum—and she enters the front doors, smells cigarette smoke, and hears the tinny bells, the trilling of adrenaline that sings to her from the worldly world.

Inside, the Stockmen's opens cavernously. Footpaths are worn in the center of the brocade carpet, and the decor suggests a fake barn—all lassos and riverine wood grain. It is lit up like midday, but nearly deserted. The long check-in desk has five stations, though only one person sits there now, a young man with a bolo tie and boils along the temples who glances at Loretta as though she has startled him.

The hum is at full speed when she approaches the desk. She stops, acts confused and embarrassed, and says, as though she doesn't know where to begin, "I'm in kind of a jam here, and I wonder if you can help me."

She explains herself, and shows him a blank check.

"I don't know," the night clerk says slowly.

He is holding the check between his thumb and forefinger, as if it might be tainted. He looks at the name and information—Dean Harder, d/b/a Zion's Harvest—and then at Loretta, and then back.

"I swear," she says. "He's my father, and he gave me these. For emergencies. It's completely good, I promise."

The boy exhales loudly and screws up his face.

"I don't know," he says.

She doesn't have a driver's license or an ID. She's got nothing to prove anything. She looks at him beseechingly, and says, "Please?"

"I'll have to ask my manager," he says. He leaves and returns with a tall, thin woman, who is made taller by the hair swooped upon her head like an ice cream cone. She has wrinkled skin and golden hair that strikes Loretta as unnatural, almost orange, and she smells strongly of perfume, and she is smoking a long, thin cigarette. She puts her big brown eyes on Loretta and sucks hard on the cigarette, and the wrinkles on her face centralize.

"We might have to give the bank a call Monday," she says—she pronounces it "Mondee." Loretta feels certain she will not do this, and says, "Of course. Sure," and the manager shrugs and says, "Okay," and hands the check back to the boy and leaves without another word.

And then Loretta—flying again, just flying—asks, "Can I make it for a little over?"

Walking back to the car, she spots the first pale hint of morning along the horizon rim to the east. A mere lightening of the dark. It is approaching four A.M. Back home, she thinks, no one is even awake yet. No one even knows they're gone.

Becky

She wakes with Lou, as she does every morning, and as Lou leaves to begin milking, she slides to her knees at the side of the bed and prays. She thanks the Lord for this day, this life, for her husband and son, Louis and Jason, their farm here in Gooding, their faith, their friends, their family, even the newly arrived woes and strife of family. She prays and prays, not thinking words—not the way Lou prays, in carefully selected, familiar phrases—so much as images and sensations. She finds herself filled, as always, with a warmth, a reaction in her body that she can only believe is the arrival of a presence, prickling her nerve ends, adding substance to her flesh, joining her. It is the sensory manifestation of the Lord, the weight of Him in the body, and it fills her with the knowledge of God, the knowledge that brought her into this church. It was not be-lief or faith, she thought. It was physics. Force and mass. It was *knowledge.* And so she is strong in the face of everyone she left behind—her faithless family in Wyoming, her Catholic friends from college—because she knows that they can't help what they don't know.

She had come to Gooding to teach school and met Lou through a fellow teacher, and her conversion was quick: she felt the weight of the Lord the second time she attended sacrament meeting. She knows her family can't help but tell the tales they have been told, repeat the heresies and bigotries against Mormons, and though they long ago stopped trying to get her to change, she knows it is always there, their sense of having lost her to this thing they call a cult. Now, though, something new has flamed inside her since the arrival of Dean and Ruth and their children and that girl, and she must pray against it, must pray to drive from her body the fear that they prove the doubters right, they illustrate the worst of what the ignorant already believe. *Polygamy,* her friends and family always said to her. *The Mormons are polygamists.* And she had insisted they were not. But here the polygamists were. In her own family. She prays against Dean and Ruth, prays not just that they will leave but that they will never have been, that they and what they are will be undone.

It is dark. Five A.M. She puts on her slippers and robe, and descends the stairs. Turns on the kitchen lights, and one bulb in the overhead fixture fritzes out. She changes it standing on a kitchen chair, and washes the dust and bugs out of the frosted glass bowl of the fixture at the sink. Outside, in the paling dark, the lights of the milking barn look supple and thick. The milking machine hums. Cows low. Becky starts a pan of sausage links, and beats together eggs and milk and cinnamon, and slices the last half of a loaf of wheat bread. She pours a splash of apple juice into the pan with the sausage links and covers it, and then goes to wake up Jason. He will grumble and growl, she knows, complain, ask to sleep in, whine that it's a Sunday, it's a weekend, just a little longer, just a little longer, and Becky prepares to resist him, because she loves him so, this boy, because she wants him to be happy in every small moment, and it has been her lifelong challenge to fight the desire to satisfy him, to soften him with pleasures. There is nothing that feels more vital to Becky than rising early, earlier than the flesh wishes, to thrust herself into life, and she must teach Jason this, she must force him, over and over, to wake and to go forth, to train the sloth out of him, the way she trained it out of herself, morning after morning.

When she knocks, there is no answer. She knocks again, and again there is no answer—no grumbling, no moaning. She cracks open the door and peeks in, and then she simply stares at the empty bed, the empty room, without understanding, at first, what isn't there.

Bradshaw

Bradshaw wakes on the cot in the basement, surrounded by the walls of jarred preserves aligned on new wood shelves, some bright with color, peach yellow, beet red, and others gone gray and furred with dusk. Right where Lori was sleeping, until he showed up. It is winter cold down there, concrete and exposed pipe and invisible shuffling in the corners, and each new morning briefly confuses Bradshaw, who must absorb and remember.

Upstairs, he hears footsteps in the kitchen. Ruth's making her horse food. They will go now any day, he and Lori. He is ready. He tells Lori they don't need a thing. He tells her he was wrong, down in The Crick, when he said to wait for money, just as he was wrong to let her tell him no. He mutters and whispers to her whenever he gets a chance, and he knows it now, without a doubt, that Ruth has seen. Loretta says wait, wait, soon now, soon. She knows something, she wants something, but they can never talk much.

He was wrong when he said they should wait for money. Everything had already changed, the landscape shifted, by the time he told her that, but he didn't realize it until their moment had passed. How had it changed? What had she said? No. *No.* He had never allowed a girl to tell him no. Never. And there had been plenty of them, starting back in Vegas. High school. His dad off on oil rigs for weeks at a time, his mom who knows where, the house his own. And there were plenty of them in Cedar City later, girls who would do what he wanted them to. Like it or not. The Mormon girls— half were as fast as hell, and the others would keep their mouths shut. At a certain point, limbs and mouths entangled, no was not something Bradshaw was willing to accept.

But with Loretta, he had. She was *that kind* of Mormon. A whole new territory. He took no for an answer, knowing that yes was up ahead somewhere. What do you call that, if not love? Surely she knows that, Lori does. Surely she knows what he has done for her, what part of himself he has given up, and what she owes him because of it.

Footsteps on the top three stairs, and Ruth's voice.

"Mr. Baker? Good morning."

Steps retreating. Upstairs, the sounds of the house: chairs dragging, forks on plates. And then heavier steps and a deeper voice: Dean.

Bradshaw pulls on his jeans and chamois work shirt, and steps into his boots. Sitting on the cot, he ties the boots and considers one of the surprises of this journey: He likes Dean. Kind of admires him. Enjoys the fact that Dean seems to trust and admire him in turn, seems to feel that Bradshaw is becoming a loyal lieutenant in Zion's Harvest, and maybe in his wider battles—his battles with the brethren down in Short Creek, his constant inner battle with the worldly world. It's not that Bradshaw won't do what he's come here to do. But sometimes he imagines having a life like Dean's, and the idea draws him in: all those people orbiting you, women and children and women, all yours, all turning toward your light as if you were the sun itself.

Breakfast is mush. That's what Ruth calls it, the oatmeal cooked to spongy softness: mush. Raisins and honey for sweetness. Some whole wheat toast with her homemade jam and no butter. Eating these meals makes Bradshaw desperate for a diner, a cafeteria somewhere with coffee and greasy eggs and glistening hash browns, big bowls of sugar, a drift of cigarette smoke. The only consolation is Lori, every morning, ducking her head toward the food, hiding those eyes. Love, he thinks every morning, love, love. He was not one who accepted love—not like that, not the way they say, the giving over, the loss of control—it was not something he sought or even believed in, necessarily, until Lori seeped into his mind.

Only she is not at the table today. The kids are crowded around, slurping and banging. Dean looms above everyone else, knees wide and head bowed, and he spoons mush into his mouth steadily and purposefully, as though he were hammering a nail.

He looks up when Bradshaw enters and says, "Morning," and turns back to the mush. Samuel—a zitty little shit who Bradshaw can tell will grow into meanness—looks to Bradshaw and nods, but no one else says a word or turns his way. Bradshaw wants more talk than this house provides. He says, "And a fine morning it is, with this lovely spread for breakfast. Thank you, Sister Ruth."

She says, "You're welcome," as she puts a bowl before him. He considers asking where Loretta is, and decides against it.

After several minutes of silent eating, Dean says to Ruth, "Perhaps she needs a little nudging," and Ruth wipes her hands on a towel and leaves. Bradshaw hears her going up, and then down the small hall, to where he knows Loretta's room is—the one she moved into when he arrived, displacing the kids into sleeping bags in the living room—and he hears, faintly, a knock and a murmur, another knock and another murmur, and then Ruth's returning steps, down the hall, down the stairs, into the kitchen. She leans over Dean's shoulder, whispers in his ear, and they leave together, and Bradshaw knows something has gone rotten. When he learns that Loretta is not in that room and that no one knows where she has gone, he thinks back on how he knew it—how he felt it—when Dean and Ruth left the kitchen together, how the knowledge came to him like a wrenching of the guts, because that, too, was love.

No one is talking to him. No one is looking at him. Dean and Ruth whisper loudly, the anger audible but not the words. The kids are hustled away to the living room, and Ruth tells Samuel, "I need you all in there and I need you quiet," and then she turns to Bradshaw, still sitting there before his mush. Ruth seems unsure what to say as she looks at him, face livid, and after forever she simply holds up a hand, as if to say, *Stay right there.*

Dean stomps upstairs and down, whispers with Ruth, and stomps back up. Soon come four loud pounding sounds, accompanied by some splintering. Bradshaw stands, and Ruth checks him with a glance.

"Can I help with anything?" he asks.

Ruth shakes her head tightly. "Thank you, no. Thank you."

"I'll go out, then."

He pulls on his wool-lined denim jacket, and steps out the back door, letting the screen door slam. He just knows. Not everything. Not the how and why. But he knows, and there is a rot in his chest. His mind moves like a hummingbird, too fast, and he feels strangely exposed—fooled and foolish—and trudges through the fallow hayfield, through frozen clod and chaff.

When he goes back in, Ruth is speaking on the telephone while Dean is seated at the kitchen table, looking calm, meditative. A rush of affection floods Bradshaw; here is how a man holds himself. Here is a right man. Ruth cuts her eyes at Bradshaw, phone tucked against the side of her head, and then turns her back and lowers her voice.

She hangs up and says to Dean, "Jason, too," and confusion ripples the stillness of Dean's calm face, and he asks, "What?" and then everything in Dean's visage—forehead, eyes, beard—contracts around the center of his face, and he says, "What?" again, louder, and Ruth doesn't answer.

He's going after her. It's the only thing he knows. He walks out and stops in the yard. Considers Dean's pickup, white with a scurf of dirt splattered upward from below. The tempest in his mind clears and he hears his own voice: *What in the fuck is wrong with me?* How had she done this to him, and what should he do about it?

He walks to his Nova. Gets in and sits, squeezing the steering wheel. Some of his things are still in the basement, but nothing important. They've gotten ahead of him, Lori and this little shit, and he needs to hurry.

A cloudy pressure in his head makes it hard for him to feel he is thinking correctly. This has never been his thing. Foresight, strategy. *He had let her tell him no.* He squeezes the steering wheel and locks his jaw and howls. Then he gets out. Slams the door. Says, jaw clamped, "Fuckity fuckity *fuck*." If he leaves here now, he will have no idea where to go.

Loretta

The hot water stays hot. It flows over her head, through her hair, sliding over her body in streams and tendrils, and it stays hot, clogging the air with steam. *This is how life will be now,* she thinks. No one monitoring the minutes of her showers, and the water always hot. No more Ruth lecturing them on toilet paper usage, giving screeds on the Lucifer's sugar. No more Dean at dinner, scolding about showers, instructing them all to wet themselves, turn off the water to soap up, and then rinse briefly—saying there was no reason a shower should take any longer than two minutes, and that it was wasteful and selfish to stand there and warm up.

Now the drowsy, narcotic comfort of the water gives her the next idea.

A knock on the door.

"Did you drown?"

Boyd. That interesting boy.

"I might've," she shouts.

"Should I mount a rescue?"

She turns off the water. Steam turns the room into a cloud. She trembles. The very idea that he might come in now.

She says, "I think I'll make it."

She dries herself vigorously, like rubbing the skin from a roasted beet. She dresses and comes out into the room, hair scraggly and wet. Boyd sits on one bed and Jason sits on the other, watching *The $10,000 Pyramid* on TV. It's the final round. The category is "Things in a Discotheque." It is almost three in the afternoon, and this is luxurious and transgressive, like the hot water—to have slept this late, well into the productive hours of the day. Loretta wants to dance. She wants to spin around and jump. On TV, a woman is giving clues: "A mirror ball. Dance music." Loretta wants to dance. Is this her future? Her Tussy future—lipstick and fast cars? On TV, the contestant says, "Things in a disco!" Loretta thinks: *A disco!* She wants to dance. She wants to curse. She wants to *drink*. She used to sip at the beers that Bradshaw kept on the floorboard of his Nova while they drove the desert a million years ago. Back when she thought Bradshaw was the way out.

Boyd and Jason smile at her sleepily. Jason's dense helmet of hair is smudged to one side. She runs into the bathroom for a bar of soap, and returns to scrawl on the mirror: *October 19, 1975, HAPPY BIRTHDAY!*

"It's whose birthday?" Jason asks her.

Boyd says, "It's all of our birthdays."

He gets it. She finds she simply likes to look at Boyd—she likes the strange color of his skin, brown and rich and with a pale, dry, almost translucent layer over it; she likes his black hair, blacker than any hair she has seen, so black it shines bluely; and she likes his enormous, alert, luminous eyes.

Boyd says, "Happy birthday, Lori!"

He comes at her, smiling wickedly, like Bradshaw might smile at her, handsome and strange, ready to wrap her up, arms out like Christ in the clouds.

Jason

It is a Sunday afternoon, and it feels like it. Deadened. Emptied of possibility. Strange, Jason thinks, that they are here, having done this, and he feels this way. *Lori? Hugs?* He rises to change the channel, and Loretta says, "Come on, Jason, you, too," but he doesn't want to.

Click, click. A nature show. On the soundless TV, a lion chases a rabbit across an African desert. The camera cuts away as it closes its paws in slow motion upon its prey.

Why did he bring Boyd? They go back a long way. They were safety buddies in elementary school. Jason can still picture the black rasp of Boyd's third-grade buzz cut. The strange smells of his house were familiar and warm to Jason, and he had taken in the oddities and embarrassments of Boyd's life—his drunken mother, his fatherlessness, his Indian-ness—and shared them. He brought Boyd with them, brought him here, and now Jason feels guilty because he wishes that he hadn't.

Boyd is in the bathroom. The shower runs. Loretta is sort of dancing around, humming. Some awful country song. "I'm Not Lisa." She catches him looking and smiles. It's still there, he thinks, whatever is between them. If he can only figure out how to unlock it.

She flops heavily onto the bed, props her chin in her hands.

"We should do something," she says.

"Aren't we driving on?"

"We should have fun. Think of something fun."

Jason tries very hard to think of something fun. The shower stops.

"We could go drive around town," he says.

"Yeah," she says, meaning *Naw*.

Boyd comes out dressed in yesterday's clothes—jeans, a three-quarter-sleeve T-shirt with a sepia-toned picture of Foghat.

"What are you kids talking about?" he asks.

Loretta says, "What to do. We could go check out the casino."

"*You* want to go to the casino?" he says.

She shrugs. "We could. We could get some beer." She sits up on the bed. Jason sits on the end of the other bed, three feet from the TV—where a jaguar now pursues a springing antelope—and Boyd stands in the bathroom doorway. Loretta bounces. "You guys wanna get some beer?"

Jason says, "I don't know," and Boyd says, "I like you old-fashioned Mormons," and Loretta is looking back and forth between them, and she says, "You guys need to learn to have fun!"

"We could check out a brothel," Boyd says.

"Check out?" Loretta says.

"Jason could stake us," Boyd says.

"What's that cost?" Jason asks.

Loretta says, "It depends," and Boyd slaps his thigh.

"I don't get you," he says. "How do you become you, living the way you've lived?"

"I'm creative," she says. "I'm smart."

And now this, Jason thinks. So much, so fast. The beer tastes sour and wheaty, and it rises instantly to his head, like it was always there waiting for him. The world warms and welcomes. He becomes garrulous. All anxiety slips away, and this becomes a world unto itself: this room, the three of them, the beer Loretta has ordered from the casino bar, because she is the one who knows how to do things.

He tells a story, and Loretta laughs. He mocks Boyd, teases him, and she laughs again. All of them seem half drunk before the first cans of Coors are empty. Tipsy and giggling. Jason sips at the beer and tries not to make faces. He feels himself begin to race. He has tasted beer a time or two before, and hasn't liked it. That seems to be changing. All of the problems and anxieties of the world—all of the past and all of the future—are somewhere outside the warm, cozy bubble of this room. Boyd belches. Loretta says, "Gross," but then she chugs what must be half a beer and follows suit. When she laughs, her eyes fill with tears.

Loretta pulls a second beer from the paper bag sitting beside the TV. She tells them stories about sneaking out at night, about the party boys down in Short Creek. "Them kids were wild," she says, admiringly. She has a farmy accent that Jason hasn't noticed before. Boyd tells a story about finding his mom passed out in the bathroom with puke in her hair, and Loretta says, "Gross," and Jason feels a warm flood of gratitude that it is Boyd's shitty life and not his that she is saying this about. He stands and goes to the windows and looks out on the mountains rising over Elko, over the whitening day.

"Seriously, though, Jason," Loretta says, flopping onto the bed and spilling beer. "We owe you one. Big time."

"I don't owe him one," Boyd says.

She acts as if she didn't hear him, just looks at Jason in that stoned way.

"Well, I owe you one," she says. "I can't believe we did it."

She rises and crosses over to him and places a hand, as light as balsa, on his forearm and taps his cheek with a kiss.

Louis

The stout, red-faced deputy at the counter is telling Louis that technically his son is not yet a runaway.

"Hafta wait forty-eight hours before we can do a thing," he says, a little embarrassed, maybe, but still chewing his gum, and for that alone, Louis wants to climb over the counter.

"Who would you find yourself in trouble with if you acted like an officer of the law before forty-eight hours expired?" Louis says carefully. "Seeing how it's me, the boy's father, who's asking you to do so."

"Now, Brother Harder," says the deputy, Sid Moody, who comes to church in Louis's ward about half the time, "I don't make—"

"You have a car. You have the keys to that car. You have a radio. You have a gun and a badge and the authority of the law, and you have the knowledge that my minor son has taken my car and run away overnight, with another minor child under the care of her guardians, and all you can manage is to tell me about the rules that allow you to sit here in the office and do nothing? Is that about it, Sidney?"

The clock makes the V of 1:50. Louis should have been here hours ago. But first there was the matter with Dean—Dean arguing, and then insisting, that he not bring in the police, and then Becky recoiling when he told her he had agreed to that and shaming him into coming here at last. And now that he's here, he's being told he is *too early*. He is recalling now what it had been like to be a brawling youngster—he and Dean swinging it out on the front lawn as kids, he and any number of other boys, his friends, even, back in those days of high school and youth, the days of drag racing the dirt roads around Gooding, the days before he settled down, as he always knew he would—recalling what it had been like in the moments before a fight, the pressure about to burst.

"I know this is hard, Louis," Moody says, watching one of his hands idly scratching the back of the other.

"How would you know that, Sidney? By what possible means would you know this is hard?"

Louis senses that he has recomposed himself.

"Maybe you ought to speak to the sheriff."

"Maybe I should, Sidney. Maybe I damn well should."

Apparently, his voice has risen. The sheriff comes out from the warren of fluorescent-lit linoleum hallways, holding up both hands and smiling amicably, a peacemaker.

Louis has been immersed in other people's problems for so long that he's almost forgotten what the hot pain of crisis feels like firsthand. He had served as the ward's bishop for almost five years, and most recently has been the head of the young men's program. People approach him constantly for advice and solace. *My husband is spending all of our money gambling. I am struggling with sexually impure thoughts. My boss is asking me to work on Sundays. My wife won't tell me where she's been going on Saturday afternoons. My son is stealing money from his grandmother.*

What do these people want? He would simply tell them what he thought they should do—*leave your husband, forgive your husband, report your son to the police*—but that was never what they wanted. People almost always know what they should do. What they come for is comfort. To have the difficult thing done for them. They want to be confirmed as the kind of person they think themselves to be, while doing something that person would not do. Or to extract themselves from the situation that proves they are not the kind of person they think themselves to be. To retract, to undo, to redo. Years and years of listening to people has hardened this sense in Louis—this notion that people come to him for love and repair only, never for advice about what to do—and has also hardened his sense that he can do neither, that he cannot fix them and he cannot love them, not really love them, not enough to fix them.

And so he has become distant from them, one by one, with their heartbreaks and hypocrisies, wanting to be relieved of the things that are rightfully theirs. He has become just as distant as Sid Moody, the deputy, and because he understands Moody's detachment, he understands how Moody is calculating his own—Louis's—pain and need and impossibility, and he understands that Moody had put him at a distance before they even began.

He and Becky drive the roads around Gooding. He tells her it's because the kids might be out there somewhere, crashed and hurt, or worse, but he doesn't think the kids are out there. He just wants to move. To avoid sitting. Becky has entered a stunned silence at last, but she bombarded him with questions, with expectations, when he returned from the sheriff's office. The sheriff had agreed to put out a dispatch to other law enforcement agencies, and to put in a few calls to sheriffs in neighboring counties.

"And what else?" Becky asked.

"What else what?"

"Is that it?"

"I don't think there's anything else to do."

He can hear the rage in the watery notes of her voice. It is a sticking point between them—his passivity—and she is feasting on this, filling herself with all that he is not, though they will speak of it, as ever, in the measured tones of people in control.

"There has to be more, Louis. There has to be."

So they are driving. They drive east on Old Shoshone Road, and south on Pole Line, and back west on Highway 26, and then south on 46, and then he begins simply cruising every country block, through the fields and farms. She asks him again where he thinks Jason has gone, and he tells her again that he doesn't know. No ideas? No, he says. Does she have any? She does not.

They return when it's time for milking. There, inside the noise of the barn, the wet suck of the machines and the milky, cow-shitty odor, Louis feels a measure of relief, and stops thinking for the moment, tries his very best to vanish inside the things that make this day like any other day.

Loretta

All things begin to seem possible. Loretta says, "Who wants to gamble?" and Jason, who seems to be stumbling and slurring even while sitting silently, burps and grins, and Boyd says, "How are we supposed to get away with that?" and Loretta rolls her eyes. "Jeez. I thought I was the sheltered one," she says, thinking maybe they could just live here, like this, the three of them. Or just two of them—she and Boyd. Every worldly thing is here. Every sinful thing.

They go to the casino, and she is right, no one bothers them. She gets tokens for the slots at the window—shows them her room key, and they ask no questions. The casino is mostly deserted; the ringing of slots and the thick haze of cigarette smoke fill the room. Now and then the reek of liquor wafts by, and Loretta breathes it in. She sits at a slot machine, and Jason and Boyd flank her. At one point, Boyd reaches across and says, "Let me try," and pulls the lever, and she smells him, soap and beer and something sweetly foreign, and she looks at his skin and finds that she wants to look at it closely, wants to examine his dark skin—she has never been so close to it, never touched it, and now she finds it exotic and interesting, the way it pales at the elbow and finger joints and worn places, the way it lightens on his palms, and she thinks about what this skin is, in the world that she has left behind, she thinks about the fact that the skin is the punishment of God, in the world she has left behind, and it makes her want to touch that skin and smell that skin. It makes her want to know what that skin means—that difference. She wonders about demons and men; she wonders why she believes in demons, beings beyond the world of people. She cannot understand why she believes in this, when so much of everything else from that world she has left behind she has simply left behind. What if Boyd were a demon? What if that was what his dark skin meant? And what if she wanted it anyway?

The waitress roaming the casino asks them if they want drinks, and Loretta answers for all of them: "Three beers and three shots," and the waitress jots and leaves. Loretta pulls the handle—cherry, banana, cherry—and the waitress returns. Loretta shows the boys how to throw back the shots, though she has never done it. How does she know how to do it? Her future is teaching her how.

Jason seems the drunkest, but they're all drunk. It's almost six. From the speakers comes rowdy music. *"I . . . wanna rock and roll all night and party e-ve-ry day."* Loretta keeps pulling the slot handle, and keeps losing. Behind her, Boyd and Jason bicker.

Jason says, "I'd be happy to buy you a bus ticket home," and Boyd says, "I bet you would."

Loretta moves to a roulette table, asks the man in the white shirt and black vest what to do and he explains it to her, but she doesn't understand. She puts chips on thirteen. She thinks that everything is reversed now, opposite, so thirteen is her lucky number, but she doesn't win. The man in the black vest gathers in the money. Boyd says, "This is fucked up." The roulette wheel spins and flashes, the ball bounces and lands in a black chute, and the man in the vest sweeps Loretta's chips toward himself across the felt table. Boyd leaves and returns. Loretta hears him telling Jason, "I hurled like a motherfucker in there. All over the seat."

A different song comes on. Slower. Sadder. *"And it's one more beer / and I don't hear you anymore . . ."*

Loretta puts chips on black thirteen. Boyd says to Jason, "What are we doing, exactly? I mean, what are *you* doing?"

Loretta loses. The chips slide away. Jason says something she can't hear.

"What I mean," Boyd says, belching, "is, I can see why she would want to leave. And I can see why I would want to leave. But I can't see why you would want to leave."

"Well."

The singer sings, *"And someone saved my life tonight sugar bear . . ."*

Boyd says, "I mean, you had it pretty good."

Something wordless is happening between the two of them behind her back. Loretta wins, and cheers, and Boyd says, "Dude, I used to think you were smart."

They go to eat in the bar. Loretta shows the key, and everything is fine, everything is good, they order drinks and cheeseburgers deluxe. On the wall are photos of cattle drives and cowboys. Longhorns everywhere. Knotty-wood paneling and red vinyl seats. Red glass candleholders glow on each table, little bowls of fire. A bartender in an ornate Western shirt and bolo tie, hair wet and tight against his head. There are just the three of them and one other group of customers—four men. Every so often, one of the men lets out a whoop, or a cloudburst of laughter erupts.

Jason says, "We probably should be careful with money."

Loretta says, "Don't worry about money."

One of the guys from the other table gets up and begins walking across the bar, toward the bathroom past where the three of them sit. Loretta sees something happen to Jason—something freezes his attention. His head pivots, following the man.

"Holy shit," Jason says.

Loretta turns to the man now. He's a hitch-gaited walker, a bit bowlegged like Bradshaw, with a thieving look. Jason says it again, whispers to himself, as if he were praying. *"Holy shit."*

"What?" Loretta says, and Jason says, "I don't think I can believe this," and she says again, "What, Jason?" and he says, "Watch this guy when he comes out of the john," and she says, "What about him?" and he says, "Just watch," and he takes a trembling sip of beer and nods toward the man now returning from the restroom and says, "See?" and she says, "What?" and Boyd says, "What, already?" and Jason says, "Stop saying that," and then the man notices them, notices them noticing him, and he stops, smiles a head-cocked smile, the smile of an explorer spying a new path through the jungle, and the man says, "What?" and Jason asks, "Are you who I think you are?" and the man says, "That depends, buddy. Who do you think I am?"

Jason

"Grab life, I guess is what I'm saying," Evel Knievel is telling them. "You kids need to take life by the balls, if you'll pardon my French, just grab it by the sack and give it a big squeeze. 'Cause that's what it's all about—just how much of life you can hold on to. Jobs, families, reputations—fuck all that. What it comes down to, at the end of the day when the horses are back in the barn, is just *taking* things, *taking* life, *taking* what-have-you, whatever, and just holding it. Just . . . *seizing* it."

He is holding both hands before him and squeezing his fists like he's draining lemons, and the look on his face tightens in conjunction with his hands. He has joined them here at their table, a round of golden beers arrayed before them. Boyd acts half amused, and Loretta seems intrigued, but Jason is awestruck, and full of the sense that this is life as it is supposed to be, right here, this exact moment, and that he must pay strict attention.

"You know?" Evel says. "You know what I'm saying? Of course, you don't. How could you? I'm not saying I did it all right or anything, not saying I'm some kind of hero, but I did try to *grab life*. I *do* try to grab it. You gotta say that for me, whatever else kind of slander and bullshit you want to peddle, at least give me that. Huh?"

He has been sitting at their table in the Stockmen's lounge for ten minutes or so, and he hasn't stopped talking. He's left his table of buddies across the bar, and seems to be settling in.

"That's just what we're trying to do, Mr. Knievel," Jason says. "We're trying to grab life, just like you say."

"What did I say about Mr. Knievel?"

Evel Knievel's words are thick, stuck to his tongue. When he isn't speaking, he breathes heavily through his mouth.

"Evel," Jason says. "Sorry."

"I mean, look around you. Look at people."

There are not many other people in the bar to look at, but for a couple of small groups and the bartender watching an episode of *Emergency!* on TV. Sirens sound; someone is being saved.

"All around you. Just look at them," he says, leaning forward and hissing in a hostile whisper. "It is flat pathetic. People living puny lives, never trying for anything real. Anything authentic. Anything that might give 'em a little goose, a little pucker in the hoo-ha. Let me tell you—when I land that bike, it's real. When I'm up there in the air, and the sound of all those people just vanishes— just disappears—that's real as a motherfucker." He looks at Loretta. "Pardon my French, hon. When I land and break those bones, you can bet your ass that's real. I'm not perfect. I'm not saying I'm perfect. Who's perfect? Nobody's perfect. I'm not some kind of, whaddya call, example and whatnot. I'm not saying you should be like me, necessarily. Not everyone's cut out for this."

He says this in a minor key, as though it were a simple, painful truth. Now he has ordered a round of Wild Turkey. The colors in his glass are beautiful, the amber glow and the angles off the cut glass and the ice cubes. Jason is trying his damnedest not to sip too slowly, but it's burning his throat. Acid is trying to crawl out of his stomach. The room tilts and reels, and Jason closes his eyes and places a hand on the table.

"He's a lightweight," he hears Loretta tell Evel Knievel, who answers, "Nothing wrong with that, kiddo."

Jason opens his eyes. Loretta sips and watches Evel Knievel, a flame on her cheeks and neck. Boyd reclines against the seat, drink cupped in his hand. Everything in his skeptical aspect angers Jason.

"You know, people always think it must be something else to be me, just something else. But what you forget is that most of those people who come to my shows, most of those *adoring crowds,* only show up to see me die. That's right"—he holds up a hand to ward off their protests—"they want to see me die. They want to see me crash, break my bones, die. I mean, that's a great story to tell your friends, right? I was there the night Evel Knievel ran up against the thing he couldn't do."

He empties his glass and raises his hand like a bull rider signaling to open the chute. The bartender starts pouring. Evel leans onto his elbows.

"Look, kids, I'm tired. I'm sore. Some days I think I might just cash it all in." Jason wants to say no, you can't, but he sees Loretta nodding empathetically. "I am only human. Only human. There are things that I cannot do, try as I might. And I might die out there some night. It could happen. It could very well happen."

He exhales loudly. He smells like booze and Old Spice, and his hair is redder and less blond than Jason remembers it. All told, he presents a picture that is less superhero than the one in Jason's mind, but he seems hard, tough, worn. Or at least he had seemed that way before he started talking.

"And I think if it did happen, if I did die out there someday, trying to push myself too far, trying too hard to satisfy what everybody wants from me, I think it would make most people happy. It would make them feel like they were right all along, never to do anything risky or adventurous. See what happens when you get a little too crazy, honey? See what comes your way when you try to grab life by the balls? Old Evel did it. He grabbed life with both hands and look what it got him. Look where he ended up."

"I don't want to see you die," Jason says, and Loretta says, "Yeah, I don't, either," and Boyd says, "I don't want anyone to die." Loretta places her hand on Evel's for two seconds, pats, and withdraws. The downy hair behind her ear glows, pale against her bright skin.

Evel stares at his hand where she touched it, and smiles wearily at the center of the table. He wears his self-pity like a star-spangled suit.

"You kids are nice. You know that? You're nice kids. Let's have another one. Should we? Can I get you another one? What'll you have, darling?"

Boyd says, "Not me," and gets up to leave. Evel shrugs and Loretta says, "Okay, then, good night, Boyd," and again Jason spots it—something between them, something in her attitude toward Boyd—and he doesn't say anything as Boyd leaves.

Here are some of the things Jason finds surprising about Evel Knievel:

He is short, and not physically imposing in any way. Jason towers over him.

His eyes are amazing, totally unforeseen, cool lime slivered with yellow. There seems to be a dying light behind them, a weak glow.

When he first sat down, his eyes locked on Jason's while he gave him a curious half-smile, and that bright, shifting color—Jason took it for intelligence, for kindness, for wisdom, for love.

He is completely unsatisfied. All he does is complain.

He is not limping, though he could not have even been out of the hospital for all that long after the Wembley jump—that spectacular crash that Jason had missed while eating dinner with Dean's family, the afternoon he met Loretta.

He wears ordinary clothing, much like any man Jason might know in Gooding or Twin Falls or Boise: blue jeans with a leather belt and metal buckle, long-sleeved snap-button shirt over a T-shirt, cowboy boots curled up at the toe from wear.

He is kind of dumb, but thinks he is brilliant. Also like most every man Jason might know back home.

His eyes steal immediately toward any hint of womanhood. The fiftysomething with the piled white hair, alone in a veil of smoke at the bar. The two middle-aged women who sat two tables over for about an hour, giggling at his every leer. Cheryl Tiegs on a TV commercial for underarm deodorant, which he watched in its entirety from twenty feet away. And Loretta, of course. Loretta.

He is older than Jason's father, and looks it, his skin pebbled like a football.

He is drunker than anyone Jason has ever seen in person, Dean Martin drunk. He had bumped into a chair as he first walked toward their table, and then corrected too far the other way and had to catch himself, stop, and hold out his hands like he was balancing on a wire.

None of that matters to Jason. He doesn't love him any less—and that's the only word for it, love—because running into him like this floods Jason with energy and hope. This is what life can be. Casual drinks with lifelong heroes. Evel Knievel in Elko, and then who knows? Farrah Fawcett in Boise? Lee Majors in Twin Falls? Life glows with possibility. His life—his and Loretta's lives. Their life.

They have done the right thing. Jason has done the right thing: surveyed the ass-end quality of his life—of milking barns and morning feedings and church and school pageants and rabbit massacres and sexlessness and sweat-stained polyester and wood-paneled station wagons and AM radio and cattle futures and three prayers a day, every day, knees aching from submission, and the never-ending boredom of the righteous and the self-righteous, prayers and prayers and cow shit and prayers—and gone out and found another world, and Evel Knievel sits in it, Evel fucking Knievel, a mad handsome demon, he sits in it with a whiskey in hand and talks to Jason, talks to Jason and Loretta, pinning them together in space and time, pinning Loretta and Jason together in space and time, no two other people anywhere, ever, able to share this memory, to own this story.

Ruth

The children are in bed, and Dean is on the phone with Loretta's father down in Short Creek, and Ruth is heartsick with the dishonesty of the day. *Aunt Loretta has driven home to Short Creek on some errand.* Samuel looked at her knowing she was false, but what could she tell him?

The girl was not right from the start. Never once right, but Dean was blind. Ruth had prayed and been answered. She felt a certainty about the answer: the girl was not right. Yet when she had told Dean this, all those months ago, he had taken her hands in his quietly, and he thought carefully before he said a word, and so she knew it was done before he spoke, knew he had arranged it in his mind, and that this was her lot now, as it was her lot always, to submit. Even knowing what she knew. It was her lot to submit to the will of one so full of human frailty, and through submission to find her eternal blessing.

It is the only way to see it. And when she prays about it, when she asks the Lord, in her moments of rebellion, how it is that *she* is supposed to obey *him,* why it is that she must turn away whatever wisdom thrives in her own bosom to heed his folly, she receives no answer but one: she must.

She believes it as fervently as she hates it. She accepts it though everything inside her strains toward her own mind, her own way, and has always done so. But her obedience to Dean is obedience to the Lord, and in obeying, in overcoming her own vain resistance, she is fulfilling her promise.

The girl has taken the gold—or some of it. The coins, not the Sutter Creek ore. Not the gold that Dean seems to worship, the filthy lucre that she believes has stained his soul. There, too, Ruth has been ignored, as he has ignored her in everything these days, in every step along this misbegotten road that brought them to this breach: a break with the prophet and brethren in Short Creek, the ambition that had overtaken Dean with the prosperity of Zion's Harvest and with his marriage to Loretta, his greed in buying the Sutter Creek gold and his pride in it, the lust that he had to have it, to touch it, to look at it, to see it. She hadn't wanted him to get it at all, had urged him to keep the Law of Consecration, to give all to the brotherhood, until he had stopped asking her about it, and then, when he did it anyway and she urged him to hide it from Loretta, he said he would.

And then he didn't.

Still, she will submit. She will carry her burden. She will care for her own soul and the souls of her children, and she will stand proud before the Lord on the day of judgment. Her Book of Mormon is open on her lap and her eyes are closed, she is deep in meditation— it is not prayer, exactly, what she does in these moments when she must turn inward for strength, when she must look toward her soul to erase the negativity that is creeping toward her, when she feels she must battle Satan and his whispers of pridefulness, of anger, of judgment against Dean and others. She breathes and concentrates on the discomfort of the moment, focuses on whatever the discomfort of the moment may be, and she reminds herself that it is a promise of salvation, that the earthly pain is but a price to pay for an eternal glory if she is righteous, if she is obedient, if she submits.

Dean hangs up and sits next to her on the couch. She does not open her eyes. It is below freezing outside, and the cold seeps upward from the basement, swirls around their ankles. Everything here feels foreign to her. It is but the second time in her life that she has left Short Creek; the first was the raid of the Federal Men who took her from her home, and it is Satan that she feels now just as it was Satan that she felt then, Satan in the atmosphere, in the air and water. She does not open her eyes, even when he speaks.

"Mother," he says.

"Yes."

"Her parents are saddened, Mother. If not altogether surprised."

Ruth nods calmly.

"She has taken the coins?"

"Yes, Mother." He endures this.

"But not the strongbox?"

"No."

It doesn't square. Why would the girl take the sack—that vain, incautious sack of gold coins—and not the locked metal box right behind it in the drawer?

She can tell that he is merely enduring her questions. Bearing them, as an obligation he must meet. It is the same for her. She imagines this conversation is part of the price she will pay to live in the celestial kingdom, in the glory of the Lord. She imagines the Lord's pleasure in her passage of this trial. Ruth does not know, still, what they are doing here in Idaho, whether they have left Short Creek for good, and when she inquires Dean tells her he doesn't know, he is still praying about it, and never once does he inquire about her opinion or ask her whether she has prayed about it, though she has, and though she has been answered.

Ruth opens her eyes and says, "Perhaps it is the Lord's will that she has taken the gold."

"I cannot see it so, Mother."

"Perhaps the Lord will use these events to remind us."

"Remind us of what?"

Ruth whispers, "That we have lost our hold on the iron rod."

"Forgive me, Mother. Perhaps I was blinded. Perhaps I have erred."

Ruth knows that Dean does not believe he has erred. She hears his swallowing of grievance, his pride in his humility. His satisfaction with himself, that he is able to so patiently pretend to accept her criticism.

"Erred in which way, Father?"

Dean does not speak for a long time. The darkness in the living room has deepened against the weak light from the kitchen, gleaming on the glass bell of the lamps, on the wood-grained arms of the couch, casting thin shadows in the nap of the carpet. He leans forward, elbows on knees, hands folded together, very nearly in the aspect of prayer. He lowers his head, raises it as if to speak, and lowers it again.

Dean says at last, "Perhaps everything, Mother. Perhaps everything I have ever tried to do," and this, too, his self-pity, is but another part of her lot in this earthly life.

The girl has never been right. And Dean's man has never been right. She opposed that from the start as well, and Dean insisted that Mr. Baker was trustworthy, that he had shown his reliability, and Ruth recognized the truth: that was how the world and its values seeped into your life and corroded it, one harmless step at a time, one innocent inch at a time, one arrogant Gentile at a time, until you could not recognize the damned from the saved.

She submits, submits. Dean sleeps beside her. She becomes more alert with each passing minute. It comes to her every night, this wakefulness. She thinks that perhaps the Lord's will is aligning with her own. Perhaps a humbling is what Dean requires. Perhaps those who have left them now will never return, just as she wishes.

Loretta

Somewhere deep in the rocking recesses of the night, Loretta tells Evel she wants to call him by his real name. She feels this must be a secret that he shares with few people, a talisman, his Sampson hair.

"Come on," she says. "What is it?"

"You don't know what it is?"

He seems genuinely surprised.

"I know it!" Jason says, erupting like a bubble in thick stew. "Robert Craig Knievel!"

Evel Knievel stares heavily at Jason, as though trying to will him away, and says, "Good for you, kiddo."

"I've seen every one of your jumps but one," Jason says, head wobbling, eyes misfocused. "I missed the last one. Wembley. My fuckin' parents wouldn't let me watch it. They made me go to a family dinner." He turns to Loretta suddenly. "Dinner with *your* family. Hey."

She pretends to smile. For Evel. She and Evel smile, patiently, together at Jason.

"My fuckin' parents," Jason says again. "They didn't want me to watch the Snake River jump."

"Uh-huh," Evel Knievel says.

"Are you sure you don't remember me? You said, 'Thanks for coming, buddy.'"

"Yeah, no," Evel says. He grins at Loretta.

"But my parents! Can you believe that? Can you fuckin' believe it? Greatest thing ever. Biggest day we ever saw." He looks at Evel, lets it sink in. "Didn't want me to go. Didn't want me to do it."

"It's not exactly my favorite thing to talk about, bud."

"Ah, hell," Jason says. "Man, don't let that get to you. Everybody makes mistakes."

They are all wasted, Loretta knows—she is blissfully drunk, protected from the world, narrowed down to the essences—and yet there is something in Jason's drunkenness that is distasteful, something loose and undisciplined and helpless, as if he were a marionette with half his strings cut. Evel leers at her. No one has ever looked at her so frankly. Not even Bradshaw.

Jason burps, and holds himself urgently still, then takes huge, steadying breaths through his nose. Evel sits back, swirls his drink.

Jason says, "Good Lord, you're amazing."

Evel shifts in his seat, frowns at Loretta.

"No, seriously, man, you are," Jason says. "I've never met anyone like you."

Evel stares hard at him—like, *Stop it*—then turns toward Loretta, who barks once, a laugh escaping from a herd of laughs within. Evel Knievel smiles at her, and in his smile there seems to be some form of original light, something shining from within. Jason stifles a burp, and looks again like he might be sick, and Evel says, "You okay, buddy? Everything gonna stay inside?" and he smiles at her, a smile of pure light. A sour, sickening smell wafts in. She realizes: this is what her future is like. Not like the magazine ads. Not something static and pretty—but something beautiful and ugly at once. It includes a famous man, a worldly man, just showing up at your table, and it includes the possibility that you might find yourself cleaning up the vomit of a boy.

Loretta starts telling Evel the truth about them, sort of, saying they'd gotten tired of their families and run away. She leaves out Dean and all that. At one point, Jason snaps to attention and slurs, "And that's not the fuckin' half of it," but she reaches under the table, grabs a thick inch of skin above his knee, and twists it, hard.

"Holy crap," Jason yelps. "Knock that off."

Loretta smiles sweetly at Evel.

"How old are you kids?" he asks her.

"I'm eighteen," Loretta says.

He begins to spout advice. *Always be true to yourself. Never let the bastards win. Don't be afraid to fail. Fail your asses off. That is how you will succeed. Be nice. That is the most important thing—be nice.*

"Couple kids like you," he says, lowering his head and waving his hand as though he were giving a blessing. "Be good to each other."

"Yes," Jason says.

"No," Loretta says. "It's not that way."

Jason looks at her, astonished.

"Be good to each other," Jason says, and reaches for her hands, which she pulls into her lap.

"It's not like that," she says to Evel Knievel.

"It is like that," Jason says loudly. "Come on. Yes, it is."

She ignores him, doesn't even look his way. Just keeps her eyes on Evel, and shakes her head.

Jason

Jason has slumped back on the seat. He sees little burn holes in the fake red leather, little blackened edges. It reminds him of the start of *Gunsmoke,* when the paper is burning away. He believes he will sleep here. The whiskey has gotten inside his nose, inside his eyes. It is making everything strange. Loretta and Evel are ignoring him, and that makes him wonder if he is even here anymore, or if he is dreaming this, and then he notices the burn holes again, and he thinks about *Gunsmoke* again, and cowboys, and heroes, and Sunday afternoons.

He wakes with a start at the sound of Loretta laughing so hard she cannot catch her breath. "You're so *funny,*" she screams.

The bar is empty but for them and the bartender, who watches TV, leaning on an elbow.

Evel says, "You're a real cute girl."

Jason musters himself into a sitting position and says, "You can say that again."

Loretta rolls her eyes and says, "Thank you, Robert."

Evel says something Jason can't understand because the words are too low. When he next opens his eyes, Evel is whispering in her ear, and she is squinching up her shoulder like he's tickling her, and he says, "You grind me up, silly," or maybe he says, "You're firing me up, Jilly," or maybe he is calling her a filly, and Jason doesn't like that, but it seems as if his eyes are stuck closed.

At some point, Jason says, "Maybe we should take this party up to the room."

Or maybe he doesn't say that. Maybe he hears it. Maybe Evel says, "Maybe we should take this party up to your room." Or it might have been Loretta. "Maybe we should take this party up to our room."

Is Boyd angry that they return, loud and drunk, at two A.M., with a bottle and a bucket of ice? Does he wake and, seeing their guest, leap from bed and join in the fun? Does he storm out in a rage? Do they sit around and listen to Evel tell stories about Caesars Palace, Wembley Stadium, Reno, Twin Falls? Do he and Loretta sit together on her bed, while Boyd and Jason sit on theirs? Is that the conversational layout? Do the people in the neighboring room call the front desk to complain about their raucous laughter, their shouts of joy? Does Jason regale Evel Knievel with all the ways that he has worshipped him? Does Boyd tell him stories about their attempts to jump bicycles and minibikes off ramps Jason built with two-by-fours and cinder blocks? Is Jason the butt of the joke in those stories? Do they tell Evel Knievel the story of the bunny bash? And what does he have to say about that? Does he say to Boyd, "Good for you. I hate those little fuckers." And does that affect Loretta in any way? Does she recoil at his heartlessness? Or does she spark up, move toward it? For isn't there something attractive in cruelty? Something essential and manly and gorgeous? Does Jason realize this as they talk—does he recognize his lack and regret it? Does he mope about it? Does Evel Knievel pull a small bindle from his shirt pocket and snort from it? Does Loretta do the same? Does Jason say no thanks? And does Evel Knievel sneer? And does Jason finally vomit, or does he make it through?

Jason comes out of the bathroom feeling lighter, relieved, but still weaving. Loretta and Evel are in hysterics, while Boyd watches them, bemused. Jason thinks: *That man is not Evel Knievel. The hair's wrong. The attitude.* At some point, he opens his eyes and finds he is lying on his side, fully dressed, feet itching hotly inside his tennis shoes, and the room lights are still on and he can hear the sound of someone sloshing the ice bucket. Then he is back in the yard at the farm, outside the milking barn in the middle of the night, and his father is yelling at him from inside the barn. "Jason Reed Harder! Have you got all that miffling done?" And he looks down to see that he has a carrier full of bottles for the calves, and the bottles are full of beer, and he has to haul them to the calves and get them to drink, but the calves don't want to drink, they gum the bottles and leave them slick with mucus, and Jason's father shouts again, "I better not find that you haven't finished that miffling!" and so he drinks from the bottles himself, tasting the slick, grassy slime of the calves' mouths on the nipples, and Evel Knievel, who is sitting in the back of one of the calf pens, says, "Come on, kiddo. You can drink one more." And Jason is standing in a circle of men in the desert behind Dean's house, and he is surrounded by bloody, misshapen bunnies, a sticky mound of fur and flesh, and a faceless man wearing a Scotch cap and a denim jacket says, "How are we going to eat all these fucking jackrabbits?" and Jason turns to find Boyd standing there, face and T-shirt bleary with blood, working on a large mouthful of something and holding a jackrabbit with a bite taken out of its side, and he says, "Aren't you going to get that miffling done?" and Jason wants to cry, he wants to drop to his knees and sleep everything away. He says, "I don't know how," and Boyd says, "*That* figures." And there is a pounding in Jason's temples and an ache inside the bone of his skull, burning like a bed of embers, and his mouth is dry, so dry, and he hears a squeaking, a metal bouncing, and Loretta's voice slithers from the dark, saying, "No," and then, more softly, "Shhhh," and Jason thinks she is talking to him, and he prepares to say, "No what?" when he hears a voice, no words, just the deep baritone music of it, and she snickers, and Jason keeps his eyes closed tight now, will not open his eyes now, because he knows it is Loretta and Evel out there together, and a soft, steady squeaking begins, a working of the bedsprings, and then a groan and Loretta says again, "Shhhhh," a note of delight and alarm, and Jason feels Boyd poke him in the back, once, hard, with his finger, and then there is nothing but the compression of the springs like a metronome, like the ticker Jason's mother kept on the piano, *tick-tick-tick-tick-tick,* for an hour, for seven hours, for nine days, for months and months, for the rest of Jason's life, *tick-tick-tick-tick-tick-tick,* and then a freeze, a seizing, and one loud *sproing* and squeak, and a final "Shhh."

Jason feels sick in his flesh. The death of something is stinking him up. He peeks through his eyelids. The room is sunk in blackness, but for a band of bright light falling through a slit in the curtains, slicing across two shapes in Loretta's bed and a ball of cloth on the nightstand a few inches from Jason's face. He lies on his side, back to Boyd. Tiny sprung fibers glow on the cloth in the light, and Jason realizes it is Loretta's lavender underwear just as her hand emerges from the darkness to grab it. Evel Knievel begins to snore like a gasping engine, deep, shuddering blasts, followed by long, wheezing inhalations. The way Boyd snores. Or Jason's grandfather. It carries the precise tone and rhythm of his dead grandfather, rending the peace of the night, the room like a grave.

Dean

Just when you feel abandoned by the Lord, He reminds you of His love.

The bank calls for Dean at around eleven A.M. on Monday. Right as Baker is getting ready to hop in that truck and pull out of the driveway to make the deliveries. What do you call that? Divine intervention?

Dean tells Ruth to stop Baker, and when she gives him a questioning look, he waves her out urgently.

A casino? A stolen check?

Dean feels scooped out. His knees wobble and weaken. He places his hand on the wall before him and imagines sliding to the floor. He's a fool. Someone is trying to make everything he stands for foolish. To make God himself foolish. Someone. Loretta. He had been so sure of her. So sure that he had turned her toward his path. The Lord's path.

He says pay the check. It's okay. He does not want anyone else to know anything.

He cannot control the trembling in his hands, and his stomach growls loudly, wrenches against him. He feels as if he might lose control of his bowels. He has to force himself to stand absolutely still, absolutely clenched against this humiliation, his stomach writhing and twisting and a sudden sharp pain that makes Dean feel like an animal, like a filthy beast that will foul itself. When the tremor passes, and he has not fouled himself, everything coheres into a single desire: that this horrific disarray be repaired.

He tells Baker only what he needs to know: Elko, the Stockmen's Hotel, the two kids, the Short Creek address, in case it comes to that.

Telling it, Dean seizes with shame and tension. He feels bare before Baker.

Baker, though, seems to have relaxed. To be unspooling, comfortably.

"You want me to do anything to the kid?" he asks.

"Do anything?"

Baker shrugs and smiles.

Dean very much does want Baker to do something like that. He very much does want to do something like that himself. He waits before answering. He wants to say the right thing, and he wants to be the right person, and he wants to have what he wants.

"Maybe not," he says.

EVEL KNIEVEL ADDRESSES
AN ADORING NATION

Were we magic, America? Were gods lifting us as we flew, carrying us over those buses, those cars, those imitation Conestoga wagons?

That's not for us to say. If we ever were magic, we're not now, now that we're dead. It's not what we expected here, nothing like anyone said it would be, but at least it goes on, boring as it is, awful as it is. We live in a plain room and eat in a cafeteria and there is nothing to do here but that—eat and remember, eat and remember.

Death used to be so important to us. Every time we put on that jumpsuit, the red, white, and blue, every time we sat at the bottom of the ramp before a jump, twisting the throttle, feeling the foam seat snug between our legs, insides rattling, breath too quick, remembering the crashes, the black fury of them, the feeling of our spine giving way and the instant knowledge that we're holding hands with death in a way that none of those people in the grandstands can ever know, not even if they go to war, not even if they're murdered at gunpoint, the moment so specific to us that it can't even exist in the imagination of anybody else.

Death was our partner. Our friend. For a while, anyway. Now it's turned on us, too.

We might have shown up anywhere in the good years. Any little shithole bar. Any Podunk store or restaurant. Anywhere we went became a temple, and we were a god, and the worship was love, the purest sweetest love, and it was as all things were then—the more we were granted, the more we hungered. The more we starved. Until there was nothing that could ever feed us.

You didn't know us, not really, but, America, we dwelled in every part of you. We lived in Butte and Las Vegas. Spokane and Reno. Boise and Grand Rapids and Tuscaloosa and Elmira. We were everywhere. Sometimes we were in a particular place and couldn't be in other places where we were needed. Where the country had an ebb in courage or confidence, and needed its daredevil. We did the best we could. Don't say we didn't.

Years and years and years passed. Just gone. When we went to Spokane, people would ask about the time we punched a cop in the Davenport Hotel. Down in Reno, some asshole would come up and remind us about the time we were thrown out of the Sands for taking out our dick at the craps table. They sold toys in our image, wrote comic books about us—showed us flying down from the sky to disrupt robberies and capture evildoers. They made us forever twenty-five years old, throbbing with muscle.

By the end, though, it got fucking weird, America. On the Internet, the computer tubes and such, there are fan sites—evelrocks .com, evelsavestheuniverse.com—where people write stories about us. Stories about "us." Craziest shit. Superhero fantasies. We fly around the world and fire amazing weapons from the air. We hold off nuclear annihilation. We turn back floods and tsunamis, stabilize the earth during quakes, send doomsday bombs spinning into space. And then there are the other stories. The villain tales. In these we are a criminal and worse. We stick up banks and fly through the shadows of the night. We run tables and women in inner cities. We are killed, explosively, spectacularly, by other superheroes—the X-Men, Spider-Man, Captain America.

The craziest shit got crazier. That is just basic American gravity, the primary force of the whole damn country, crazy pulled toward crazier. One of the Web sites had a link called "Evel Erotica." Seriously. The world is full of more stupid shit than anyone could ever guess, and every bit of it comes from other people. Other people. You spend your whole life trying to do something in relation to them—impress them, get their love and attention—and then it somehow all gets turned into stories, then lies, and then something like this:

Cherry leaned forward and Evel drove into her from behind. "You're in for the ride of your life," the handsome daredevil exclaimed, thrusting while he ran the bike up the ramp and off into the air, fucking and flying, until the bike landed with a violent lurch and they crashed and came, breaking their bones, spilling their blood . . .

It is a fucked-up world, America. Even the love is all wrong.

PIONEER DAY

It is Pioneer Day, and almost raining, thick clouds ready to burst during the morning parade and services. Everyone is ready for rain. Dust rises with every step. The wheat and barley wilt. But everyone prays for the storm to hold off, just through tonight, through the dance. Everyone tries to read the sky as a signal from the Lord, and Ruth is doing that, too, Ruth is watching the sky and hoping it will do as she asks, that it *will* open up and pour down upon them so there will be no dancing. She is hoping this even as she knows it will not happen, that even if it rains there will be dancing, in the wardhouse or in the school, and that she will be there for the dancing, and that Brother Billy will be there for the dancing, and that Brother Billy will be there to dance with her, and that he will know what that means, and she will know what that means, and everyone around them—right down to the children—will know what it means, too.

In the afternoon, the brothers and sisters pick corn for the dinner. The clouds move off and return but nothing falls. Ruth stays in the rows as long as she can, breathing dust and corn silk, relishing the close, shady tunnels, hoping not to see Brother Billy or her parents. She snaps the ears downward and tucks them into a burlap sack held by her sisters, Alma and Sarah. They are singing a song together, under their breath, the way they do, as though their hushed singing were a secret. *"'Father, I will rev'rent be / And in thy house walk quietly.'"* They are always quiet, these two, always together, and usually near Ruth, ever since the days when it was unclear if they would ever return home, the days they spent in the house of the man and woman whose name Ruth cannot remember—though it is more true to say that Ruth will not allow herself to remember the name. They all came back with different experiences. Ruth's father spent four days in jail. Her mother and aunts had spent the days here with no word about their children. *"'Listen to the words I hear, / For in thy house I feel thee near.'"* And the children had all gone to different families, to Gentiles and apostate Mormons in Hurricane and Cedar City and St. George, each to a different home that was not home. Ruth and Sarah and Alma had spent the quiet days in the home of the family in Hurricane with the television and the fancy plates and the gentle whispering. That had been their exile. Ruth knew to feel fortunate, because some children did not return, children who were kept away by the Federal Men, kept in other families, and their parents live on in Short Creek, moving among them like ghosts. *"'May my thoughts more perfect be, / That I may speak more rev'rently.'"*

Ruth stuffs two more ears into the bag. "Okay, run these down," she says, and Alma and Sarah shuffle away down the row.

She steps through cornstalks into a new row and stumbles into someone, and she apologizes, and a man answers in a deep voice and turns to face her. A new person. An unfamiliar person. He is tall and he is young—a young man, the rarest of people around here—and he is handsome, despite a pair of large, flappy ears. Ruth feels as if she has been pleasantly tricked. She would like to stare at him. Study him. The back of her neck flushes.

"Hello, young lady," he says, arms full of corn, bowing in a manner that might be mischievous, and she says, "Hello, old man." Ruth steps back through the cornstalks to the row she had come from, and she can hear him chuckling. She stands there, catching her breath as if recovering from a fright, until her sisters come running down the row, laughing.

Walking home, Ruth's sisters needle her about Brother Billy. They're supposed to call him Brother Adler, but he is too familiar from the days when he was younger and would sometimes watch them while they played with his younger sisters. Ruth cannot think of him by any other name.

"You'll need to watch out for his elbows," Sarah says quietly, and Alma giggles, and adds, "He'll give you a black eye." Ruth hisses, "You shut your mouth," and Sarah gasps in mock astonishment, and Alma says, "I'm telling," and Ruth says, "You go right ahead," and the girls giggle harder.

His dancing is but one of the many ways in which Ruth finds Brother Billy unacceptable. The main one she cannot express, or feels she is not supposed to express: he simply does not attract her.

He does not draw her, does not please her senses, does not appeal. She does not want to dance with him. She is a precise and excellent dancer, Ruth is, and Brother Billy's laughing, loose way of dancing is embarrassing—bumping into the others, mixing up his feet, coming in late on calls. And she does not want to do any of the other things a girl might want to do in courtship. She does not want to hold his hand, and she does not—definitely, absolutely—want to do the many unthinkable things she has been thinking about doing. Not with him.

Every time her father speaks to her these days, she dreads the possibility that he will tell her Brother Billy has asked to begin courtship. She tries to imagine her father allowing her to say no. Ruth had been the last to see it, and the sting of feeling foolish is still fresh. Brother Billy came to Sunday dinner three times in May and June, each time without his young wife and their two children. Ruth's mother had paid extra attention to her dress and her hair those days, and her father had been unusually generous and kind to her in front of Brother Billy, thanking her warmly, calling her sweetheart, smiling lovingly, a charade that was obvious to everyone but Ruth, somehow. After dinner in the kitchen it was Sarah, young Sarah, just eleven years old, who said, "Looks like someone's courting," and giggled with the others while Ruth's face burned. How had she not seen this? Everything about it was obvious, and still, she had not. Ruth is sixteen. Three of the girls she grew up with have married already, two of them as sister wives. The world around her works in just this way—the sideways courtship, the arrangements made offstage—and yet she is offended: she feels omitted from her own life. She believes in the Principle. She does. Believes it is ordained by God, believes she will eventually be joined in a celestial marriage with sister wives and her future husband.

But not like this. Not without her choosing.

The clouds have drifted south, and so the picnic goes ahead as planned, in the field behind the schoolhouse. The long tables are covered with food, with corn and salads and chicken and pies. In the shorn grass beyond is the place for the dancing, squared by four poles strung with lights. Ruth and her mother arrive early to help with the food, and she watches carefully as the families show up, as the children race off to join the other children, and the men and women fall into groups, and she watches for Brother Billy until he arrives with his family. He seems shined up. Combed and brushed. She feels his eyes roving for her. She sees the man from the cornfield arrive. The unfamiliar man. He arrives with the Barlows, and Ruth wonders who he is and where he came from and why he's here. He, too, seems shined up, combed and brushed, and Ruth wants to stand and watch him.

People fill their plates and crowd the tables. Ruth carries food and dishes between the schoolhouse and the field. She watches Brother Billy as he goes to the table for food, his eyes roving, and she ducks to the other side of the crowd as he finds a seat with his family. She watches Brother Billy, and she watches the man from the cornfield, that tall handsome man.

Uncle Elden moves to the front and the crowd hushes. He gazes upon them placidly, and lets the silence linger. Ruth wonders if he is waiting for the Lord to arrive in his mind. He begins to tell the story of the pioneers and their handcarts, of the arduous journey of the Saints, fleeing their persecutors in Nauvoo, Illinois, for a land where they could practice their religion in peace.

"Driven from their . . . *homes*," he says. "Their prophet murdered by a mob. They traveled in fear and in . . . faith, trusting God would lead them."

Days and nights on the trail. The fatal winter. Death stalking them all—children, the elderly, the young and strong.

"Can you imagine . . . the powerful *doubt,* brothers and sisters?" the prophet asks. "Can you imagine the difficulties of sustaining your faith in a wilderness, surrounded by death, and told . . . to put your trust in the Lord?"

The Saints persevered, following Brother Brigham until he arrived in the valley of the Great Salt Lake, on this very date in 1847.

"Still . . . the Gentiles went to war against us, brothers and sisters, to war against *this priesthood*. They tried to stop us from voting. Burned our homes, destroyed our fields. Until even the . . . church . . . *itself* . . . turned its back on the sacred principles.

"Still, they persecuted us. Still, we would not yield."

He pauses. Everyone knows what is coming.

"There was a man," he says, "named Governor . . . *Pyle*. The governor of Arizona, who set forth a special effort to persecute this people."

The raid of '53. Five years later, Ruth is thinking of her return home, her mother's desperate embrace. She recalls the way the children came back to their families, a few one day, a few the next, the community slowly restored. Ruth and her sisters shadowed their mother's every step for weeks, from garden to kitchen to church and back—and it felt wrong to talk about where they had been and what had happened there, so she didn't. Everyone else seemed to feel the same. Almost nothing was ever said about the raid except in church, where the brethren spoke of it constantly as a lesson in persecution and salvation.

"They wanted to carry the children away, to adopt . . . them out and destroy the records, so the children would not know their lineage. This was in the hearts of many men."

Ruth sees that the man from the cornfield has closed his eyes.

"We look back now and rejoice at the deliverance . . . the Lord brought us. But we did not know, at the time, what would happen . . . and what the end would be."

He pauses and beams at the crowd, gazing up and down the tables. Brother Billy is taking a fussing infant from his wife's arms. The man from the cornfield is watching Uncle Elden, rapt. Ruth can sense his passionate response—everyone else, it seems, is so familiar with these words that they land without much effect. As the raid has been turned into a story, it has come to feel less real. But to the man from the cornfield, Ruth thinks, the story is devastating. She says a silent prayer of thanks that she has been chosen to be among the Lord's servants here in Short Creek.

"And so now," the prophet says, smiling and opening his arms, "let's dance."

The crowd erupts in applause. Ruth watches as the man from the cornfield stands. Handsome. Righteous. New and unfamiliar. He looks at her and nods, grandly. She realizes what's going on inside of her: She does not want to stare at him. She does not want to watch him. She does not want to dance with him or talk to him. She wants to touch him. She wants to touch every part of him.

At the dance, her father approaches with Brother Billy. Ruth considers saying that she is sick. She considers saying she sprained her ankle picking corn. She considers saying she does not know how to dance. That she does not know what dancing even is. Here they come, her father leading the way, Brother Billy as an applicant or supplicant, all of it outside of her control, all of it a dance in itself, the steps already laid out, invented and drawn up by others, by her father and Brother Billy, yes, but also by others long before her who wrote the music and named the steps, all of it beyond her.

"Good evening, Ruth," Brother Billy says.

"Good evening, Brother Adler."

"I was hoping I might request the pleasure of the next dance."

Over her father's shoulder, several yards away, stands the tall young man from the cornfield. Ruth thinks he might be looking at her. He looms above the others.

"Little sister?" her father asks.

"I'm afraid," she starts, but no words come, and she clears her throat and starts again. "I'm afraid that I have already promised the next dance to someone else."

"Oh?" Brother Billy asks, glancing at her father, who narrows his eyes in puzzlement, and asks, "To whom have you promised the next dance?"

Ruth points to the tall young man. They turn to look at him, and her father says, "Ah. The new man. The convert."

"Brother Harder?" Brother Billy asks, and her father nods.

Brother Billy tips his head, and says, "Perhaps the next dance, then?"

"Unfortunately," Ruth says, "all of my dances have been spoken for tonight. Every one of them."

SHORT CREEK

October 20, 1975

ELKO, NEVADA

Loretta wakes, parched, no sense of time. It might be any time. The back of Boyd's head is six inches away, a wing of shiny black hair. Across the gap between the beds are the two lumps that are Jason and that motorcycle guy. Shades drawn. Light slips through an open slice of curtain. The room is ripe with body smell. A disorienting ache pulses from her head down her body, and acid sears the back of her throat. She feels like she must stay perfectly still. Something cloudy hangs between her and whatever brought her to this moment—something that does not quite blot out memory, but presses it out of the immediate range.

She gets up and pees. The sound embarrasses her. She sits on the toilet for so long, face propped in her hands, that her legs fall asleep. When she stands and flushes the toilet thunderously, she has to wait for the blood to return to her legs, tingling and prickling, before she can walk. When she does, Evel Knievel is sitting up,

scratching the back of his neck, and he says, "Mornin', darlin',"
and Loretta looks away from him and mutters, "Darlin'."

Every decision has been wrong. Last night she had thought he
was so cool. So interesting. And then with Boyd. Every decision.
Wrong. Every bit of her life must come off of her, must be stripped
like worn paint.

She showers. Stays in the hot water until it cools. When she
emerges, Jason is saying something she can't quite make out and
Boyd snorts, says, "Oh, please." Everyone is awake. Evel Knievel is
stepping into his jeans. Boyd and Jason are both sitting up, bedcov-
ers piled around them. Jason looks as though he has been shot or
stabbed. He looks at Loretta and then back to Boyd, who is gazing
grumpily into his lap.

"If you boys are gonna be friends," Evel Knievel says, standing
there holding his shirt in front of him, "you're going to have to
learn to keep the ladies in their place."

Jason ignores him. "I'm the one who let you come along in the
first place, you fucker," he whispers. "You came to my birthdays.
Grandpa's funeral. You were my goddamn motherfucking safety
buddy."

Boyd stares into the sheets.

Jason sputters, "It's *my car*!"

Boyd nods wearily. "Yeah. I know. Your dad's car."

Loretta wishes for a back door. She sits on the bed with a towel,
absently rubbing her hair, and Boyd lifts his eyes at her, smiles
shyly. She hates the hope she sees there. She cannot quite remember
how she ended up doing what she did but now, in the headachy,
sick new day, she imagines her parents knowing about this, she
imagines the brothers and sisters back home in the ward, she imag-

ines Dean and even Ruth, and despite whatever she thinks she knows about herself and her future, she feels stamped by sin.

Evel Knievel finishes snapping up his shirt, and slaps his thighs loudly. "We sure had us a party," he says.

Jason turns to him and stares. Evaluates. Jason's tight curly hair has been slept flat on one side. Confused emotion splotches his face and neck.

"You don't seem very scarred up," he says.

Evel looks at Boyd and winks.

"Who *are* you?" Jason asks.

"You know who I am, bud," he says.

"Your hero," Loretta says. "Remember?"

She can't stand his hurt.

Evel stops pulling on his boots and squints at Jason. Boyd walks into the bathroom.

"Why would you even ask me that?" Evel Knievel says.

The shower comes on.

"Can I see one of your scars?" Jason asks.

"You wanna see my driver's license?" Evel Knievel asks.

"Okay," Jason says, and Evel Knievel laughs.

"Look, bud, I don't give a shit whether you believe me or not," he says. "Who needs some breakfast?"

"I do," Jason says.

"Not me," Loretta says.

Jason says, "Tell me this. How do you keep from getting scared?"

"God, this again," Evel Knievel says. "All right. You just have to force it down." He stands and stomps his heels into his boots. He drops into a karate stance. "Cram that fear down to the ground, sit on it, kick it, punch it in the face, take it by the neck and squeeze it until it's dead, and know that you'll have to do the same thing again the next time and the next. You just kill it and kill it and kill it again. Ride that fucker into the ground."

He strikes at it with the ax edges of his hands—kills fear and kills it and kills it.

"Kill it!" he shouts, then stands straight. "Breakfast!"

Jason walks with him downstairs. The carpet sponges underfoot. Fifty years of cigarettes and fried food haunt the air. Jason feels so many things that he cannot pin them down as anything other than: bad. He wants breakfast very much, and yet he doubts he'll be able to get any down. Why did he change his mind about this guy? It was something in the morning muss of him. Something in the oily glaze on his face. Not Evel Knievel. Also: the guy in the bed next to him was not the guy who is not Evel Knievel. Not Evel Knievel, and not with Loretta. It was Boyd. He could not add it up, but it added up to him being a fool, fooled maliciously by everyone, by his hero, by his love, and by his best friend, conspiring to bring him to this dull vomit of a day.

Evel Knievel clicks his tongue happily as they walk down the maroon and gold carpet. When they pass the smoky, ringing bells of the casino entrance, a voice calls: "Hey, man, we've been looking for you."

Evel Knievel looks around, and then spots his buddies hailing him from a blackjack table. "Guess I gotta go," he says, offering his hand. Jason shakes it. How should he act?

"It was nice to meet you," Jason says.

Evel Knievel claps Jason on the shoulder.

"Buddy, that was a hell of a party," he says. "Do you remember running around the room naked? 'Bout three in the A.M.?"

"What? No. *No*."

There is no way he did that. There is no way he would do that. There is no way this guy is Evel Knievel.

"Okay," Evel Knievel says. "Just asking."

"Wait," Jason says. "Are you shitting me? I didn't do that."

Evel Knievel cackles. He punches Jason on the shoulder.

"You don't remember that? Really? Huh. Well, I gotta hit it. You take care."

He walks off and joins his buddies, and they laugh and slap backs, and Jason thinks he hears one of the guys calling him Bob or maybe John or maybe he doesn't hear it right. The others wear jeans and cowboy boots, just like Evel Knievel, and one of them wears a John Deere cap, and they seem like ordinary Idaho-type men, and Jason feels a blush warm his whole body. The men gather around Evel Knievel and he vanishes.

Jason eats breakfast alone, sheeny eggs and soggy hash browns and wet toast, looking over the *Elko Daily Free Press* and listening to the ringing of the slots. The food sits like a fist in his stomach, until it becomes clear that it will no longer sit in his stomach at all, and he rushes across the café to the bathrooms—GUYS and GALS— and into a stall, where everything comes up, still warm. Jason can see a pair of auburn polyester pants swaddled around cowboy boots in the next stall, and he flushes and waits for them to disappear. He walks back through the café, pays his check, and assesses the thin leaves of cash in his wallet—his FFA livestock sale money, his mission money—and finds a twenty, a ten, a five, a five, a five, and seven ones.

In the casino, people hunch over the tables, and thin columns of smoke rise from ashtrays, like a planetary surface pocked with asteroid strikes. Jason walks out the front doors and stands under the huge awning, out of the bright sun. It is clear and cold. He feels like he is six, and he's gotten lost at the carnival, and what he wants to do is cry.

He goes back to the room. How will he face them? What will they say? He turns the key in the door and opens it on a dark room. The counters sit empty. Their bags are gone. A piece of paper lies on the television, weighed down by a water glass:

Catch you later. B & L.

The world rushes away from Jason in every direction, untouching him. He becomes the last person. The final one.

Boyd sleeps, slumped against the passenger door. Loretta tries not to look at the odometer too frequently. It is already dusky, the sun vanished somewhere she cannot see, either behind the gray stain of clouds or one of the mountain spines that flank them on their journey south. She hasn't seen a building in what feels like forever. She likes this sensation—everyone behind her but Boyd—and she is untroubled about Jason. He will be fine. He will be taken care of.

But it is only now—now that she and Boyd have put a couple of hours behind them, now that she has piloted Jason's big old bucket of wobble long enough to predict its drifts and fades—that she fully turns her mind to the gold. Dean's gold. The gold she's gotten, and the gold she's going for. Sutter Creek gold. It had hung out there, behind the scrim of impossibility, for long enough that she failed to contend with the practical problems it might raise. For example: how do you even turn gold into money?

And then there is this: She might not even care anymore. She can't decide if she even wants it anymore, or why she wanted it to begin with. This is her mission but now she feels trapped in it.

Boyd wakes, moaning.

"Mornin'," she says. "Feel any better?"

"No."

"Maybe you need more shut-eye," she says. "We've got a ways to go."

Sleep, she thinks. *Go away.*

Boyd flips a heater vent up and down with a finger. He turns to her and says, "This is the worst thing I have ever done."

"Stop it."

"No. The worst."

He is pouting. Are they all like this? Every single one of them, just a big hurt baby?

"Then why'd you do it?"

"For you."

"For me?"

"To be with you."

"And now you're with me. And now you're miserable."

He flips the vent up and down.

"Don't you feel at least a little shitty?" he says.

"A little shitty, yes. A little."

"Then why'd you do it?"

"I don't know."

"Not to be with me."

"Okay. To be with you."

She can hardly say it. What had she felt for this boy? Had she just tricked herself? Because he clearly could not have been the one who tricked her. Not like Bradshaw. Tricky Bradshaw. No, she knows what she was thinking: that here was a chance to do the worst thing—the worst to Dean, the worst to all that she was leaving behind—the worst thing, with this Indian, this Lamanite, this child of sin, for that is what the elders taught, that the brown skin was a punishment for immorality, and in the cloud of drink she was thrilled by the entire idea of giving herself to that. But now he's here and he's just another one of them.

She puts on the headlights. Boyd is looking at her now, moon-faced, eyes black in the shadows of the car, waiting for a declaration of purpose, a statement, she knows, like those she made back in the hotel room before they left—*It will be me and you. Isn't that the way you want it, too? Don't you want to be alone with me, Boyd?*—and now those statements feel like a nest of tethers around her feet, ready to tangle her up any way she tries to move.

"We'll get to Short Creek. We'll figure this out," she says at last.

"He was my best friend. Really my only friend. In the whole world there's just my mom and him and nothing else. Nobody. Assholes. What kind of a person does that to his friend?"

"Boyd, he's going to be fine."

"That's not exactly what I'm wanting to hear from you right now, Loretta. I wish it was him I was worried about, but it's not."

"You're not a bad person."

"That's not it, either."

A tiny cluster of lights appears, far ahead in the cave of darkness. Ely, Nevada. Halfway.

Boyd says, "What happened to the you from yesterday?"

"Right here."

"The you from last night?"

Loretta is visited by a pang of conscience regarding her sexual sin—for doing that with someone she had just met, like some

whore. Her father had talked about her purity constantly. She remembers him counseling her, giving her bedtime chats, reading her
verses about her virtue, the talk of righteousness flooding her
mind with thoughts of sin. "The Lord delights in the chastity of
His children." Does she still believe that, though she thinks she
does not? Is she wrong that she can simply decide what she believes?

"Same me," she says.

Jason sits in the room at the Stockmen's with the note. Seventy-five
hours pass. One hundred forty-three hours pass. Five thousand
three hundred fifty-four hours pass. He will live in this dim room
forever. A numb, gentle throb in his cranium. He remembers the
LeBaron. His father's car. The keys are no longer on the countertop
by the TV. He looks around, digs through pockets. Goes downstairs and out into the parking lot, where there is no longer a pea-
green 1970 Chrysler Imperial LeBaron. The sky blazes, summer
blue and winter cold.

He will live here. At the Stockmen's. Maid service. Buffets.
Perfect.

He has fifty-two dollars and fifty-two cents. He goes inside and
pays for another night. Eleven dollars. There is a mirror behind the
counter and he assesses himself: gawky and tall, monster ears, hair
starting to frizz out of its bun, a bright rash of freckled self-
consciousness on his cheeks. He hates the way he looks. It is all
there, every time he examines himself for the signs. The failure is
all right there.

He sits on the lobby couch, a burnt-red leather with a fake rustic
wood frame. He wants to lie down. Someday, this will be a story.

Maybe it will develop a moral. His mom could figure that out. He wonders if he will ever tell her this story and listen as she makes it a lesson. He wonders if he will ever tell his father and listen as he identifies the mistakes Jason made, looking backward for the blame.

He can afford three more days here.

He thinks of his grandfather. Crusty old Grandpa. How did such a tough guy create the family line that leads to Jason? When he was Jason's age he left home and went to kill people in another country. But Jason—a little pain makes him cry. When Boyd shot him in the arm with a BB gun last summer, burying the BB in a gray lump under his skin, they'd gone to Grandpa for help. Jason's lower lip trembled, and when Grandpa saw it he turned away, embarrassed. "Don't start bawling," he said as he squeezed out the BB like a pimple.

Jason opens his eyes to bright sunlight. Lying on the couch in the lobby, head on a big leather pillow. The high afternoon sun slants in, pushing a boundary of sunlight across the ornate maroon and gold carpet. A loud ringing bursts from the casino. Somebody's luck has gone right.

Good luck. This will be the place to wait for it.

He walks outside. For some reason, his head doesn't hurt, though the hangover slows him down. Bile burns the back of his throat. The cold tightens his face. Feels good. His clothing is huge, heavy. He has been physically shrunken. What a preposterous person he is, to shrink like this. He thinks of heaven, of the idea that our lives will be played out for all to see. In heaven, on the movie screen, will everyone see this? His shrinking? He used to live in terror that everyone in heaven—his family and friends, the angels and the heavenly host, God himself—would be forced to watch him masturbate seven thousand times. And now, though he is done with God, bored with God, the idea of that heavenly scrutiny reenters his mind with the force of pure belief.

Everyone in heaven who watches his movie will be stronger than him. Everyone he knows is stronger. Boyd and Loretta are stronger. Evel Knievel is stronger. That guy from last night, whoever he was. Stronger. Mom and Dad. Every kid at school, every dull old farmer at church and his wife—stronger. Uncle Dean, that crazy fuck: way stronger.

Jason decides to pray.

"Our Father in Heaven," he whispers, standing on the bright concrete outside the Stockmen's, folding his arms and bowing his head.

His eyes burn and fill. *Naturally,* he thinks.

He stops. Opens his eyes. Unfolds his arms. What could he even ask for? Make me happy, please. Give me what I want.

He eats alone in the Stockmen's. Cheeseburger deluxe and fries—$1.95. He remembers when the idea of eating hamburgers every day was thrilling, but this tastes like feed. Like fodder. Goes to his room. Takes off his shoes. Turns on the TV. *Baretta* rerun, in the middle of the afternoon. Strange. Lies on the bed, head propped on two pillows, and watches the screen between his feet. Baretta talks to his cockatoo. The loosened toes of Jason's white socks are pooched up, like tiny elf hats. He thinks of the elves in *The Lord of the Rings,* fleet and deadly with bow, light and magical, and he thinks of Samwise Gamgee, the loyal friend, and he thinks maybe he ought to get that book out and vanish into Middle Earth. Remembers that the book is in the box in the trunk of the LeBaron. With his Evel Knievel scrapbook and his box of eight-tracks.

Someone bangs on the door and calls, "Jason?"

Is that Boyd? Sounds like Boyd. It's Boyd and Loretta. A massive flood pours out of Jason, tumbles him off the bed, carries him to the door. "Catch you later" meant later today. It meant now. They are back, it is them at the door. Of course they didn't leave him. They wouldn't do that.

Another knock, rapid, impatient.

Jason pulls open the door. A man he knows but can't place stands in the hall, one thumb in a belt loop and a cocky grin filling his face like stones in a bag. Who is he? Why is he so familiar? He wears a hat that reads "Sandy Excavation."

"Hey, bud," the man says, peering past Jason into the room. "Where's Lori?"

By the time they reach Hurricane, Boyd is asleep. The dusk, the wintry landscape of red hills, pine, and scarves of snow, the familiar pattern of lights, and then the town itself as they draw into it—every mile nearer to home, nearer to Short Creek—feeds Loretta's anxiety as it becomes more familiar. Hurricane is where they came for supplies. It's where she came with Tonaya when they were chasing around after the party boys. She pilots the LeBaron carefully down Main Street, twenty-three miles per hour. She passes the bright Texaco station where she met Bradshaw. She passes the Safeway, where she spots a Chevrolet van that she realizes is probably the one that Brother Gardner and his two wives and eight children pilot around town.

They're out of Hurricane and back on the highway. Almost there now. She will be driving past her home inside of an hour, past the home where she grew up and to the home where she moved in with Dean and Ruth. Her mother will be sitting somewhere, mending or a book in her lap, and her father will be in the lighted garage, space heater at his feet, planing or sanding a piece of wood. She barely knows her parents. She barely understands them as people. She thinks of the things that Jason and Boyd said about their parents on the way down here—for them, their parents are individuals, with characteristics. Boyd's mom is funny and irresponsible and permissive and, occasionally, unexpectedly cruel—she'd had his dog put down after it shit on the carpet. Jason's dad is serious and punctual, dour and dull; he turns everything into a lesson about some form of looming danger, whether it is moral disaster or pink-eye in the herd. His mother is, somehow, he had said, exactly the same, except that where his father sees doom, she sees joy; where he is grim about the dangers of life, she is optimistic. She remembers thinking how wonderful they sounded.

The sprinkled lights of Short Creek emerge. She can identify two thirds of the lights by family name. A tiny constellation, spinning around itself. She could find Dean's place with her eyes closed. She remembers moving there. The ache of disaster in her heart. She remembers his visitation the night of their wedding. His hand on her knee. Holding her in place.

Baker says, "I guess you pups thought you were pretty smart."

Jason doesn't want to answer. He wants to throw up from somewhere deep inside his bones.

Baker says, "Pret-ty smart." He acts very happy, pepped up. The smell of liquor fills the car. Baker taps a ring on the steering wheel, chews gum like he's trying to kill it. The front end of his Nova shimmies, shaking the steering wheel, but he keeps the gas pedal pinned to the floor. The needle flutters past ninety.

He says, "Got balls, though. Gotta say."

Every now and then they pass a semi, but mostly the freeway is deserted. The sun droops behind them, a blurred white disk with a golden rind. Far ahead, hanging above the horizon, a blurry gray storm smears the sky. They drive past Wells, and the next sign reads: WENDOVER 59, SALT LAKE CITY 179.

Back in Elko, Baker came into the hotel room asking questions, scanning the place. Jason felt groggy, stoned. It took him a long time to remember who Baker was. He kept saying, I don't know, I don't know, and Baker would ask again, screwing his head to one side while he squinted at Jason. *Where's Lori? Where's your Indian buddy? Sure, you know. I guess I'm not as stupid as you might think, bud. Why'd they leave? What happened? You all have a falling-out? The road crew broke up? Answer me. I ain't such a bad guy if you just answer me. Here.* He took Jason's ear between thumb and forefinger and twisted it so hard Jason thought it might rip. *Jog your memory? No? Okay, try this: Where were you going before the breakup of the fun-time crew? Where were you pups headed? Nowhere? Just going nowhere?* He wrenched the ear again, stretching the skin like taffy, and Jason howled in complete surrender. He kept saying, I don't know, I don't know, which was true, but he was also getting ready to say something else. It didn't take much. Jason was lying on his side on the bed, trying to squirm away, and Baker was kneeling over him, the liquor smell making Jason sick. Baker wrenched again. *Hush up now, Jason. So, were you all headed down to Hilldale?* Jason shook his head. He said, I really don't know, I really don't know, they left me. *Down to Nephi?* He shook his head. *Back to Short Creek?* Jason doesn't know what his face did then, but Baker let go, clapped briskly, and said, *The Crick. All right.* He stepped to the door, stopped with his hand on the knob, and looked back at Jason, curled on the bed. Pondered him for fifteen seconds, ticktocked his head sideways, made an aggravated face, shrugged, said, *Get your crap.* And then they were in his Nova, and they were going.

"Only thing is, you were not that smart," Baker says now, waving his index finger back and forth like a windshield wiper. "There was a flaw in the design. Can you tell me what it was?"

"No."

"Guess."

"I don't know," Jason says, holding wadded-up toilet paper from the Stockmen's against his ear.

"Jesus, you're a baby." He says this the way he's been saying everything, as though nothing could puncture his happy mood. "I'd have guessed you were a little tougher."

A thin, cold draft whines in along the door. The rearview mirror blazes with reflected sun, and the Nova's shadow races ahead of them on the pale asphalt, veined and crossed with black tar. It will take seven hours or so, Jason knows, to get to Short Creek.

"The fatal error," Baker says, "was the checks."

"The checks?"

"The checks."

"What do you mean?"

Baker laughs out loud.

"Are you shitting me?" He looks at Jason again with that screwed-in focus, as though he could auger the truth out of him, and then relaxes and laughs, deep and real. "Lori, Lori."

"What?"

"Let me tell you something about our Loretta," he says. He

cocks his head and looks at the road thoughtfully. He smiles, starts to speak, then stops, frowns, smiles, scratches his jaw. "Naw. Never mind."

"No, what?"

"Naw. So. They really ditched you. Just split."

Jason doesn't answer.

"That is unfortunate. That does suck."

He hasn't stopped smiling. He fidgets, snaps his fingers. He lifts a silver flask from his shirt pocket, unscrews, tips it, and gasps happily.

"She ain't so great with the promises, little Loretta," he says. "So, yeah, that does suck. But your deal was gonna go bad eventually, one way or another."

Jason thinks about checks. Dean's checks? Tries to piece it together.

"So you're here for Dean?" he asks.

"Some for him, some for me."

They drive. They pass West Wendover, a tiny town before the Utah border, and as they come to the state line, a white, flat plain opens, a cracked moonscape running so far and so flat that Jason thinks he can see the earth curve. It could be purgatory, with Baker as guide. Jason has died and is being ferried to hell.

A sign says: BONNEVILLE SALT FLATS VISITORS CENTER 1.

"I love this place," Baker says. "This is where the Donner Party got itself shitwise. Didn't bring enough water. Lost livestock. Got weak and sick. Took too long crossing, so they were still in the mountains when winter came."

He laughs. They round a bend and town lights appear, yellow in the dusk.

"Remember this for your next big adventure, kid," he says. "Things don't go bad at the end. That's just when it becomes obvious. First, you cross a desert of salt without enough to drink. Then your oxes die. Your kids get scurvy."

He laughs again. "Next thing, you've eaten all your horses and it won't stop snowing."

The lilac light on the salt pan is turning black, grain by grain. The world seems too large, too empty, for them to simply drive a few hours and catch up with Boyd and Loretta, but the car's velocity and Baker's focus convinces Jason that they will find them, and that it will be bad for Loretta, maybe very bad, and it will be bad for Boyd and bad for Jason. And that it is entirely Jason's fault.

Baker says, "You hungry? I could eat the ass out of a cow."

In the café, Baker gathers huge mouthfuls of hamburger and chews mightily, like he is working a hand crank. Every so often he yawns. The café hums with table noise, plate and fork, the talk of truckers and country people. The waitress tops Baker's coffee.

"Looks like somebody's got a long drive," she says. "You hauling a load?"

"Naw," he says, and winks. "In a rush to meet a gal."

Baker looks at Jason's plate and says, "Your hamburger ain't gonna eat itself."

"What happens if we find them?" Jason asks.

"*When* we find them. Think positive."

He reaches over and grabs Jason's burger. Bites off a third of it, chews and chews, staring at Jason, then takes another bite, then says, "One step at a time."

The snow starts as they drive past the southern tip of the Great Salt Lake, which lies like a great blankness under the cloudy night.

Everywhere else, the valley between the mountain spines glitters with light, and a thickening layer of white covers the freeway but for the parallel lines of wheel paths. The Nova slides and spins, but Baker doesn't ease up on the gas. He grips the wheel with both hands and leans forward, as if he can keep them on track with sheer will.

Jason wishes for a crash. He might be praying for one. He's not sure he really understands the difference between wishing and praying. But he notices—here, where the Mormon Trail ground to a halt, where the pioneer handcarts stopped and Brigham Young declared this was the place, where God sent the seagulls to save the crops, and where a shining new city was built, where the church settled and grew, where the temple and the tabernacle arose, where the Saints gathered twice a year to worship, to separate themselves from the world; here, where his parents would bring him every couple of years, to visit Temple Square and stay at the Hotel Utah, their capital, their Mecca—even here, feeling desperate and forsaken, he is not turning to prayer. Not really. He remembers the long-ago game of Yes or No?, Boyd and him playacting at a serious business, and realizes that he has arrived at an answer that is really just a feeling. A guess. Just another kind of faith.

They pass semis in a blind wash of white. Station wagons and pickup trucks. The Nova swishes but stays road bound. Sometimes Baker lets out a little whoop, and sometimes he yawns and then shakes his head violently, as if to drive away his fatigue, but mostly he stays clenched, focused, two hands on the wheel, leading with his chin. The flask stays in his pocket.

An hour south of Salt Lake, the snow stops and the freeway clears. Baker slowly relaxes, sits back, and holds the wheel with one hand, but he still seems agitated. It is past ten.

"So, tell me," Baker says. "Were you fucking her? Was this other kid fucking her? The Indian? God, let's hope not. Let's hope not for her sake. I mean, she's in a big enough shit storm already without fucking some mongrel dog."

"Don't say that," Jason says—and Baker pounds him on the shoulder, fist like stone driving him into the door.

"Don't start giving me advice about what to say."

Jason rubs and rubs his arm, and the moment he releases it, Baker pounds him again. The new pain vacuums up Jason's breath, leaves him cringing and wincing, close to tears.

"Okay, goddammit?" Baker says.

"Okay." Jason says. *"Okay."*

"So. Who was fucking her? Somebody was fucking her."

"No."

"Kid, you must be the stupidest guy on the face of this earth. Your buddy was fucking her. Is fucking her. I mean, that's the way this works: you ate all your horses, it won't stop snowing, and somebody else is fucking your girl."

He pounds the steering wheel with the heel of his hand. Fear seeps through Jason. He tries to sort out the message in the story: Who ate the horses? What was the snow?

"Get it?" Baker says. "You're fucked, is what it is."

They pass a sign that glares in the Nova's headlights: CEDAR CITY 112. Jason knows that is where they will leave the freeway and head down, into the desert, to Short Creek.

Baker yawns—the yawn swamps him, against his will, large and powerful—and then shakes his head violently, as if to drive it away. He sniffs. Nods.

"Yeah, I'm afraid Lori was fucking your little redskin. Worse than I even thought. I mean, you live your life, you make your plans, you try to do the right thing, and what happens? What happens, kid? I'm asking you."

"I don't know."

"You do know! You do know because I just told you! What happens," Baker says, "is you ate all the horses and it won't stop snowing and the girl you love is fucking some dirty Indian nigger and you have to figure out what to do about it."

He whistles and clicks his tongue.

"Gotta figure out who to eat."

She feels almost sick going back into that house. A little dulled and confused. An unplugged lamp sits on the floor, cord like a tail, and trapezoids of moonlight, cast through the windows, hang on the bare walls. Ghosts of missing furniture haunt the carpet.

"This place is huge," Boyd says, flipping on a light. Loretta flips it back off. "Let's not go announcing ourselves," she says. She sets down her duffel bag. The gold inside—the coins in the canvas sack, rolled tightly inside one of her denim skirts—clangs dully on the linoleum entry. She kicks off her shoes. Force of habit. Ruth's rules. Boyd wanders the carpet in his dirty gray tennis shoes, gazing up at the high ceiling like he's in a cathedral. It's past ten, late for around here, but who knows who might see a light and get interested. She's not sure whether the United Order might stop by. The God Squad. She's not sure it isn't officially Uncle Elden's house or the Order's house. They own everything. But Dean's key worked on the front door, and she's soon to see about the others. She's gripping them so tightly they might be cutting into her palm.

It's time to tell Boyd, probably. She looks at him to begin and sees he is coming her way, his best attempt at a romantic look on his face, eyebrows raised. It never ends, these men coming at her. She can tell he is nervous, half embarrassed. She misses Bradshaw and his crazy confidence.

"Stop it," she says, though she smiles to soften it. "I've got something to show you. To tell you."

They sit on the floor in the darkened, moonlit room. She explains about the coins she has. She explains about the gold that is still, now, she thinks, locked in Dean's office. "Gold!" Boyd says. "Fuckin'-A!" She unwraps and shows him the coins, thick and heavy, gleaming richly, almost amber in the dim light, and she lets him hold them, and he seems awestruck. He keeps saying it, a prayer or a curse: "Gold!" She tells him about the Sutter Creek gold, how important it is to Dean, and how important that is to her.

"I want to take it from him, and I want him to know I took it from him, and I want him to know that I knew how important it was to him when I took it," she says.

Boyd is looking at her strangely.

"Lori," he whispers. "Why did he leave that gold down here? In an empty house?"

"What?"

"Why did he leave it here? Why would he?"

It does not dawn on her slowly. She does not have to think it over. It reminds her of a crash she once had on a bicycle; one moment she was moving along one way, and then she abruptly was not, and the blow that struck her felt not like it came from a specific direction but from everywhere at once. Why had she ever thought the gold was here? She couldn't remember.

"Lori?"

She takes the coins and wraps them back up, then goes to the door to Dean's office, the white cube at the back of the room off the kitchen. The key slides and turns. She puts on the light in the windowless room. It's half emptied, too—some of Dean's books remain, some files, a pair of his Red Wings on the floor beside the chair, one tipped on its side. She goes to the cabinet, to the bottom drawer, and takes the smaller key between her thumb and forefinger. The key slides and turns, and the drawer pulls out, and the drawer is empty.

"Well, shit," Boyd says.

She sits in the chair heavily.

"Who cares?" Boyd says.

She cares. This is not his to judge, to care about or not care about. She kicks idly at the metal drawer, and then again, harder. She thinks back: The Sutter Creek gold wasn't with the coins, she knew that. Didn't she know that? And she had looked everywhere through that house up in Idaho, everywhere she could think of, every chance she had. And then—what? Why had she decided it was here? He told her. Hadn't he? The idea seems so ludicrous now. So clearly, obviously ludicrous. She feels stupid. As stupid as Jason. As stupid as Boyd.

"We should get out of here," she says.

"We've still got the coins, though," Boyd says.

She doesn't answer. *We.* His big hurt brown eyes. How could she have done what she did with him? She feels a pang of judgment about herself: whore. Boyd flops onto the couch, arms outstretched, exhausted. She goes to the carpeted, banistered staircase and starts up. She will get her things, her shoebox, and they will go, and that will be okay, it will be all right, it will still be great that she has done this, that she has fled Dean and that life.

Boyd shouts, "Maybe we could just live here. Join the brethren."

We. She reaches the top of the stairs, pads to the end of the hallway. Two small framed things remain on the walls, quotations Ruth has embroidered: "David's wives and concubines were given unto him of me . . ."

She goes to her room. The sagging queen under the denim quilt. The dresser and its grimy mirror, where she watched Ruth braid her hair for the wedding. Out the window she sees the occasional farm light, spread thinly toward the spiny desert mountains. Loretta opens the drawers, empty, empty, empty. Then, in the bottom drawer, she finds her shoebox. Her eyes have become hot. She lifts out the box, opens it. Her throat feels thick and her scalp prickles. She sits on the padded stool before the dresser, and looks through the box. Her grandmother's Christmas ornaments. Her diary. "The man I will marry." Earrings. Arrowheads. A hazy photograph of herself as an infant, her parents huddled around her. She looks up and is startled by her image in the mirror: grief stricken, gunshot. She feels dimmed with a sorrow for all that is bygone and impossible and flown away. For all that has to be the way it is simply because it is over now, it has happened, and is never to be gotten back.

Jason wakes to a shove from Baker. "It's go time," he says.

The Nova creeps with its lights off, down a dirt road lined in ditch grass. Forms take shape. Ahead is a barny, big-shouldered house. They're in the country somewhere. The stars look tiny and still, as though racing away from the earth.

"You snore like a girl," Baker says.

"What time is it?"

Baker chuckles.

"You're a funny kid. It's late."

"Where are we?"

"We're there, buddy. The Crick. We are there."

They stop in front of the house. It is dark, but for thin light through curtains in the biggest window. Ahead, sharked crooked-lyonto the border where the lawn peters out into dirt, sits the Le-Baron. Baker leans on the steering wheel and works his chin against a knuckle, staring at the house. Jason can see now that it is cheap, simple—wood siding in dirty cream paint, asphalt shingles. Small, dark, gabled windows. One thick strip of paint has peeled loose and bowed to the ground. A tricycle lies on its side on the grass.

"I don't know what to do here," Baker says. "What do you think I should do?"

"Maybe we ought to just leave."

"Good one. Okay." He pops the steering wheel with both palms. "Let's go see our friends."

Frosty grass crackles underfoot. The concrete step has a worn mat with the words WELCOME TO OUR HOME. Scuff marks cover the bottom of the wooden door. Baker looks around, thinking. He seems unconcerned about Jason and what Jason might do, and Jason wonders why it is so obvious that he will do nothing. Baker takes the doorknob. When it turns, he gives Jason a look of happy surprise and pushes it open. Inside, a linoleum entryway opens onto a carpeted cavern of a living room, half empty, that opens onto a kitchen at the back, where a single light is on. A disassembled living space remains—a love seat and end table that suggest where the rest of the missing furniture used to be. A couple of lumps—duffel bags, piles of clothes, a pair of tennis shoes that he recognizes as Loretta's—sit on the floor. Baker walks in. Yawns. He stares out the kitchen window. The refrigerator hums. Baker turns and steps back through the kitchen quietly, and as he is doing so a door along the side of the room opens, and Boyd walks out, looking down as he buttons his jeans.

Baker's face opens brightly, delighted. Just as Boyd is noticing there is something amiss, Baker says, "Hello, shitbird," and takes three rapid strides across the room and slaps Boyd against the side of his head with such force that Boyd stumbles, then sits on the ground. Baker strikes him again, a meaty clout on the ear, and Boyd topples over, covers his head with his hands. From upstairs comes a voice. "Boyd?" Loretta's voice.

Baker looks toward the stairs and bellows in answer, wordlessly, a joyous animal roar that he seems to draw upward from somewhere deep and black and far below the earth.

Then he's taking the stairs, two by two.

Bradshaw? What? *Bradshaw?* Loretta can't put together an idea of why Bradshaw is here, but there he is, Bradshaw, barging in the door while she sits there, shoebox in her lap, and he is smiling and moving so forcefully that her body knows to be terrified even before her mind does: it drains and parches and trembles.

Bradshaw knocks the shoebox from her lap.

"Hey, baby. Surprise."

She shakes her head. He stands over her. His fury fills the room.

"You're not? You're not surprised?"

"Brad," she starts.

He leans down, puts his face so close she feels his nose tickling the hairs of her nose, and bellows: "SHUT UP!" A blast of liquor. He stands and inhales vigorously through his nostrils, and then says, almost dreamily, almost as if he were talking to himself, "Just shut up, Lori. Let that be your plan. Now get your lousy faithless ass downstairs."

Out the door and down the hall and down the stairs, and there is the next surprise: Jason. He stands in the kitchen, with the aspect of a jackrabbit staying perfectly still to avoid the eye of the hawk. Boyd is curled on the ground, hands to his head.

Bradshaw says, "What a couple of chickenshits."

Jason thinks he doesn't recognize Loretta, though he does. She has lost control of her face. She called him Brad. Why is she calling him Brad, and why is she calling him Brad in that way?

"Thought you two might take off while you had the chance," Baker says. "I guess you must like me."

He takes Loretta by the arm and guides her to the love seat and shoves her into it.

"You two come on over and sit here, too," he says.

When they are arrayed—Loretta in the love seat, Boyd and Jason sitting on the carpet in a kind of triangle—Baker makes a show of looking from Boyd to Loretta, from Loretta to Boyd. He makes a show of trying to think it through, sort it out.

Finally, he looks at Jason, waggles his thumb between Boyd and Loretta, and says, "Told ya, stupid."

Bradshaw takes a deep breath. Pulls the flask from his back pocket and tips it up until it's empty. He tilts his head back and forth, as though carrying on a debate within himself.

Loretta says, "I was getting ready to call you."

"Yeah?"

He begins to pace. Heavy on the boot heels.

She says, "Yeah," and he nods and stomps, and says, blearily, "Your plan was that you'd leave without telling me, take off with these jokers, come down and get it, and then call me?"

They are talking secrets and plans, Loretta and Baker are, and Jason feels yet another hot spear of jealousy. How wrong he has been, about everything.

Loretta says, "Yeah. Yes, Brad," her voice a vibrato of fear. Brad again. What does it mean that she's calling him that? Baker says, "Yeah?" like he's genuinely, deeply curious. He steps to Boyd and kicks him in the ribs so hard Boyd lifts up and falls onto his side. He moans and says, "Goddammit," and Baker adjusts his angle and kicks him again, and says, "No more from you, you red fucking nigger." Boyd retches, a wet, beery mess pooling on the shag. "A kick for every single fucking word," Baker says, and Boyd coughs and whispers, "Okay," and Baker kicks him again. Boyd begins to quietly cry.

Bradshaw resumes pacing, pounding his heels. At last he says to Lori, "So where is it?" and she doesn't know why she does this but she says, "I've got it. I was getting ready to call and tell you." She is trying to get his eyes, to share a look, to go to that place where he will do what she wants him to do.

"I got it for us," she says.

"That is so great," he says.

He yawns, hugely. He will not join her in that look.

What in the fuck are they talking about? Jason wants Loretta to look at him, but she does not. Her eyes follow Baker, and she is terrified, and she does not give Jason a glance.

"I don't know," Baker says. He comes over, pulls Loretta to her feet by an arm. "I'm sorely disappointed, Lori, but maybe you can make it up to me."

Now she looks at Jason, and then Boyd, and her face crumbles. Her look makes Jason feel like one of her captors.

"Upstairs," Baker says.

She heads toward the stairs. She's in her socks. She wishes she could grab her shoes. They are right there, in the doorway. But she goes up. Behind her, Bradshaw pauses. He says, "I don't really care what you shitheels do," and Loretta speeds up a tiny bit, and Bradshaw's still behind her, at the base of the stairs, saying to the boys, "Maybe you ought to just walk on out of here," and now she's at the top of the stairs, and now she's in the hallway, and now she's sprinting toward her room.

Jason thinks: *Just leave?*

"Lori and I are going to take it from here," Baker says, smiling, and then, as if he cannot help himself, adds, "If you know what I mean," and he winks and clicks his tongue, like he's spurring a horse into motion, and starts up the steps.

———

She shuts and locks the door, and runs to the window, but it won't slide open. The thick wooden dowel that Dean had put there blocks it. The doorknob rattles furiously. "Lori?" Bradshaw calls. She takes up the stool from the dresser.

Jason and Boyd do not move. Jason says, "Come on. It's two against one."

Boyd snorts. "That's right, big shot. Two of us, one of him." Upstairs, Baker is howling her name and banging banging banging, and then there is a sharp, brittle shatter.

Loretta sets the stool back down before the window and steps up on it. Thick, icy air seeps into the room. Bradshaw is pounding, pounding, now kicking the door. She can hear it splinter. She steps onto the windowsill, feels the glass sink hotly into her foot as she ducks through the window and pushes off into the sky.

She feels it in her left ankle when she lands. An explosion. A demolition. She rolls away from it, breath punched out of her. One foot bloody, one broken. The LeBaron sits fifteen yards away. The keys are in her hand. She stands and begins to hop.

Something whooshes onto the front lawn outside. Baker howls, "God-*damn* it!" and now come his thundering boot heels down the stairs. Jason says to Boyd, "Come *on*."

Jason rises. Baker is racing toward the front door, and Jason, without thinking, without making a decision, cuts toward him, Baker glancing in his direction in irritated surprise, and Jason hurls himself toward Baker's legs, and wraps them up as Baker bowls him over.

Loretta hops and hops on her cut foot. She waits for the door to burst open behind her. In her broken ankle, she can feel the pieces of bone shift with each hop. It screams with a pain that is almost a comfort, a hot distraction, a welcome elsewhere. She makes it to the LeBaron and puts her hand on it, hops, hops, reaches for the door.

Jason holds Baker's struggling thighs, his right hand gripping his left wrist, while Baker rains down blows on his back. "You're dead, you little fucker," Baker spits, and he grabs Jason's ear and turns it hard again, sending a bright flame of pain along Jason's scalp along with the certainty that what he says is true, that Jason really is now going to be dead, and soon. "You are super fucking dead." Outside, the LeBaron chugs into life. The engine noise rises, and then it begins to diminish, and Jason feels that he will lose control of Baker's legs at any moment. His knees, loosening, are knocking Jason in the chest, and soon he will be fucked, truly fucked. Baker starts to heave his knees powerfully, and one cracks Jason in the mouth, and the iron taste of blood arrives, and Jason thinks that Baker will get loose now, and he'll be in his car in seconds, following, and Loretta will never get away. Then he feels a heavy thump. Boyd. Boyd has a knee on Baker's back and one on his neck, mashing Baker's face into the carpet. Baker stops flailing and Jason gets a better grip around his thighs, face pressed against his hip. Baker says, "Guys," into the carpet, smush-mouthed, and then again, "Guys," and the LeBaron is already distant, already who knows where, and Baker screams like an animal into the carpet. They sit there like that, the three of them locked together, until all Jason knows for sure is that they can no longer hear the LeBaron anywhere. It's all the way gone.

She can do this with one foot. It is just a matter of deciding to do it. Like Ruth would do. She presses the gas pedal to the floor with her blood-damp sock, ignoring the pain. Gravel growls under the tires. Dust fills the cab. She breathes and breathes and breathes. Loretta reaches the paved county road, and turns onto it. She can't stop shivering, though she isn't registering the cold. The LeBaron's heater is blasting and she knows it will soon be too warm in here. She passes through Short Creek at just above the speed limit—the huge brick church, the walls of the prophet's compound, the small post office and store, the United Order warehouse. She thinks about the kids. She wishes she could see Benjamin one more time. Read *The Poky Little Puppy*. When she reaches the outskirts she presses the accelerator and the car surges loosely. Her ankle howls. It rests at an impossible angle, swollen tight. The pierced sticky bottom of her pedal foot burns and throbs. The first pink signs of day are lining those dusky orange walls of stone that rise from the desert. The rear end fishtails and stabilizes, and she holds down the pedal. Her left ankle is a bag of bones, and sometime—out far away, in the time that comes after this time—she knows she will need to do something about it, but for now she tells herself just this: She can do this with one foot. It's an automatic, this old boat. She can drive it forever with just one foot.

Jason thinks the end might come any minute. Once Baker is free, he will kill them. With his own two hands. He told them he would, and Jason believes him. Carpet fibers tickle his face. He can feel his arms and hands weakening, but Boyd has Baker perfectly pinned, facedown, one knee on the back of his neck and one in the middle of his back. Jason lies on his side, arms wrapped around Baker's thighs and face against his hip. Jason and Boyd don't talk until not talking seems like the way to do it. They lie there for what feels like hours, the scent of mud and old oatmeal and dirty socks and home-made bread radiating. Baker's anger dies second by second, then surges, fades, surges. Jason stares at the bundle of electrical wires hanging from the ceiling. His shoulders rage. He feels far away from himself.

Baker says, "Guys. Come on. It's over. Just let me up. Seriously now. Come on." Then he tries thrashing violently. Boyd tips and catches himself on his hands, but keeps his weight on Baker's neck, and Baker stops. "All right," he says. "Enough. I give. Just let me up." Nobody answers him. "I can't breathe," he says.

Boyd says, "You can breathe."

Baker says, "I can't breathe very well." Jason thinks that any moment now he will lose his grip. Baker says, "Just let me up and we'll all go our separate ways."

Jason says, "Boyd?"

"No way," Boyd says. "My ribs are in pieces."

"Then what?"

"I don't know," he says. Dead voiced.

"Guys," Baker says to the carpet. "Guys."

Then he laughs, a long manic outburst that fades to silence.

Jason wonders where Loretta is now, and can't block the wish to be with her. Boyd makes wincy noises. Jason looks up from his half-obscured angle at his friend, his oldest and only friend, and sees Boyd staring vacantly. They have each lost the same thing: not Loretta, but an idea of her. A faith.

"Seriously, guys," Baker says.

It is almost six A.M.

"Boyd," Jason says.

"I know."

"There's two of us."

"Yeah."

"Guys, I mean it, let me up and let's just call it over."

"Shut up, fucko," Boyd says.

A long silence follows.

Baker begins to take deep, regular breaths.

"Right," Boyd says. "Sure, man."

Baker's body loses its tension. The muscles in his legs slacken.

"I don't know," Jason whispers. "It feels real."

One of Baker's feet kicks weakly, lifts and drops on its toe, involuntary. He snorts, begins to wheeze.

"I think it's real," Jason says.

"No way."

Baker snores noisily into the carpet. Jason loosens his grip. Nothing. He slides his arms free—fiery with pins and needles—and Baker snorts wetly, pauses, resumes snoring. If he's faking, Jason thinks, he's doing a good job of it. Then he thinks: *How hard would it be to fool me?* He rolls away and stands slowly. When he sees Boyd's face, he grows worried—he is ashen, stunned, and Jason knows from his Boy Scout first-aid training that Boyd is in shock. Boyd looks like he is about to tip over, breath shallow and eyes drooping. Jason reaches out and takes his elbow and helps him stand, watching Baker and knowing that they are committed now, they'll never get hold of him in that way again, and as Boyd's knees come off his neck, Baker lifts and turns his head and lays it down again and sleeps, astonishingly, sleeps.

"No way," Boyd says.

They walk out. No keys in the Nova, and they're not going back to root around in Baker's pockets and risk waking him. Boyd's coat is in the LeBaron, so they take turns wearing Jason's as they walk into town, looking back nervously all the way. Boyd limps from the pain in his ribs. They barely speak, and Jason wonders: How do you start? What do you say first?

"What do we do now?" he asks.

Boyd shrugs. "Go until we get someplace."

It is warmer than it's been in days. Trucks pass, drivers stare. Every house is huge, stamped from the same mold. There are no stores. No stop signs. No normal town things. They walk past a huge walled compound; the gabled roofs of two enormous homes, larger than Dean's, loom above. The desert spreads, flat and dusty red, toward the jutting mountains that seem to shelter the place. Curtains part as they pass; a woman in her yard, in a long dress, ankle to wrist, turns away from them watchfully.

"This place is the weirdest," Boyd says.

Why does Jason not think Baker is coming? He simply doesn't. They reach a small country store. Two rusting gas pumps out front and a Greyhound bus sign in the window. They go in without speaking. Jason has enough money for two tickets home and four packages of Ho Hos. After he pays, he looks at the change in his palm: $2.13. His mission money.

They stand outside by the ice machine and the dented garbage can in the radiant morning sun and eat like they're starving, until Boyd begins to laugh. A wet glob of Ho Ho flies out. He stops, gains control, and then begins again, shaking uncontrollably, eyes pinched shut, and then watering over. Jason just watches him, waiting, chewing. He is visited by a powerful urge to be home. To be a child. Boyd stops, takes a breath, wipes his eyes, and says, "He fell asleep," and starts all over again, the force of it smearing his face around, bending him over. Jason finally has no choice. It is beyond him, it always has been beyond him. He joins in.

Loretta turns north on Highway 59, heading toward Cedar. Spokes of light radiate from the low morning sun, and she thinks she will turn toward it, drive through the red rock canyons, through Zion and Bryce Canyon, and head to Colorado. Or maybe north to Wyoming. Or maybe southeast to New Mexico. An understanding dawns: Her future is not pictures of other places and other things and other people. It is not pictures of anything, and it is not one place. It is the absence of pictures, a void, and this fills her with elation. She wants to bow down before the absence. She wants to worship it.

She is wearing everything she has: the jeans she wore to seminary with Jason, a Led Zeppelin T-shirt of Boyd's, a pair of cotton socks, one of which is torn and bloody, and three one-dollar bills, folded in her front pocket. The gold and the checks and her clothes and money and everything else are behind her. The LeBaron's heater hums waves of hot air, and the inside of the car feels spacious and welcoming, a kind of home. The adrenaline of the past hours has fled, and a warm, happy weariness settles. She will need to sleep somewhere, and she has nowhere to sleep. She will need to do something about her ankle, and she has no way to pay a doctor. She needs shoes. She needs food. She needs gas. She has no idea how she will get any of it.

It is the happiest she has ever been, the best moment of her life, but only so far.

ACKNOWLEDGMENTS

My deepest thanks are due to friends who read early versions of this novel and gave me guidance. Sam Ligon, in particular, read every scrap of this and repeatedly helped me expand the world of the book. Mike Baccam, Stephen Knezovich, and Jess Walter also provided valuable help—as did the brilliant Ed Park, whom I am lucky to have as an editor. I have been so fortunate to call Renée Zuckerbrot my agent, and her editorial insights and patience through the various drafts helped me discover the story hidden there.

I would like to express my gratitude to PEN and the family of Robert W. Bingham, as well as the Washington Artists Trust. Their support made it possible for me to devote time to this novel that I would not have otherwise had.

I relied upon several sources of historical information while writing this novel but also took certain dramatic liberties. (These include changing the date of Evel Knievel's London bus jump, which actually occurred in May 1975, and retaining the name Short Creek for the fundamentalist community in northern Arizona, even though the community has actually changed its name to Colorado City.)

Leigh Montville's biography *Evel* was particularly useful in understanding the history and mythology surrounding Knievel, and the History channel documentary *Absolute Evel* was valuable as a resource in attempting to reproduce the man's voice. Several accounts of the Short Creek raids were helpful in describing that day, but it was the *Life* magazine photographs of the raid that I returned to repeatedly when I wanted to try to imagine my way inside those events.

Among the many others to whom I owe thanks are:

The members of my "church," fellow squires of the night's body: Chris, Dan, Jess, Sam, Tony.

The faculty and students of Eastern Washington University's MFA program, where I learned and where I sometimes teach.

The gang at the *Spokesman-Review,* where it has been my privilege to work since 1999.

The Internet, which makes it so easy to find useful information about everything from the mating patterns of jackrabbits to the dashboard of a 1970 Chrysler LeBaron.

And, most of all, my family: my mother, brothers, and sisters; my wife, Amy, and son, Cole.

AN IMPRINT OF PUSHKIN PRESS

ONE, an imprint of Pushkin Press, publishes one exceptional fiction or non-fiction title a season. Its list is commissioned and edited by the writer and editor Elena Lappin, who selects the best writing by authors whose extraordinary voices, talent and vision deserve a wide readership and media focus.

THREE GRAVES FULL
Jamie Mason

"Incredibly entertaining and suspenseful... brilliant" *The Times*

A SENSE OF DIRECTION
PILGRIMAGE FOR THE RESTLESS AND THE HOPEFUL
Gideon Lewis-Kraus

"A winning blend of earnestness, wit and high-octane intellect" *Observer*

A REPLACEMENT LIFE
Boris Fishman

"Piercing, witty and enviably well written" *New Statesman*

THE FISHERMEN
Chigozie Obioma

"Striking, controlled and masterfully taut… timeless" *Financial Times*

WHISPERS THROUGH A MEGAPHONE
Rachel Elliott

"Sharp, realistic… charming" *Daily Mail*

THE MINOR OUTSIDER
Ted McDermott

"A spirited, audacious, and drolly funny debut" Patrick deWitt, author of *Undermajordomo Minor*

DAREDEVILS
Shawn Vestal

"Electrifying… a major new voice in fiction" Jess Walter, author of *Beautiful Ruins*

DON'T LET MY BABY DO RODEO
Boris Fishman

"An eloquent and uncynical tale of how far people must travel to find out what they truly want and who they truly are" *Chicago Tribune*

www.pushkinpress.com/one